Vision of the Grail

A Spiritual Adventure
at the Dawn of the 21st Century

Kathleen Jacoby

Lightlines Publishing Company
Palm Springs • San Mateo
2001

Published in the United States by:

Lightlines Publishing Company
760 Vella Road
Palm Springs, CA 92264
(760) 325-9200

E-mail: info@lightlinespublishingco.com
Website: http://lightlinespublishingco.com

Cover design and layout by Steve Freier

Library of Congress Cataloging-In-Publication Data

Jacoby, Kathleen
    Vision of the Grail / Kathleen Jacoby
    ISBN 1-930126-07-7 (paperback : alk. paper)
    1. Fiction - Spiritual Life 2. Visionary 3. Metaphysical I. Title

    PS 3568.BT 685.8.J17 2001   2001088464
    813'.54 – dc21   CIP

                ISBN 1-930126-07-7
        10 9 8 7 6 5 4 3 2 1

    First Printing, Mouse The Publisher, 1996
    Second Printing, Lightlines Publishing Co., 2001
    Printed in the United States of America

Also by Kathleen Jacoby:

Where You Live Is What You Learn
A guidebook to understanding how your address
affects your life.

A Call To Prayer
An inner guide to help you live a prayerful life and reap
the ensuing rewards. (Available as an e-book.)

Seasons of the Soul
An inspiring newsletter available by subscription
from the author.

Numbers by Design
A syndicated monthly numerology column.

Visions
An inspirational syndicated column.

For more information, please see order form
at the back of this book, or visit the author's website:
http://theinnervoice.com/VOG.htm
e-mail: VisionoftheGrail@aol.com

Dedication...
To the guidance that prompted me,
and to the ones who paved the way so
there was a road to follow.

Acknowledgements...
To my wonderful family and friends
who cheered and encouraged me
every step of the way...
and to Jacquelyn, without whom this
would never have been finished.

I also wish to thank Jim Clark and
Nancy Freier of Lightlines Publishing Co.
for sharing the Vision.

Contents

*For Holly and all children
who represent the future.*

Chapter 1
❧ A Strange Assignment ❧

As I trudged up the hill noting my breath, I felt an overwhelming sense of gratitude for life, and had a strange sensation that things were about to change in a most remarkable way. Because of the work I did as a writer and consultant, I was able to live in an area that was ideal for me, and had the luxury to take time to enjoy nature when I wanted, rather than on fixed days off.

Good hiking trails were plentiful on the San Francisco Peninsula, and I often went with a friend who lived close to the nature preserves we enjoyed so much. These walks in the hills allowed us to exercise amidst the beauty and temperate climate of the area, enjoying the scenery and animated conversation without interruption.

This was a valuable friendship, and more and more, I was aware of the need to choose companions wisely, to reflect the best of myself and my possibilities rather than my limitations. Once long ago, I had a teacher who summed it up very simply. "How do you know what your own liver looks like unless you look at the liver of somebody else?" I thought that was a strange statement at the time, but realized the truth of what she said as the years went by.

We see ourselves constantly in everybody around us. They are mirrors, reflecting parts of ourselves back to us, and sometimes it's hard to believe that because they may represent our blind spots or our judgments. Through the years, whenever I would get upset at my friends or relatives, I always had to ask myself, "What are they showing me about me?"

That same teacher would look at the sea of faces in front of her and challenge us to write a list of all our grievances against someone who caused us suffering. At the end of the exercise, when we felt smug and self-satisfied, she'd smile, like the Cheshire Cat, and say, "Now, put your name in the place of the one you are condemning." Everyone groaned. Instead of, "She never listens to me," we had to turn it around. "I never listen to her." "He doesn't appreciate me" became, "I don't appreciate him." And then beyond that, "I never listen to me." "I don't appreciate myself." She had a way of getting to the heart of an issue and making us look at our own part in the process. It was great training, and I carried it with me through the years.

She counseled us to pay attention to the quality of our relationships. Gradually, I recognized people in my life who encouraged me to grow, as well as the ones who were threatened whenever I would take a step forward. It wasn't easy to give up old friendships that had been established during a time when my needs were different, and when love was involved, it was even harder. But I found myself imprisoned by lack of growth, and for me, relationships had to involve the component of a search for meaning and hold compatible goals of unfoldment.

I was thankful for my friends like Bonita, and coming back to the present moment, we completed our hike up the hill, and stood at the summit looking over the valley in quiet appreciation. Bonita let out a hearty 'whoop' as we moved toward her home, nestled amidst the trees. Behind the main house was a beautiful octagonal structure that had been built on what she and her husband were told was a sacred site, and the work she did there with groups helped them get in touch with the sacred parts of themselves through sound, meditation, and music.

As we walked into what was called the Center, I could feel the sense of peace and ease that it always gave me. There was a welcoming presence that encouraged insights and reflection.

"Would you like some tea?" Bonita asked.

I responded that I would, but that I'd like to meditate first. We each found comfortable spaces in which to sit, and as I eased into a state of relaxation, moving away from the personal me to a greater collective sense of unity, I felt the presence of what I came to regard as the inner teacher. As I became still and listened, a message seemed to imprint itself upon my mind: "Find the Holy Grail."

"Find the what?" I thought. The Presence receded, and I was left with the cryptic message. "Find the Holy Grail."

Bonita and I always shared our insights after meditation, and I paused as if trying to find the right words. I told her what I'd received and asked her what she knew about the Holy Grail.

"Not much," she replied, "but I do know that there has to be a book about it. Wasn't that connected to the myth of King Arthur?"

I nodded my head, because that seemed right, and mentally noted that I would go to my favorite bookstore to investigate further. After we finished our tea and made arrangements for our next walk, I drove down the hill, questioning what I knew about the Grail. Very little. What an odd message, I thought, and wondered what it meant... but recognized from experience that this was the way I was led to grow. I felt the Presence many years ago when I learned to meditate, and it had taken me on a number of journeys, each insight or directive leading to something more that rounded out a part of my education, adding dimension to my understanding.

When I thought about it, what I called the Presence had been there when I was little. One day at about age four, I was playing in my bedroom, when I noticed a file of ants marching across the floor. In a fit of anger, I began to step on them. As I did this, I could feel the color red inside me and a swelling of something that I now recognize as power. The killing of them inflated a part of me that wanted dominion, and in the midst of my action, I was suddenly overwhelmed by a voice that came from beyond the lustful sensation, and lodged itself in front of me.

"Stop!" it commanded.

I halted in the midst of my frenzy and looked around. Again, the voice spoke again. "Stop! You are never to do that again."

My attention diverted from the act of killing the ants to this compelling presence. I stood quietly and listened. "It's not your right to kill anything. You must never do that again because it is wrong." The voice was not judgmental in tone. It was the voice of a loving parent, explaining right from wrong.

In that moment my guilt was so great, I looked at

what I'd done. Ants were scurrying everywhere, confused from my messing up their pattern. I immediately went to the kitchen and brought the sugar bowl, leaving little clumps of it for the remaining ones who had escaped my rampage. I cleaned up the dead ants and asked forgiveness for my action. From that point, I knew the Presence was with me. It remained evident until I became self-conscious at the time of puberty, and then it seemed to disappear until such time as I consciously brought myself into prayer, meditation and reflection.

So here again, it had surfaced, and I was being set on a course to investigate what finding the Holy Grail meant. I knew this venture would have to wait until tomorrow, because I had deadlines to meet. As the editor of a quarterly newsletter, I was determined to finish the spring issue before it was summer!

I awoke the next morning, remembering a dream from the night before. It was strange in its implication. A man came to meet with a friend of mine who had a little software company that I helped manage in the past, so I was standing with my friend as this other individual approached us. He wanted to buy some of John's software, and his assistant seemed very nervous and asked us if we knew how wealthy his boss really was. In effect, he said to us, "Don't you know who Russell Steitz is? He's one of the wealthiest men in the United States!"

As I looked back at the man referred to, he appeared to be someone who would go to whatever means necessary to get what he wanted. I felt he was not to be trusted, nor to be trifled with. He had a strong need to exert power and control over others.

In the next scene of my dream, we were in another room, and this man, Russell, was talking to a group of us. He was standing over us and seemed to be in an adversarial position. His actions confirmed my earlier suspicions of his need to control.

All of a sudden, I looked up and saw him... the real him who dwelt inside, and I blurted out, "Oh, Russell, have you forgotten who you really are?"

He looked toward me, infuriated at the perceived attack, and began to launch into a tirade. However, when he saw who had spoken, and observed the look of pure love and clarity on my face, his whole demeanor shifted, and his expression softened. Remembrance replaced anger, and he asked if we had gone to school together.

I knew we hadn't been to school together... that I was just to remind him of the original intention and vision for his life. This man who had been embroiled by his position released the veil that kept him from himself. My calling him out had opened that possibility.

The dream was over, and I shook myself after writing it down. I wondered what it meant, and how it fit into the message I received yesterday. It brought up a related thought in the Bible... about the rich man going to heaven. In the English versions translated from Greek, the admonition is given that it is easier for a camel to go through the eye of a needle than for a rich man to go through the gates of heaven. However, in the original Aramaic, which was the language of Jesus, the translation states that it is easier for a rope to go through the eye of a needle than for a rich man to go through the gates of heaven, the implication being that if a rope is reduced to its simplest strand, it can pass through the eye. However, it cannot get through while it is in an inflated state because it is encumbered by accumulation.

Somehow that tied into the dream, and I vowed to get a copy of the Lamsa Bible which was the Aramaic translation that more accurately reflected what the New Testament actually stated. I thought there might be other important differences in translation that I would need later.

From years past, I became aware of synchronicity, the act of meaningful coincidence. The eminent Swiss psychiatrist, Carl Jung, had done a lot of work in the field, as had others, and I found that coincidence meant "coinciding events that brought an important moment together." Those meaningful coincidences were never to be discarded, for they contained valuable clues to the future.

After dressing, I decided my first stop would be Wisdom Books. The store was located in an old house on the peninsula and it had an air of magic about it. I was friends with the owner and had actually participated in its creation fifteen years before. Now, I worked there on Sundays as part of my service to others. I often bought more books than I made in salary, but it was worth it. For me, this was a place of meaningful coincidence.

As I walked up the steps and opened the door, I was greeted by my friend Matthew, the store's owner. "Matt, what books do you have on the Holy Grail?" I asked, never being one for beating around the bush.

He looked at me strangely and asked why I was curious. "Because I had a message in my meditation yesterday that I was supposed to find the Holy Grail."

"That's funny, you're the third person this morning to come in and ask the same question!"

He got up and walked to a section in the store that had books related to myth and King Arthur. "Too bad, they bought what I had, but let's see what we can find." As he rummaged through the shelves, I thought about our used book room and said Iíd go back there. Wondering why others had also gotten the message, I was more curious than ever to find the meaning of the directive. Poking amidst the used books, I could find nothing, and he came around, shaking his head. "No luck, but I'll have more books coming in within the week. I'll place an order today."

Disappointed, I thought how, in the past, I never seemed to find what I needed through a class, or in books alone. It was as though I had to find truth through the clues life presented. Once during the '70s, when having a spiritual teacher was especially popular, the Inner Presence told me that I was not to attach myself to one view only, because Life was my teacher. I laughed as I recalled this and shared it with Matt, who was not only a great resource, but a good friend.

"Well, Matt, what do you know about the Holy Grail? How would you define it?"

He thought for a moment. "It's actually quite complex, but what it boils down to is that each of us is a Grail, and the quest for the Holy Grail is a search for unity and wholeness within ourselves. It goes way beyond the Arthurian legends and can be traced back to Hermetic philosophy."

What he told me intrigued me. I thought about a poster I had on a door in my study. It was of Hermes, the Ancient Egyptian personification of wisdom. Now I was feeling excited, for I was looking at clues and needed to put them together. I spent a little more time in the store, looking through some dictionaries of symbols, jotting down notes, and then I left.

At home I looked at the poster. Inscribed on it was, "The supreme mind – being light and life, fashioned a glorious universal man in its own image. A man of earth and a man of heaven, dwelling in the light of God. Understand, O Hermes, and meditate deeply upon the mystery. That, which in you sees and hears, is not of the world, but is the mind of God, incarnate... Divine Light dwells in the midst of mortal darkness, and ignorance cannot divide them. Learn deeply of the mind and its mystery, for therein lies the secret of eternal life!"

The poster went on to tell of Hermes' writing which personified universal wisdom with sacred eloquence. That wisdom was dormant for ages, but was now stirring in the hearts and minds of the people of the world as a spiritual awakening was taking place. The Great Pyramid, which was a symbol of eternity, was said to be dedicated to this new humanity.

Here was an ancient writer who saw the human being as potentially divine, and that the key to that divinity was within the mind. It wasn't a lot, but that gave me a piece that might fit into a larger puzzle later.

I looked at my notes from the bookstore. The dictionary of symbols had information about the Grail. It originated from pre-Christian religions and was later translated within Christianity as the vessel for the holy sacraments.

It was interesting to note that Carl Jung regarded the Grail as symbolizing the inner wholeness for which humans have always been searching. He felt it was difficult to achieve this state because people were more caught in the material pursuit, than in the inner pursuit, and often missed the opportunity for insight.

I was particularly taken by his idea that the 'quest for the inaccessible Grail symbolized the spiritual risks and demands of the interior life, which alone can open the Gates of the heavenly space where the divine chalice stands in the light of its own radiance.' The prize to be found for each individual would be a fundamental transformation of heart and soul.

Here again was reference to light, as in the paragraph written about Hermes. They were saying the same thing in different ways.

I had two clues that involved methods to finding our inner light. For now, I would have to let that be enough. There was more work to do on the newsletter.

Chapter 2
❧ The Labyrinth ❧

The next morning, as I worked on the newsletter, the phone rang. It was my friend Luke, who had been a priest in the Catholic Church for 17 years before recognizing that he had a different path to take. We talked about our upcoming plans for a walk on the Labyrinth at Grace Cathedral in San Francisco. The Labyrinth is a sacred geometrical pattern found on the floor of Chartres Cathedral in France, and copied for use by pilgrims in the United States.

Luke had been a customer at the bookstore for years, and the way he and I became friends was another coincidental occurrence. I read an article about the Labyrinth in San Francisco a couple of years before and felt immediate excitement, sensing this was something I had to learn more about. The Labyrinth is a circle about forty feet in diameter, with a path that leads through a maze-like pattern to a central space that looks like a flower. The six petals, or stations in the center, represent the inner portion of oneself.

I remembered that Luke had talked about the Labyrinth once when he came into the store, so I called him to find out more information. When I expressed interest in walking on it, he offered to take me. That was the beginning of a special friendship that involved pilgrimages to Grace Cathedral, and beyond.

I recalled our first venture to the Labyrinth. It was a Monday morning when Luke came to pick me up, and as we were pulling out of my driveway, he commented that he wished we had asked our mutual friend Helen to join us. "Why not try now?" I said, and jumped out of the car to call her.

Helen was a wonderful friend who worked spiritually with people to help ease their suffering. She was a minister and a clairvoyant who had helped many. She was also a lot of fun.

As the phone rang, I thought if it was right that she join us, she would be there.

"Hello? I heard Helen say.

"Helen, it's me. What are you doing right now? I asked.

"Well, nothing really. Why?"

"How would you like to go with Luke and me on an adventure for the day?"

She paused and then said she'd be delighted. "When must I be ready?"

"Now! We are nearing your street."

"Oh, my," she said. "Give me 10 minutes."

We circled the block a few times and then picked her up. We gave her only cryptic details of what our adventure entailed.

We drove up the Peninsula to San Francisco in perfect weather. The rain had finally cleared from the past two weeks storms. The sky was crystal blue, as only it could be in northern California. I remember thinking that I could always tell when our football team, the 49ers were playing at home. The sky was a color here that it wasn't in other cities, and you could actually see the difference on the television.

When we arrived at Grace Cathedral, a parking space miraculously appeared so that we only had to walk a short distance to the main entrance of the Cathedral. Stairs were not always easy for Helen, as she had a troublesome case of arthritis. As we walked into the vestibule of the church, we could see the Labyrinth lying in repose, beautifully placed behind the pews. It fit perfectly in the space provided. We walked through the magnificent cathedral and found places to spend alone with our thoughts and prayers, preparing for the experience of the Labyrinth.

In reading about it, I learned that the Labyrinth was an ancient tool for finding oneself. It contained a vibrational field that emerged through walking the geometric pattern. Different than a maze, there was only one way to go into the center of the Labyrinth and one way to come out. The path was clearly defined on the purple and gray carpet that lay on the floor of the Cathedral, and individuals had reported many different reactions when walking on it, from deep insight to euphoria, depression and anxiety, deferred understanding, tears, laughter, joy, sorrow and bliss. People moved at varying paces. Some were slow and reflective, others quick and purposeful, a few dancing and swaying. There was no right or wrong way to engage in the process.

We wanted to prepare ourselves for a sacrament. As we saw it, the Labyrinth is truly a sacred reminder from the ancients to remember who we are. After our individual prayer time, we approached the Labyrinth as we felt moved to walk it. Without shoes, the texture of the carpet was evident, and as I walked the first time, I felt the presence of calm and connection in the face of a much larger unfolding mystery we call life, and was awed by the forces we don't understand, that affect us in spite of our ignorance.

As we completed the process, we took time to sit and digest what we'd received. Leaving the Cathedral, we had lunch at a wonderful place on the ocean's edge. It seemed fitting to end the walk with a ceremonial luncheon and good conversation. Each of us had been deepened and had questions answered. Helen felt she had lost her way, because she became disoriented in the process of walking the Labyrinth, and Luke told her this happened sometimes when people release themselves to the process. We drove back on the coastal route, and the water reflected in places like a jewel twinkling in the sunlight. Thus began our monthly adventures to the Labyrinth as a threesome.

Returning to the present, Luke and I confirmed our arrangements for a trip to the Cathedral the following Monday, I decided it would be wise to go back over my notes from each of our previous walks to see if there were further clues related to the Holy Grail. I had a habit of writing down whatever was presented after walking on the Labyrinth, and in pulling out the calendar from the past year, I thumbed through each month since we started our journey. There in my November notes was inscribed, *You must uphold the sacred in a profane world… not exclude humor, or take yourself so seriously.*

The Cathedral had stained glass windows, and in the first few panels were also embedded words that would leap out to me and make a phrase as I put the disconnected pieces together. *Nations among freedom employ love.* In the last entry from January, I received *Maintain after the Rapture.* I wasn't able to see how these applied to the present directive, but knew from past experience that things had a way of tying together, so no clue was ever wasted.

The phone rang. One of my subscribers was calling to see if I'd completed the newsletter. I told her I'd gotten momentarily sidetracked, but I would get it out before spring was over.

She paused for a moment and then continued. "You know, this newsletter means a lot to people. I don't know if you really are aware how much the ideas contribute to their lives, and I just want you to know that. You really are a vessel of light."

I thanked her and chuckled aloud. "Yes, and a reluctant one at that!" She said a few more encouraging words and we hung up. I thought about how well meaning people were, but sometimes the pressure caught me in a rebellious space that didn't want the responsibility for making things clear and lighter for others. Yet, as I thought about it, what was the idea behind the Holy Grail? In fact, weren't those words "a vessel of light" something I'd read in conjunction to it? Was this a coincidence? ...Synchronicity in front of our faces all the time, we just need to pay attention?

As I rummaged through my notes for some of the articles, I found a notice for a lecture later in the week, titled *After The Rapture,* to be held at a local bookstore. Another tie-in, this time to my Labyrinth experience. I jotted down the details on my calendar and made a mental note to be there. The newsletter was shaping up, and as the afternoon was winding down, I decided to go for a walk.

Walking was a wonderful way of clearing the cob-webs. It revitalized and renewed me, and I enjoyed the seasonal variety of trees and flowers in my area. It was also a way of distilling thought. Taking the time to move my body and allow my mind to follow, instead of the other way around, gave a different per-spective. There seemed to be partnership that wasn't always evident, especially since I spent so much time in front of my computer. A walk of two or three miles gave me just what I needed.

The next day, I had brunch with my friend John, who'd been in my dream a couple of nights before. Aside from being a brilliant software engineer, he was an accomplished musician, artist/photographer, gourmet cook, and had a keen interest in religion.

John had done a lot of inner work, trying to recon-cile his fundamentalist Christian roots with an emerg-ing awareness of unity through Buddhism and other mystical traditions.

After a delicious meal of crab soufflé and chilled melon, I told him about my exploration of the Holy Grail, and asked what he knew about it. He went over to one of the bookshelves housing some rare editions of ancient manuscripts, and thumbed through several until he found what he thought might interest me.

"Here's something you might be able to use. Looks like there is a tie to not only Hermetic tradition, but shades of the Grail in India, China and Ethiopia. In fact, it says that the Grail, as it moved through the ages, became adapted to Christianity and was the underpinning of the Knights Templar. Interestingly enough, they were organized in approximately 1111 and were later hunted down, disbanded and were found amidst the Gnostics."

John handed me the book, and as I read, I thought the correspondences were really intriguing. There were tie-ins to the Ark of the Covenant and a physical Grail that may have ended in Ethiopia. The date 1111 seemed somehow timely, what with so much recent interest in 11:11. What I thought would be an intriguing little hunt seemed to have become a multi-pronged search.

I had heard of the Gnostics and the Knights Templar, but had no idea what they were. The Ark of the Covenant had also floated around in various things I read, but I knew very little about what that really meant either. 11:11 was a phenomenon that had begun to occur when digital clocks became popular, and I knew there was significance related to timing and an awakening it supposedly represented. Could it have something to do with the Grail? I didn't know.

After brunch, I went to the bookstore for the Sunday shift. This was my place of repose, one of my sacred spaces. Everyone who came into the store commented on the feeling of its being a place of renewal in the midst of chaos... a sanctuary in an ocean of activity. I agreed. Often there were serendipitous meetings or gatherings with interesting people who happened to converge at the same time. We'd had many a glorious discussion group that developed spontaneously, and in review, I acknowledged how many of my friends I'd met through the store.

I thought perhaps someone would come in who had more knowledge about the Grail. At this point, I was thoroughly engaged because it was like a detective story. I was looking forward to what the next clue might be. The day went along without much activity, and I became engrossed in some of my regular chores. The phone rang, and it was one of our customers who called periodically with interesting bits of information related to where the world was going. I told him about my quest and he said I ought to check it out on the Internet. Of course! Why didn't I think of that? I finished up the day and headed for home, eager to get on the World Wide Web.

As I typed in my password, I wondered if there was a forum I hadn't seen about the Grail. Scrolling through the various offerings in a Metaphysical section, there it was, *The Grail Quest*, with about 49 messages. How strange we are, I thought. We only see what we want to see, and as many times as I'd logged on to the forums, I'd never noticed that one.

Starting at the top, there were interesting messages... some reiterating what I'd already found, but one in particular intrigued me. Someone referred to a book tying the Labyrinth to the Grail, only available to members of a secret society. How fascinating, especially since I was planning to go with my friends to walk it the next day.

After checking out what was available, I left my own message asking for any information that would add to what I already knew, and then moved over to the section on Labyrinths, where I left a general message asking if anyone knew about the connection between the two. There were enough authorities in the field who checked in. Someone was bound to know something.

That night I had another dream. In it I saw a vision of a cup outside my window. It was resting in midair, and was the form of a Silver Chalice. At first I didn't give it much attention, but realized that I must look carefully, because it wouldn't always be there. As I viewed it in the dream, I became filled with light, to the point where I knew I could fly, and gradually I lifted off the ground and moved gracefully around the room, doing somersaults in the air and swooping down between the furniture, never hitting anything. Gently, I landed on my feet and I knew that I could do this at will as long as I remembered the message of the Grail.

In the dream, there was another person doing yoga, who was rolled up like a pretzel on a bed. She was so intent in her practice that she didn't see the Chalice, for she was facing the wall. I sensed I didn't have to be involved in a complex process, for through the Grail, I would gain everything I needed.

Waking, I jotted down my perception of the dream. It seemed to clearly indicate that when I looked at the Chalice and concentrated on its content, I was transformed into something no longer earthbound. It was on the other side of the window, signifying to me that it was not in the same realm as I was. Therefore, I couldn't find it in physical reality, but there was a window that would allow me to view it, if I would look.

Also, I had to be aware of when it was there, for it wasn't always evident. This implied the need to pay attention to my intuition, which is the bridge between the two worlds. The scene with the person doing yoga on the bed seemed to indicate that we have to be careful not to get lulled by the various disciplines we are involved with to the point of missing opportunities that are presented through a different view.

At 10 o'clock Luke arrived. We picked up Helen and then headed for San Francisco. It was May, when the weather would alternate between hot and cool. Weather could be 80 degrees on the peninsula, while the city was blanketed in fog, driving the temperature down to the high '50s or low '60s, so in summer, going to San Francisco always required taking a jacket, just in case.

This day was no exception. As we drove north, the fog crept over the coastal mountains, significantly cooling everything. Downtown San Francisco was immune to dense fog for the most part, and as we climbed Nob Hill, the weather was glorious with the fresh blue sky I'd come to associate with the city. Again, we found a parking space close to the entrance of the church and proceeded in our normal fashion to ready ourselves for the Labyrinth experience.

Helen and Luke walked first this time. I felt the need to walk later, as something was bubbling under the surface, and I looked up at the stained glass windows. Open to Light's Radiance, streamed down upon me and I jotted it on a small notepad so I wouldn't forget. As my friends completed the Labyrinth, so did others who had been walking it. I moved forward and took my shoes off as requested, and placed each foot upon the path for another round of insight.

As I walked, I held the Holy Grail within my consciousness, open to whatever it might want me to know, and as I moved thoughtfully along the path, I had the insight that I needed to clear the way... to make of myself a perfected vessel and attune to the light that was presenting itself on earth now. This was not a request, it was a mandate, and I was being told to refine my ways, as it was a requirement for the continuance of life. Some were called to act as forerunners, but what was given would apply to all life and would become more evident as the new millennium unfolded.

I felt responsibility for what I'd heard and sat afterward in quiet contemplation, trying to digest the implications, and then sought out Helen and Luke who were ready to make our customary browse through the church gift shop.

"Well," Luke asked, "did you get an insight?"

"More than I wanted. How about you?" He nodded. "Mm-hum. Helen did, too."

She looked at me seriously. "They aren't fooling around anymore," she said. "We don't have time."

I knew what she meant. This was a very different feeling from our past visits, and from the response of my two friends, each of us was being pushed to make adjustments in our lives that would allow for attunement to something greater.

"Well, I certainly didn't expect this." Luke shook his head in wonder. None of us were novices in the presence of Spirit, each having our share of experiences, and tests of faith. The intensity of this time period had come upon us suddenly, however, and I don't think any of us was prepared for the urgency of the directives we were given.

"What did you get, Luke?" I asked.

"Well, I'm told that I must change my patterns of eating. As I perceived the message, I have to eat food that is consciously cultivated."

Helen chuckled. "Yes, they told me that, too. In addition, I have to stop smoking, because it's blocking

my metabolism and interfering with the proper function of my liver."

Helen was of an age where cigarettes had been the
"in" thing to do. It was a pastime that she thoroughly
enjoyed and had tried repeatedly to give up because
of pressure from her family and younger friends.
Now, she seemed to have a different perspective, and
was quiet as she reflected upon the full meaning of
this directive for her.

Luke was equally still. He loved good food and at
times tended to binge on his favorite "goodies." Now
he was being directed to be aware of his eating habits,
and to eat only what was raised consciously.

"Well," I said to them both, "if I'm supposed to be
open to the light now available, I assume what you've
been told applies to me as well." They both nodded.
We were all quiet. As we drove out of the city towards
the coastal route, fog covered the entire road.

"I think we'll take 280," Luke said. "We can't see
anything on the coast route today."

We came back to the Peninsula, and stopped at a
favorite outdoor restaurant, since the weather was
warm and the food was generally well-prepared and
top quality.

"What do you make of it all," I asked?

Helen, who had been especially quiet, spoke. "I see
this as an absolute directive. I've known that something big was happening behind the scenes, I've had
the feeling in my readings and in my meditation. I've
been agitated and unable to sleep, and felt as though I
was revved up at a high rate of speed. It's been uncomfortable because something is in the process of
shifting. It's as though it's happening, and somebody

forgot to tell us so that we'd have enough time to pack all our belongings in leisure. Now, we're given 24-hours notice. Do you know what I mean?"

We did. Both of us had also noticed that things seemed to be speeding up, and I had even commented at an earlier get together that we all knew things were going to heat up in the '90s, but nobody knew how fast it was going to happen. Now we were in the midst of it.

In the early '90s we were still crossing the threshold, but by the end of the decade, everything began to move much faster. We had been preparing for the long-awaited shift of the ages. It seemed intriguing in the past as we used to speak of it, but now it was urgent and uncomfortable, for the immanence of change was upon us.

"So, what are you both going to do," I asked?

They looked at me and answered simultaneously, "What we've been told!"

Luke added. "I'm going to do it because I know it's right, and when I got the insight, I could see the purpose for the directive. It isn't something unreasonable. I saw the whole food chain and the compromises that we are making in relation to it. There is no communion and no dignity. The plants and animals are being treated like non-entities. They are merely numbers in some game of accounting.

"There is indifference to them as living creatures, and they are being housed in pathetic conditions. We are eating animals that have been raised on fear and antibiotics!

"Vegetables from commercial farms are raised in the same framework of chemicals and pesticides, so we are eating produce that looks bigger, but has very little vitamin content in relation to the vegetables raised without artificial fertilizer. It's no small wonder there are more cancers and immune-deficiency diseases. We are slowly destroying ourselves through our indifference to our food sources."

Luke was not one to go on about things at this length, as he was a pretty practical individual. Obviously, something had touched him deeply and made an indelible impression. No one said anything for a while, and when the waiter came to ask what we'd like, we all ordered organic greens.

Helen commented about the body being a temple. "I know now why I'm being asked to stop smoking. I could see how the cigarettes are interfering with the natural repair process in my body. It is constantly stressed; having to work overtime to try to rid the toxins I keep sucking in. I never saw that before. It's as though my body is this wonderful being that's trying so hard to support me, and I'm unconsciously putting something in it that is keeping it from doing its job. Things are beginning to break down, and it doesn't have the reserves to keep up with the demand. For God's sake, I just never realized what I was doing!"

She shook her head and looked down at her hands. "I think it's part of what's contributed to the arthritis. That and coffee. I could actually see how the things that I put into my mouth were being absorbed by my body. It wasn't a pretty picture, I'll tell you! Oh, my." Again, she lapsed into quiet and it was my turn to speak.

"You know, when I got that I need to be a clear vessel, I could see myself as a cup, and I could see the importance of the quality of my choices. Things I take for granted like water and air are important. A vision of how much we compromise ecologically came home to me as it did to both of you. It was as though the contaminants keep us from being tuned to something that is important. Part of this has to do with refinement. I am just not quite sure about all the details."

After lunch, Luke dropped us off. There were calls waiting for me on the answering machine, but I felt I needed the rest of the afternoon to myself. I was tired, and wanted to close my eyes for a few moments before I tackled anything. Reflecting on the past week, it seemed that an awful lot of information was coming in with a strong sense of urgency. I wondered why. Slowly, I let go of my thoughts and drifted into sleep.

Dreaming, I found myself confronted by two cups. One was leaden in color and the other was brilliant silver. As I moved closer, the leaden one seemed lifeless and austere. Its contents were murky. The other, of brilliant silver, resonated a tone that was reminiscent of sounds I'd heard when certain bells were played in cathedrals. It was beautiful, melodic and inviting.

Also, a radiant light shone from it that seemed to have no source. It was very bright, yet comforting, and a clear liquid streamed over the sides, positively affecting everything it touched. The leaden cup was isolated, however. It was unable to benefit from the other cup's presence because it had been weakened by its contents and it couldn't be attuned.

Chapter 3
❧ *After The Rapture* ❧

The phone rang and awakened me. Wondering if it was morning, I groped my hand toward the receiver and mumbled into the telephone. It was my friend, Michele.

"Do you remember that there is a lecture tomorrow evening at the Metaphysical Bookstore?" she said. I had been so overwhelmed with everything else that I had forgotten.

"Let's go together. Would you like dinner before?" she continued, and we agreed to meet at one of our favorite little midtown restaurants, then go to hear the lecture *After the Rapture*.

Life was not letting me off the hook. Things were moving at a dizzying pace, so I decided to get a notebook that would be used specifically for jotting down the coinciding events and messages I was receiving. I found one that would serve the purpose, and gathered the bits and pieces of information I had accumulated related to this search.

• The meditation in which I was told to *find the Holy Grail.*

• Reminding someone in my dream to remember who they really were.

• The importance of translation; to get a Lamsa Bible.

• Grail and Hermetic philosophy.

• Grail and Gnosticism, Templars.

- Grail and the Ark of the Covenant.
- Grail and 11:11.

Directives at the Labyrinth, including the following in the order received:

1. Uphold the Sacred in a profane world.
2. Do not exclude humor, or take yourself too seriously.
3. Nations among freedom employ love.
4. Maintain after the Rapture.
5. Open to Light's Radiance.
6. Clear the way.
7. Make of Self a perfected vessel.
8. Attune to the Light presenting itself to earth now.
9. Eat consciously.

Now I had something to use as a base for confirming and adding to the body of knowledge I was gaining through this process.

The next evening, I met Michele at the restaurant, and we fell into easy conversation over dinner. She spoke of events she'd been involved with since our last get-together and gave me a copy of her latest newsletter. With Michele, I could share everything. We had similar experiences and a lot in common, although she was born in France and I in America.

She could recall great texture in her formative years, and then, having come to this country before World War II, she was in a unique position to blend the best of both worlds during the vital time of repair and growth that followed the war.

Having a flair for writing, she landed a job in New

York as an editor, became an accomplished author with several books to her credit, and developed a passion for philosophical pursuits. We shared many similar paths from the past that contributed to our present level of awareness. We both edited small newsletters, and had our own following in the teachings we shared with others.

Michele was a prime example of equality in friendship. We respected and admired one another and were able to talk about things that we couldn't express with many others. We were peers, even though we had a considerable age difference. I found it amazing that when individuals were kindred spirits, age had no meaning. My older and younger friends of that caliber were all one – no age, no gender, no separation based on anything other than the quality of our interactions. We were at home and had found aspects of ourselves reflected back to us in one another. These were people who were part of our soul families. I was grateful for them, as they made my journey through life a little sweeter.

Dinner over, we proceeded to the bookstore where the lecture was being given by a man named Roland Ivory. I was intrigued about him based on the title of his talk, *After The Rapture*, which matched what I received at the Labyrinth. As we approached, we could see that others were also interested in the subject. There was already a huge line of people waiting for tickets.

"My goodness, I thought we'd be early," I murmured.

Michele laughed. "Well, it looks as though we're not the only ones who want to hear what Mr. Ivory has to offer. I'd say that is a pretty good indication that something is going on, wouldn't you?"

She was right. The Bay Area often had a unique role in presenting the next step of unfoldment in whatever way was important for the future. We were on the brink of a new focus as we spoke. We nodded to other people we knew who were there, and one of the regulars to the lecture series came over. He was a transplanted Englishman from the Philippines, who had arrived in California during the heyday of the '60s. Paul knew everything that was going on, and tended to dwell on conspiracy theories and ideas.

"Did you know that the government is involved in secret testing of high frequency sound waves in Alaska?"

He didn't even wait for hellos. "This is very disturbing because it's affecting the ozone layer and the atmosphere. It's interfering with animal migration and damaging people's health."

He glowered and shook his head. I jokingly referred to him as Chief Thunder Cloud, but often he wasn't far wrong about things that were happening.

"I hope this evening isn't going to be about that," I said.

"No, not really. But Ivory is aware of it. It's having an effect on things."

Someone else who Paul recognized joined the line, and he was off to spread his concerns there.

"You know, it's very sad that this man dwells on what is wrong. It obviously causes him a great deal of suffering." Michele had compassion for him. "Did he go through the war?" she asked.

"Yes," I nodded, "I believe he was in a prisoner of

war camp in the Pacific during the latter part of World War II. He's that age."

"Well, that explains a great deal," said Michele. "You can look at people and often find that they are riveted by the events that occurred in the beginning of their lives. They tend to replay similar scenarios over and over again regardless of present circumstances."

The line moved forward as the room opened for the lecture. We paid for our tickets and inched towards the front, finding two seats in good position to see the lectern. Soon the room was filled, and as the clock struck eight o'clock, our speaker emerged from a side door, dressed casually in dark slacks and a loose fitting shirt. He had long brown/silver hair, a mustache, and compelling green eyes. He also had a smile that would disarm anyone. As he spoke, I recognized that this was someone I wanted to know.

His lecture centered around the changes that we were experiencing on Earth and how they tied in to the so called "end times" mentioned in many places, the Bible being one of them. I took some notes.

1. The *Rapture* was both a time and a process that individuals could choose to be part of through the preparation within their bodies, minds and spirits of attuning to higher vibrations.

2. There were tones and codes that would affect subtle body centers.

3. There were individuals who had been pre-encoded with the information so that there would be "trigger" events, or elements that would cause those people to remember who they really were and why they were here.

Some of those triggers were fairly simple, such as the digital clock reading of 11:11. People would respond to that number combination and wonder where they had seen it before or what it meant to them. From that point, other elements would become apparent. There would be more synchronistic events in the lives of those people, including:

• meaningful coincidences.

• fortuitous encounters.

• a sense of urgency about preparing for some event that was yet to come.

I could agree to much of what he said, having just experienced the sense of urgency with Helen and Luke. Also, since the early '80s when I'd gotten my digital clock, I always seemed to look at it when it was 11:11. It happened too often to be coincidental, and I found the number combination fascinating.

I remember asking people if they had that experience also. Some just looked at me blankly, but there were people who also noticed it, and a chance encounter in the bookstore with a flyer that asked the very question, "Are you aware of 11:11?" made me jump when I saw it. Perhaps there was something significant to it after all.

In calling the number posted, I found that it was a group whose ideas did not coincide with mine, but I was grateful to know others had also been impacted. Now Ivory was confirming the purpose for that 'contact.'

Meaningful coincidences were a constant in my life. Things were often synchronistic. Earlier in the day, I had two calls, and when talking with the first individual about my newsletter, I related the directive to find the Holy Grail, and she asked me if I'd seen the latest issue of Ariadne's Web, a quarterly magazine. She said the entire issue was dedicated to the Grail. That gave me insight as to why the two other people had gone to the bookstore searching for information about the Grail.

Later in the day, I received a call from a former colleague and mentioned to him the same directive. He said it was quite coincidental that he'd just been watching a show on the Knights Templar, and in the last episode of the investigation the focus was on the Holy Grail and its implication in relation to Jesus and Mary Magdalene. In this hypothesis, she was thought to be the Grail, and supposedly had children who transmitted the lineage of Jesus throughout history. It was to the heirs of that union that the Templars were bound to serve and protect. Because of their views, they were hunted by the orthodox church and driven underground, later to be found amidst the Gnostics, another outlawed religious group. He said he'd made a copy of the show and would loan it to me. I was curious to see it, because the implication was quite mind-boggling!

These were affirmations to me, signals that I was on the right track. I didn't yet know how Roland Ivory's lecture fit in to the whole scenario, but I'd find out when the timing was right. At this point, I was just gathering my clues. This would go into my notebook tonight with the rest.

After the lecture, people milled around Ivory during the book signing and asked more questions. The book, *After The Rapture*, presented in greater detail what he had discussed in the lecture. It looked like it would be worth owning, so I picked up a copy and waited for my turn to meet him. As we moved closer to the front of the line, I had an uncanny feeling that something of major significance was about to occur.

The man in front of us suddenly became quite agitated and launched into a tirade against aspects of Ivory's lecture. The author tried to reason with the man, who seemed to grow more and more belligerent. In one hair-raising second, the man raised his fist to assault Ivory, and with equal speed, Ivory placed his hand in a way that blocked the thrusting fist, and intoned a sound that made the man stand frozen for what seemed like eternity.

Everyone was stunned, and after the silence, the man seemed dazed and mumbled some apology. He was escorted out of the store after Ivory told the manager he did not want to involve the authorities. He closed his eyes for a moment and a pale light emanated from him. Then, it was as though nothing had happened. He sat down at the table where he had been signing books and looked up at me, fully recovered.

"How did you do that?" I asked.

"Ancient method for deflecting hostility. Works like a charm." He laughed and discarded the event as one of the things that happens when revolutionary information is presented.

I asked if he had workshops, and he looked at me thoughtfully.

"Yes, I do. But I have a hunch that you need to come down to New Mexico where I live. I'm going to have a gathering with a few selected people. I think you are one of them."

I was momentarily taken aback, but as I looked into his eyes, the intensity of connection to a much deeper purpose awakened remembrance in me. Instead of rejecting the invitation, I agreed that he was right. We exchanged phone numbers, and he wrote a few words in the book I'd handed him. After I paid for my purchase, Michele and I headed back to the car. She was reflective after the events, and I could tell she had something on her mind.

"You need to go there," she said quietly. "There is something very important waiting for you in New Mexico, and Roland Ivory is a missing piece to a much larger puzzle."

Chapter 4
❧ The New Mexico Connection ❧

I sat looking out the window of the 737 as we made our way to Albuquerque. The weather was gorgeous, and I marveled at the events that led to my departure. Everyone who knew me was amazed that I'd willingly agreed to this adventure. Physical traveling was not my favorite pastime. I much preferred mental trips!

Roland Ivory called the next afternoon following his lecture. He asked me if I'd read the inscription in the book he signed, and I realized I had not. Turning the front cover, there inscribed were the words, *'In light and remembrance of the Grail!'*

For a moment I was speechless.

"How did you know? Who are you?"

He chuckled. His voice was deep and melodious. "I recognized you the moment I looked up. You sent your defense ahead, and after the assault came grace."

"What are you talking about?" I asked. "Did you think that man had anything to do with me?"

He sighed. "Yes. He was your attempt to block the energy. You weren't consciously aware of what you were doing, but didn't you have a feeling prior to the outburst that something extraordinary was about to occur?"

Thinking back, I remembered feeling a sense of expectation. "Yes. I did," I said.

He continued. "In that split second you tapped

into a birth memory, and just as quickly, you tried to deflect it."

"Why would I do that?" I asked.

"Because you knew that the connection we were about to make would change your life forever, and you were afraid. Don't worry. I'm not blaming you for what happened, I'm just making you aware of the potency of your thoughts."

Roland told me that there were 144,000 fragments of what he called the Living Light incarnated on earth. He said each had to find links to the others and that once each and every fragment was ignited, a new template would be put in place for humanity. He believed he was one of those fragments and that I was, also. When we finished talking, I'd agreed to go to New Mexico, and spend seven days with the group he'd gathered, even though I had no logical idea what he was talking about.

I realized after we spoke that my entire body was vibrating, and there was an audible hum in my ears. I felt fully alive and filled with anticipation and excitement that I had only touched briefly before. It was as though I awakened to a distant memory that held promise of something I'd always yearned for, the feeling of home that had nothing to do with a physical location.

The stewardess came and asked each of us to put our seats in an upright position and make sure our seat belts were fastened. We were coming in to some clear air turbulence, not surprising over the mountain ranges. As we skirted the Grand Canyon, I was amazed at the depth of the crevices and the etchings like long tendrils that stretched for miles. The color was deep and rich, a shade of red that as a Californian I rarely saw.

We were suddenly buffeted by a series of sharp blasts that caused the aircraft to pitch and drop several hundred feet in a matter of seconds. I felt queasy and was becoming alarmed as the flight attendants ran to seats and lowered their heads. Several passengers shrieked as the storage lockers above them opened, sending coats and packages flying.

Nobody dared move, as we were in the grips of a force that shook us mercilessly. As suddenly as it came upon us, we passed through the clear air storm. The attendants moved to assist people, some noticeably shaken. Fortunately, there were no small children on this flight.

The pilot announced that we'd passed through a more severe version of what was a fairly common occurrence at this time of year over the mountains. He offered drinks for anyone who wanted them, and although I normally did not drink alcohol when flying, I made an exception on this trip. Looking down at the topography, I shuddered to think of us lost in that terrain. How would anyone ever be found, and would there be anything to find? The fragility of life loomed into focus. In an airplane, you become acutely aware of how little control you have over your life.

We landed in Albuquerque twenty minutes behind schedule, and as I walked through the airport toward the shuttle bus, I was moved by the openness and magnificent sculptures, rich in texture, portraying a distinctive feeling. This was the southwest, and it felt good.

The rental agency had the car I'd ordered.

Something was going right! When they brought it up,
I noted that it was silver with California license plates.
"That's quite a coincidence. How do you happen to
have California plates in New Mexico?" The attendant
told me that they had cars from all over the country.

I followed directions out of town to get to the
Interstate. I was heading northwest toward a little
town called Sulfur Springs, about 90 minutes from
Albuquerque. As I drove to the highway that would
take me north, I was overwhelmed with the expanse
and haunting beauty of this state. Two weeks ago, I
would never have believed I'd be driving in New
Mexico. Yet, here I was. How important it is for us
never to say never! At any moment, events can trigger
major alterations in our lives. An hour before, I was
facing potential disaster. Now I was approaching the
possibility of events that could change the way I
viewed life forever.

As I drove on the connecting highway, I passed
Indian Casinos that dotted the landscape. Going west,
I noted the mountain ranges, and as I got closer to the
turnoff, I had an uncanny feeling of coming home. The
narrow road toward Sulfur Springs meandered
through small towns and an Indian reservation, where
the soil changed dramatically to the red that I associated with Arizona. As I moved further up the valley,
cottonwood trees dotted the landscape near a slow-
moving river. I was amazed at the number of state
parks, one next to the other.

The little town of Sulfur Springs loomed ahead,
not much more than a few buildings on either side of
the road. I followed directions to the turnoff for
Ivory's house and climbed a dirt road that wove

round a series of mountainous curves. At one point I reached a plateau, and to my right was the smooth southwestern adobe wall with a heavy wooden gate I'd been told to look for. Beyond the gate lay a good-sized courtyard with a huge fountain dominating the center of the area.

As I parked the car, Roland emerged from the house. "Have a good flight?" He was almost smirking.

I looked at him, suddenly aware that the turbulence in the airplane may not have been the result of natural causes. "Did you do that?" I was not amused.

"No, of course not," he laughed. "You did!"

I felt agitated at the accusation and turned on him. "Look! I have enough issue traveling on airplanes without being accused of causing what I just went through. That was a dangerous situation!"

He became quiet and studied me seriously. "Yes, it was a dangerous situation. That's how much you wanted to avoid confronting this part of your journey. Fortunately, the greater part of you was not willing to cause harm to others. You did, however, cause them some discomfort."

As much as I wanted to leap to my defense, something deep inside said he was right. A part of me was resisting this experience, whatever it was going to be. I sat down on the steps and shook my head. "I never realized how powerful we are. I am so sorry."

He sat down next to me. "You don't need to apologize to me. You also need to know that you could not have caused that turbulence if the others had not been in agreement. If only one of them had held an equal, stabilizing vision, it wouldn't have happened. One light illumines the darkness. That's all that is needed.

So you had some powerful assistance in your attempt to disrupt this trip."

With that, he got up and offered his hand. "Come on. Let me show you around and where you'll be staying."

That evening I felt very self-conscious. The incident with the airplane dogged me, and I battled feelings of annoyance and negativity. The whole idea of coming to New Mexico had been a mistake. I was stiff at dinner, and I could feel that I was distancing myself from the other guests. Roland hardly paid attention to me, which only made me feel more isolated. It was almost like being an adolescent again, and I was annoyed at my own reactions and lack of self-control.

After dinner, I made excuses to go back to my room early, and Roland suggested that I spend the next day quietly to get adjusted to the altitude, which was about 7,000 feet. He said we'd meet in the early afternoon and get the agenda set for the gathering. All I wanted to do was go home. The thought of my own bed, my things, and my friends, made me feel almost panicky, because they were so far away. I tried to gather control of myself and meditate, but too much was swirling in my head.

I was staying in a small bungalow on the mountain side of the property that looked up to a hillside garden. There were places for outdoor meditation, paths for walking, and a marvelous herb garden. The smell of fresh basil and sage permeated my little dwelling, and I was glad for it. However, that night I slept fitfully.

When I got up in the morning, I found a tray outside my door filled with fresh fruit, rye toast, sweet butter, orange marmalade, Earl Grey tea and a small pitcher of cream. Coincidence? I wondered. This was similar to the breakfast I had every morning, including my favorite tea, and I only drank it with cream. How did he know I didn't drink coffee? The whole thing made me angry. Someone had psyched me out and clearly had the upper hand. All because of a stupid meditation where I was told to find the Holy Grail. Well, this was certainly not it!

After I ate everything edible on the tray, I showered and dressed. I took a few moments to gather my thoughts and to find a place of calm inside. Roland Ivory knew how to push my buttons, and the truth was that I wasn't used to anybody having an upper hand with me. I was generally the one that others turned to as the knower. Suddenly and unwittingly, I was the known.

A small digital clock next to the bed caught my eye... 11:11. Naturally! What else? As I felt myself revving up again in self-defense, I determined that if I was going to actually stay here for the seven day duration, I'd better make the most of it and get myself together. I could either indulge my limitations or reach up to a bigger possibility. I decided to extend my reach.

Sitting with myself, I reviewed the events that led me to this discomfort. Bottom line, I was engaged in a process with someone who had more knowledge and clearly had an idea of what this was about. I, on the other hand, was moving forward on blind faith, and the feeling of being out of control was very uncomfortable.

The major block to my forward movement and

inner peace was internal fear that overwhelmed me. I would have to utilize several techniques to bring myself out of this place of alienation and polarization. It was unpleasant and distressing, and I felt disconnected. Breathing deeply, I thought of unity. Inwardly, I saw myself relaxing and coming to more and more fullness. Gradually, through a combination of deep breathing and visualization, I felt calm, serene and poised. I was centered again.

Years ago, while going through group therapy, I remembered coming to a place where I was catapulted into a state of mental anguish and self-involvement. Everything became a psychological issue, and I analyzed things to death. My head became heavy as I dwelled on how everything revolved around me as the center of the universe. This period of alienation lasted about three months, and suddenly one day, I opted for a larger reality, getting off the subject of Me and moving back into We. That recognition freed me, and I returned to being a part of life, not its center.

There is nothing wrong with analysis, or coming to terms with issues that disable us. In fact, it is a necessary step in a journey toward wholeness. But the level of self-indulgence in the process has a tendency to cause isolation from the rest of the body...the rest of the system, and it is important to know when enough is enough. The very tight fixation with self closes the door to Self. When I recognized that during my process, and told the psychologist I would be leaving the group, he asked why. I told him I'd lost my spiritual center, but had regained it once again.

There was nothing for him to say. The period of analysis was finished.

At the present moment, I chose to zoom out and observe the larger picture so that I could find my part in it, rather than focusing on my viewpoint alone. When I was little and would come home from school with a grievance about what other people did to me, my mother would always ask what I had done to them. Her response used to be annoying, but it taught me to look at the whole picture in every situation, and contributed to diplomatic skills that served me well later.

Renewed, I decided to stroll through the herbal garden and take a walk on one of the hillside paths. The air was very dry, but the sky was blue and inviting. I stopped to look at the rows of herbs and marveled at the quality of growth in spite of the altitude. As I leaned down to touch the leaves of a particularly intriguing plant, a feminine voice came from behind. "They're lovely, aren't they?"

Turning, I noted a woman in her early thirties with flowing copper hair and sparkling eyes. She had alabaster skin that was almost luminous. "I'm Fiona," she said, extending her hand. I introduced myself, noting that she had an accent, and we began to chat about the garden.

"Do you live here?" I asked.

She smiled and shook her head. "Lord, no. I come for visits whenever I can. I live part time in New York and the rest in Ireland. I met Roland when I was in my late teens, and have loved him ever since."

I surmised that this meant they were a 'couple' and proceeded to ask about her interests. She told me of her involvement in ancient cultures. She was a filmmaker who had worked on a documentary project about the Celts, and developed a passion for their philosophy as a result. She belonged to a Celtic group in Ireland, and indicated that there was a great upsurge in interest of the Celts throughout the United Kingdom. I didn't know much about them, but had exposure to their resurgence in popularity because we had constant requests at the store for information about them.

Fiona told me it was the Celtic tradition that gave rise to the legend of King Arthur and the Knights of the Round Table. The Celts were very inclined toward the spirituality of earth and the feminine, with ties to Stonehenge and the Druids. Their tradition was deeply ritualistic and religious, but included groups that patriarchal religions excluded. The Celts continued the mystical traditions of their ancestors, and the tales they told were always of honor, for they forged heroes and heroines into archetypal or mythical figures, whom others could look to as ideals to follow.

Fiona turned and directed her attention to me. "Roland told me that you are one of us," she said.

The feeling of self-consciousness rose again, and I made a point to breathe deeply as I considered the implications of her statement. "I don't know,"I answered. "It's too soon for me to know anything. I've just begun a strange quest, and I'm still a little bit in shock about it all."

"You mean you're looking for the Grail?" Her tone was casual, as though she was talking about the weather.

"Yes. I am."I explained how I'd received the insight during meditation and that it led me on a journey that involved the labyrinth, the lecture, other things, and this.

"We were all called to the Grail in similar ways. It springs up within when you're ready. You must have done a lot of work on yourself prior to the insight, because the Grail doesn't summon you until you're spiritually prepared."

I thought that was somewhat elitist and said so. She responded candidly.

"Good Lord, no. This has nothing to do with snobbery. It is a calling. Once you are in pursuit of the Grail, your life changes forever, so you must have the spiritual underpinnings to provide stability for the journey. Dear woman, my comment was merely observation, for none of the Grail seekers are any better than anybody else. In fact, to someone else, this wouldn't even be of interest. We all have different roles to play in life."

We began walking, and I noted the trees were a different type of pine from the ones we had in California. They were smaller with bushier needles. But they were still pines, and the fragrance was one I truly loved. It always brought me back to special times during my childhood when I'd be in the mountains. Reflecting, I thought how much the sense of smell triggers response within us. It has an affect on the psyche and body for good or ill.

Fiona was quiet, and we enjoyed our surroundings. As she had a watch, she suggested it might be time to turn around so that we didn't miss the afternoon get-together.

One wing of Roland's U-shaped house was designed for workshops. There was a large area with comfortable chairs positioned in a semi-circle around a fireplace. One of the adobe walls had a huge marking board with an overhead screen that could be pulled down for videos. The room was spacious and angular, octagonal adobe tiles covering the floor, with southwestern area rugs placed strategically over them. A small kitchenette area at one end was suitable for drinks and snacks, with a bathroom around the corner.

There were large picture windows and thick wooden doors leading to a covered flagstone patio where chairs were arranged in a setting of beautiful clay pots filled with flowers and hanging air ferns. Vines crawled up the columns supporting the overhang, and I thought this was a perfect workshop area. I was beginning to feel at home.

It had been important for me to take the time to center myself before joining the group. Once long ago, I'd heard a popular Guru speak. She commented that people needed to take care of their personal issues prior to a workshop so that others didn't have to be responsible for them. She had cited an incident when at one of her retreats an individual came, upset because his girlfriend left him. He proceeded to smash his head against the wall in an act of frustration, and other people had to stop what they were doing to rush him to the hospital. Her point was that he had been so self-involved that he did not consider the rights of others at the conference. By indulging himself, he swept other people into his drama. She told him if he wanted a girlfriend so badly, he should just go to the relationship tree and pick another.

Now, in thinking about that incident and relating it to Roland's comment about the airplane, I wondered about the responsibility of each of those participants in the process. But then, you could peel the layers of the example endlessly. The bottom line was that we are each responsible for ourselves and our attitudes. Roland's vision must have been pretty darn clear, for I was intent on cleaning up my act before I set foot in his house again!

In addition to Fiona and myself, there were three other participants: A young man named Nathan who was a computer wizard from Massachusetts, an ageless artist from Taos by the name of Lillian, and Mark, a psychotherapist from Oregon.

Roland came in and sat quietly, looking steadily at each of us in turn. I was determined not to lose control or show surprise at anything he might say. Gradually, his gaze rested on me, or should I say in me. I looked into his eyes and was transported. My breath noticeably stopped, and I had to overcome the fear that welled up inside.

What was I afraid of? Determined, I made myself breathe deeply and hold his glance. As I did, I had the vision of a gatekeeper in my mind. The doors were thick with self-protection, and by allowing myself to ease into letting go, the wall and gate dissolved. I emerged in another space at another depth and then a wall appeared again. I was able to move through three stages of communion in his eyes, but when I reached the fourth, I had to turn away. I wasn't ready.

I could feel my body responding differently after our encounter. Everything was heightened; alive, expectant. My vision was clearer and I felt anticipation. The feeling was almost sexual, but far beyond what we think it to be. As I explored the sensation and allowed it to move through my body without judging it, I became aware of deep sobs coming from my left. Mark was holding his stomach and shaking, his body vibrating uncontrollably. Roland had touched a raw nerve, and Mark was coming unglued.

I didn't know if I should do anything to help him, but Roland motioned me to be still. He allowed Mark to continue the process and then made a series of sounds similar to the ones he'd done at the bookstore. Gradually, Mark became calm, and his breathing moved into a rhythmic pattern.

Roland completed his review of the group and sat quietly for a moment, closing his eyes as he'd done previously, and I could see light emanating from him once again. He smiled and bid us welcome. It was apparent that he had made an assessment about each one of us that we had yet to discover.

"So, how about each of you sharing the circumstances that brought you here," he suggested.

Fiona volunteered first, and said that she'd found references to the Grail in Celtic lore that propelled her to search for its source. She told of her meeting with Roland years ago through her parents and how they had a sense that someday they would do work together. I didn't get that this was necessarily a romantic relationship after all, and as she spoke, I thought of how limited our categories for one another were. We did not give latitude to relationships except in very narrow parameters, and our definitions for them tended to be black or white.

English, as a language, is perfectly structured to describe tangibles, but one must really work at it to convey feeling. The romance languages, such as

French, are filled with words that convey subtle differences for relationships. In English, the word love is a generic catchall. 'I love your hat.' 'I just love watching football.' 'I love chocolate cake.' 'I love you all.' 'I deeply love you.' It's no wonder that English is perplexing to foreigners.

Nathan expressed interest in finding correspondences through the field of quantum physics. He used computers to prove mathematical possibilities and had worked on a system that actually captured the life of a mathematical formula from onset to death. The company he worked for had been responsible for a video that presented the entire process that he planned to show us during the week.

He went on to say that the Grail represented dimensions of reality, and he was interested in finding how to prove that through a mathematical formula. Roland stopped him from going much further, as it was obviously a subject about which he could talk for hours.

I expressed my reason for being there and the odd coincidences that led me to search for the Holy Grail. The others nodded in recognition, for there were corresponding elements that marked their journeys as well.

Mark was quiet for a moment and then spoke eloquently about his background. He had come from a family in which he was the scapegoat. His punishment consisted of heavy abuse, and the result was that he spent a considerable part of his life trying to find his own healing through the process of his clients. At one point, he recognized that something inside him had "split" and discovered the need to find unity within himself.

He had experienced a mystical state after using a drug called Ecstasy, in which he saw a golden container that he thought was a chalice. For him, the words had come that he had to make peace with the Great Mother. Shortly after that, he had quite by accident gone to a lecture given by Roland. What he heard fascinated him, and he was committed to the journey.

Lillian was last to speak. She had a deep husky voice, and told of travels throughout the world that brought her to Taos. I was fascinated by her look. She was sixty something, and her face was deeply etched by time and exposure to the sun. Her raven colored hair was held up by hair sticks, and she dressed in classic southwestern garb. She was stunning, a little bawdy, and truly my idea of an uninhibited artist, rich with texture.

She told of her immersion in the Goddess culture when she was a child in the Roman Catholic church. Although they were told to pray to Jesus in school, her grandmother had a strong link to the Virgin Mary and would always tell her little granddaughter to ask the Blessed Mother for what she needed. This got her into a lot of trouble during her years in catholic school, for she was openly questioning and rebellious. She believed that Mary was the most powerful part of the church, even though her influence was hidden.

As Lillian traveled throughout the world, she found aspects of the suppressed feminine in other cultures. She became compelled to paint the Goddess figures, always through shadow or veiled, and had become quite well known for her efforts. She believed that woman and the Grail were one.

Roland thanked each of us and asked quietly, "Now, are you willing to do the work to reach the Grail?"

Chapter 5
❧ Rivers of Light ❧

As we entered the workshop area on the second day, we were welcomed by a beautiful Indian woman wearing a sari. With her hands clasped together, she bowed, intoning the sacred greeting, "Namasté" that recognizes the God in each of us. Light and grace radiated from her, as well as an unbelievable sense of inward peace and self-assuredness. This woman was, to my mind, the embodiment of the Feminine Principle.

As she glanced at each of us, her smile touched a responding chord within my own heart, and I felt bathed in her loving presence. She directed us to pillows on the floor, and as we settled down, she gracefully lifted one portion of her sari and seated herself in lotus position on a pillow facing us. I noted a ring on her toe and bracelets on her arms. It was obvious that she appreciated the decorative arts of the feminine.

She told us that she would guide us in a series of exercises designed to open the energy centers in our body, enabling us to be more receptive to subtle reality, and to help restore our bodies to full and vibrant health. These exercises were to be repeated every morning before our sessions with Roland. She said that there would be no talking after the initial explanation. She would show us by example, and we were to move in attunement to our own body rhythm through intuition, not logic.

We became quiet as she directed us to breathe. Filling the body with breath was essential to energize the cellular structure. Breath was our vehicle to life, and the correct use of it could open centers for heightened receptivity to subtle energy forces. Certain philosophies believed our biblical interpretation was in error, for their doctrines stated that, In the beginning was the Breath. Without breath, there was no life.

She directed us to focus on the movement of breath, to feel it in the various parts of our bodies. Too often, we breathed shallowly, not allowing ourselves the full benefit of oxygen as a healing and restorative gift. Breath, like everything else in our lives, was not to be taken for granted. The quality of our breath affected the quality of our life. Oxygen vitalized the bloodstream, and the bloodstream was the river of life. This was a hard concept for us as westerners to understand, because we had moved so far from the inner doctrines. Yet, in many parts of the world, working with the breath was an accepted part of daily living.

She then directed us in the use of sound. She explained that primal tones have a powerful effect on the body, and that through proper preparation with breath the body could become a tuning fork and benefit from the effects of sound vibration.

Finally, she spoke of color and its healing effect on the body. An individual in perfect health would emit a unique tonal quality. This sound corresponded to vibrant colors, radiating from the chakras or energy centers within the body. If any one center was out of alignment, it stressed the others and the tone and color were weakened as a result. Through visualization, color could be reintroduced.

The process she was teaching us, incorporating breath, sound and color, would restore the body to perfect alignment.

We were fortunate that the veil between east and west was falling. The benefits to both cultures through the health practices of the other were enormous. Here was one more example of the need to incorporate rather than deny, so that the emergence of a third, greater alternative could be born.

Our guide began intoning sound with the breath in a sequential pattern. Once we had developed a bellows effect within the body through sustained breathing techniques, it was able to act as a resonant chamber. She then introduced color to the sequence. Using appropriate tones with the sound of *'om'*, we brought the breath down to our root center first. We began visualizing colors of the rainbow sequentially that correlated to the different energy centers as we moved up the body. By the time we reached the top of our heads, we were a symphony of breath, tone, and color merging into a holy communion. I could feel the energy centers in my body bursting with light. It was not an unpleasant feeling, but it was unfamiliar. I was activating portions of myself that had rarely been used, and the sensation made me a little heady.

This process continued for approximately forty minutes, and by the time we were gently brought out of it, I was in a state of ecstasy. In Hindu terms, I was filled with Shakti, or Spirit. By our standards, I had experienced an altered state of consciousness.

The remarkable thing about this procedure was that it did not involve anything other than our own resources. Through a combination of breathing, sound and visualization, we were able to experience what I was sure in drug culture would have been considered the ultimate high. Yet, this cost nothing, and took no toll on the body. On the contrary, it renewed and replenished.

Our session completed, the beautiful lady rose and motioned us to form in a circle. Hands again pressed together, she looked at each one and bowed. We did the same. Then she moved gracefully out of the room.

Nathan was the first to speak. He was totally blown away by the quality of his experience and commented that he'd never had a high to equal it. Mark, who had explored the use of drugs, felt the caliber of this session was much more rewarding than anything he'd done before, and Lillian and Fiona just smiled.

Lillian interjected: "We have just been blessed by a very wise woman," and we all agreed. Roland entered quietly and sat down in one of the overstuffed chairs. He looked at us, nodded with pleasure, and spoke.

"I am glad you were each able to receive the gift of our guest. She is a remarkable being, and it was my good fortune to be able to extend this time with her to you."

Mark looked up from his private reverie and asked, "What is her name?"

"She is Sarasvati," said Roland.

"What does that mean in English?" asked Nathan.

Roland smiled. "Sarasvati means the Goddess of Wisdom."

After a very light lunch of organic mixed greens, we had two hours to ourselves before going to the next session. I decided to catch up on writing postcards, so I went into town. I asked at a local restaurant where I could get cards, and they referred me to the River Spa.

The River Spa looked like a nondescript building from the outside, but turned out to be a charming combination of unique gifts and bath house, offering mud, herbal, and sulfur baths, as well as massage and other wonderful natural opiates for the body. Looking at the clock, I realized I had enough time to enjoy one of them, and sensed the desire for a mineral/herbal plunge.

The dressing areas and accompanying baths were very modest, yet there was something cozy about the environment. I told the attendant how much time I had, and asked that she make sure I was out when I needed to be, so I wouldn't miss the afternoon session.

After the incredible morning, I didn't know if I would fall asleep or not. Everything had been so heightened. Colors were brighter, sound was clearer. My perceptions were sharper, and my body hummed. I still felt it. I was holding the "charge."

The water was ready and as I inched my way into the thick mineral bath with the scent of Eucalyptus embracing my nose, I felt incredibly fortunate. As I reviewed the trip, it was turning out to be a miracle, and all my initial fears and doubts were gone. By dealing with my issues in the beginning and not allowing them to intrude on others, I was able to make the best of what was offered.

With our human tendency toward sharing everything we feel, I saw the value of holding one's own counsel at times. Certain things are no one else's business, and sometimes there is a fine line between sharing and self-indulgence.

As I paid attention to my perceptions, I noted that one of the things evident to me in New Mexico was the solidity of the land. Coming from California, I never realized how much I was always prepared for earthquakes. My body was on constant alert, and I wondered how much of that affected my elevated blood pressure.

Since being in New Mexico, I'd felt the difference in the earth. It was deep and quiet, very old and wise. There was a sense of sacredness that came from it.

California was young, formative, and dynamic. Interestingly, the state of the earth seemed to reflect the state of activity; California always on the cutting edge of new thought, and New Mexico a cradle of artistic creativity. The difference between the two areas was palpable.

As I reflected, I drifted off into a space where my body was no longer a weight, but merged with the minerals, the herbs, and the water. I felt the interaction of each ingredient. We were one floating system of energy, and we became the tub, the room, the town, the world. It was an amazing feeling. Everything was a glow of oneness that continued to merge, like a river of light.

I was brought back to earth by a tap on the door and a sweet voice telling me it was time to go. Reluctantly, I climbed out of the tub and showered. Having made my purchases, I was able to return to the house just in time for the afternoon session.

Everyone had gathered by the time I arrived, and I found my seat as quietly as possible. Roland looked at me expectantly. "Have a good time?"

"I went to town, to the River Spa." I explained how

I'd gone for postcards, and decided on taking the bath, where I had the remarkable experience of merging with all life while in the tub.

Roland looked at me. "Very good. You were able to hold the energy from the morning session."

Fiona interjected, "That is one of my favorite things to do when I'm here, that and the natural sulfur springs. We should all go. They're just wonderful! How about tonight?"

Her suggestion was received with enthusiasm, and it was agreed that after dinner, we'd drive up to the springs, not far from Roland's house. As we settled down and turned our attention to Roland, he was somewhat reflective.

"What you experienced this morning was a very vital link to maintaining harmony in your life. Without this process, you are more likely to be thrown off center at one time or another and lose your vital energy force, especially as conditions of change become more and more evident externally. The one thing this process requires is an act of discipline on your part. You need to set aside forty minutes every day to do this, and I'd like you to start tomorrow morning and continue for the remainder of your stay. Any questions?"

"Yeah. I have a couple." It was Mark. "It's my understanding that each of us has a unique tone. If that's so, why is it that the sounds she made worked so well for all of us?"

"Good question." Roland looked at us carefully before speaking. "You were all brought together because at a soul level you are each part of a unit, a soul family or group, and your vibration rates are quite similar. As you work with the process you were taught, and we'll continue it each morning, you'll find your own subtle variation of the pitch. For the most part, your attunement is pretty much the same."

Lillian seemed perplexed. "How do you know that, Roland?"

"It's evident in your auras. If there were a series of patterns and we had to group them, all of you would be placed in one group, because the colors and shapes in your patterns match."

Nathan was also curious. "So just what is the implication of that?"

"As we attune ourselves to one another, and by the way, I'm part of this unit, we are forming a very large field or band of information that might be termed 'energy' in some circles. We are causing a sound or tone to form that harmonizes and creates a light source, and it is in the band waves of light that higher consciousness or information is stored. As you move into light, you are not only affected by the light wave, you are encoded by it. It is an actual physical exchange at a cellular level.

"When we band together as a united force, the light we're able to generate is that much more powerful, and we share in a process that sometimes is called the 'give away,' because it is a recognition of our interconnectedness. We not only gain individually and as a group, we are contributing something to the collective light pool for others."

Nathan wanted to know more about the process and what the connection looked like from a pure energy standpoint.

Roland got up and moved to the board. He chose a

couple of pens of different colors and began to draw lines that intersected and moved to create two triangles facing one another. One was red, the other blue.

"As we see ourselves within the casing of this field of energy, we can perceive it as two triangles. One is red and represents the electrical field moving downward with its point toward the earth, and the other is blue which would be magnetic, coming from the earth and moving toward the electrical component. As the electric and magnetic fields intersect, you enter the electromagnetic field.

"This intersection becomes a hexagram. In the texts of India, it represents the union of fire and water, and in the western tradition, it is often referred to as the Star of David. However, a lesser-known interpretation that is pertinent to this group is from the Yucatan. The hexagram is a symbol of the sun shedding its rays on the earth, the absolute requirement for life.

"As we activate each individual 'star,' and attune our vibrations to one another, the hexagrams are strengthened and add to the collective body of light. The purpose of showing this as a geometrical form is that at a subtle level, that's how the configuration of energy appears. We don't physically have to stand in it to activate it, the arc of encoded information will reshape itself because of the caliber of each of the components."

I was curious. "I have heard that when we tune into the light, we will activate a double. Do you know anything about that?"

"Yes. For every energy form in manifestation there is a double or twin component in potential. When you consciously attune yourself to the encoded information of light, the twin or "double" is activated and becomes an additional force."

"Wait!" Lillian looked perplexed. "I am dazed and confused," she quipped. "You're speaking Greek to me!"

"It's alright, Lillian." Roland laughed. "We're going to go further into this during the rest of the week. It should start to make sense by the end. Right now, we have to gather all the pieces and put them on the table. Then we'll fit them together like a jigsaw puzzle."

There was more discussion, and then it was time to break for half an hour before dinner. I was feeling slightly overwhelmed by everything I'd experienced and went back to my bungalow to lie down. I thought I'd close my eyes just for a minute, but before I knew it, I was in a deep sleep. Then I began to dream.

In my dream, I was in the center of a maze. I was running from one end to the other, and I couldn't get my bearings. There were others also in the maze trying to find out where they should be. We moved around like this for quite some time, and then all of a sudden it was as though through a series of coincidences, we had miraculously found the right spot for each of us, and the whole maze lit up, reflecting an incredible light. It was a blend of the most vibrant colors I had ever seen, but they were emerging from and moving back into an awesome white that was the foundation for everything.

As that magical instant occurred, there was a musical sound that could be heard. It was magnificent! It was as though all of us had come to the position for which we'd been created and then the moment or second passed, and we were again running everywhere, trying to find an appropriate space. However, this time none of us were frantic, because we had experienced something that fulfilled our purpose.

I was wakened by the sound of tapping on my door. Groggily, I got up and went to answer it. Lillian stood before me, smiling. "You missed dinner. Roland thought you'd probably needed your sleep, but asked if I'd bring you this." She handed a tray to me, and I accepted it gratefully.

"Are you going to join us for the sulfur springs?" she asked. I was exhausted, but hated to miss the fun. Yet, remembering situations in the past when I did not pay attention to the needs of my body, I knew the end result. This retreat was too important to miss because of a momentary want. I told Lillian that it would probably be better for me to just spend the evening quietly, so that I'd be rested in the morning.

I sat down to write some cards to friends back home. It seemed a million years since I'd been there, when indeed I'd only been here for two days. After I finished the cards, I decided to take a walk. The sky was still light and it was beautiful outside. Walking up the trail from the hillside herb garden, I took my time and stopped periodically to look at the scenery. Everything was bathed in a beautiful purple glow, sky reflecting the setting tones of sun on the red mountains. It was truly breathtaking.

As I paused, I heard the sound of a bird nearby. It was a crow or raven, very large and blue black. He was looking at me and making a lot of noise. As I walked toward him, he jumped from branch to branch, crowing all the while. He didn't seem to be trying to get away, but rather to make me aware of something. He swooped low in front of me to the left, and as I watched him, there off the trail was a shiny object that caught my eye.

Walking over, I found a small gold coin with the imprint of a sword on one side, and a cup on the other. "Imagine that!" I said aloud. Why would I be surprised by anything here? Next to the coin was a beautiful iridescent black feather with shades of blue and purple shimmering in the light. I picked them both up and took them with me.

Rather excited by my find, I stopped at the bungalow to get the tray, and then went back to the main house to see if anyone was there. Walking to the workshop area, one of Roland's dogs followed me. He was a beautiful German shepherd, very much like a dog of mine from years ago. I had never had a more loyal animal, and I cried every time I saw dogs that reminded me of him. This dog, Shep, was amazingly perceptive. He seemed to know how I felt and looked through soul-filled eyes as though to tell me something.

No one was in the workshop area, so I proceeded to the kitchen to leave the tray. As I walked in, a woman from the local tribe, who helped Roland, turned to see who had entered.

"Hello!" I said. She looked at me suspiciously, and nodded. As I set the tray down near the sink, she moved over toward me and then with a riveting glance, looked at the feather.

"Where did you get that?" she asked.

I glanced at the feather and told her that the crow had called to me and shown the place where the feather was with the gold coin. As I opened my palm to show the coin, she reached out and snatched it from my hand.

"This coin is bad medicine," she said. "You don't want to mess with it." She thrust the coin into the pocket of her apron.

I was somewhat taken aback, and asked her why the coin was negative. She looked at me and began a tirade against the Spanish, who she said had enslaved her ancestors and desecrated their sacred grounds. The gold coins were part of the system that destroyed them, and she felt it was unlucky to have one. I thanked her for the information, but told her I'd like to show it to the others. I felt in this case that the coin was more a reminder of the Grail than of the oppressors who ruined a civilization.

Reluctantly, she handed me the token. "Do what you want, but it's bad medicine. This feather is Raven. It was tricking you. Ravens like to pull people into the dark place!" Her face looked very harsh as she studied me, and then she scurried out of the kitchen without so much as a good-bye.

As I walked along the hall to return to my bungalow, I passed a door to the library, and walked in to investigate whether there was information about the coin. Roland had a fairly remarkable collection of books, and I thought he might have something that would shed light on my find. Browsing through the shelves, I saw books written in Greek, French and Latin along with the many English titles.

Thumbing through a couple that caught my eye; a book fell to my feet. As I picked it up, I laughed. The title was *Power Animals,* and I opened to a page with one bold word as a title: "Raven!"

Raven, according to the author, was the carrier of magic, and could lead the individual into the Great Mystery. Depending on the use of the gift, the individual would become enlightened or fall into bad company. Raven was able to bring gifts and messages from the Ancients to humans. Contact with a raven or raven feathers was notice that magic was afoot!

Back in my room, I went over what happened and jotted down the incidents of the day. According to Raven, there was a negative possibility implied in my find, but also a great potential. To my way of thinking, the coin represented a gift. I would take it with me in the morning and see what the others thought. I also wanted to ask Roland about the strange little woman in the kitchen.

I thought about the events of the day, with its varied texture, and noted the difference between the woman from India we had met this morning and the Native American woman I met tonight. They both came from a deep spiritual heritage, but one had chosen to embrace the vastness of love, and the other was bound by the constriction of hate.

Chapter 6
❧ Tree, Mountain, Bird, Sky ❧

Iawakened to the sound of my alarm clock. I hadn't slept well at first because I was upset by my encounter with the woman in the kitchen. However, once I fell asleep, it was deep and rich. I couldn't remember what I'd dreamt, but certain symbols seemed to recur throughout the night. I remembered the Raven, the coin, and a priest running with a golden cup toward water. Not much to go on, but perhaps others would know more.

The day was dry and cool. We did our breathing exercises with color and sound as we had been taught, and talked with one another about our various paths, gradually developing a sense of rapport as a group. Roland participated, but remained on the periphery. I could see that he was skilled at bringing people together without making himself the focal point. He had asked the right questions to each of us, piquing interest in the others to know more. He was a consummate conductor, orchestrating our full participation rather than allowing us to remain the passive recipients of his wisdom.

I mentioned the incident with the bird and coin, and the others were intrigued. Roland was especially interested in the story of the bird, however, because he had seen coins on the property before. He felt this had been a site where artifacts had been buried, and planned at some point to excavate if the mountain gave him permission. While the others looked at the coin, Roland took me aside.

"Raven tells of a change in consciousness. You truly are on the brink of a great mystery, and I think you have the strength and tenacity to handle it."

I hesitated bringing up the woman in the kitchen, but decided I needed to gain clarity about the interaction.

"The woman who comes to help you told me the coin is bad luck, and that Raven would lead me to darkness."

He smiled. "Doreen is a good woman, but she doesn't trust white people to hold the vision. In her experience, a gold coin is a magnet for exploitation, and Raven signifies the potential to misuse what you receive. So her concern was understandable, given her history, and she doesn't know you yet. When she does, her reaction will be completely different."

We gathered at mid-morning after having breakfast and taking time for our individual needs. Roland told us that the Grail concept was found in almost every philosophy, and it was important not to associate the Grail with any one tradition or background, as it was a universal symbol that had been found throughout antiquity.

He planned to take us to Native American ruins, and if time permitted, to the river that ran through town. As there were only six of us, we were all able to fit in his utility vehicle. He nosed the car down the mountain and asked us to pay attention to the silence.

For Lillian, this may not have been a treat, but for the rest of us, coming from more impacted areas, the quiet was restoring. I had already noticed it the day before, although I found myself aware of how hard it was to "come down" after being in the Bay Area. The energy was so different here.

We traveled through the mountains to an unmarked road, and turned off. The road was dirt and wound around the mountain past a series of houses, some of them quite grand. As we approached the summit, the road narrowed, and there were huge boulders embedded in the mountain that became the roadway. Nothing but a four-wheel drive would have been able to cross them. We drove to a vast clearing and Roland parked the car. Emerging from the vehicle, we were on top of the world.

From our vantage point, we could see the mountains north and east as well as the valleys and canyons that separated them. The view was spectacular, and the sky an amazing color of blue. This blue was strong. It was not the pale blue of the Bay Area that was so distinctive to me, because there was no water to diffuse its intensity. Also, we were at about 9,000 feet in altitude. Roland suggested we investigate for a while on our own, and as I looked up, there were hawks circling nearby. I was impressed by the serenity; no people, no houses, no traffic, and other than a couple of airplanes, no noise.

Walking around the area, Roland told us that this had been the secret village of Native Americans who lived in the area during the 1600's. The Spanish sent priests out to the new territories, and New Mexico had not been spared. The invasion of Europeans in the southwest left the native population displaced and their culture savaged. Viewed as sub-human, they were treated harshly by the conquerors, who enslaved them for work on churches, buildings, and roads in the area.

This village, the remnants of which we stood on, had been an attempt by the local native community to save their culture after they revolted against the Spaniards. They had taken their families and moved to this mountaintop, which was totally inaccessible to anyone but the heartiest soul. They had built dwellings and gardens, bringing their seeds and animals with them. Because of their vantage point, they were able to fend off invaders, and for some time were able to maintain their autonomy.

As we walked through the ghost village, I could feel a sense of peace and oneness that had been part of their culture. There was an exquisite connection to earth and sky, and as I looked around at the breathtaking vistas, trees beckoned. One in particular stood out. I had an uncanny feeling it was the presence of a 'she' and sensed she was the grandmother tree. I could feel her speak to me through the currents of wind that played in the air. Looking closer, I saw Kokopeli playing his flute in her branches. I felt so embraced by her that all thought of separation was erased.

As I stood watching her branches swaying in the breeze, the thought came into my mind that she was a guardian of the earth. She and the other trees were the nervous system of the planet, and the significance of our destroying the forests went way beyond the ozone layer. As we destroyed the earth's receptors, we destroyed our own. As we obliterated earth's consciousness, we guaranteed the demise of ours. There was no separation between any of us. The trees were absolutely necessary to the health of the planet, and we were slowly killing them and ourselves through our ignorance – through the myth of separation.

The others came beside me and gazed up at her also. Roland stood silently nearby. Tears welled in my eyes, knowing that we were all one – the tree, the mountain, the bird, the sky... all of us bound by one life force, indivisible except in our field of perception. And it was in that field of perception where we created our heaven and hell. It was here that we subverted and perverted the unity of life to fulfill our perspective, so often based on fear and lack.

The mountain gave fully. The trees offered without condition. The sky embraced us, and the air and water sustained our life. Yet, we continued to take without replenishing. We demanded without considering. Oh, how I yearned to sustain that feeling of connection!

I felt a gentle presence on my shoulder, and as I looked around, Roland's green eyes embraced me. He knew. He felt it, too. Looking at the rest of the group, I could see their own immersion in the spirit of Grandmother Tree's message. If only we could bottle this and give it to humanity. What could we repair and create as a result?

Roland softly called us to gather, and we found a spot that felt appropriate for group prayer and meditation. We affirmed life, the greater plan unfolding, and the spirit of these magnificent people who lived as one with the mountain and one another. We then went to separate spaces to hold our own vision. I chose a spot near flowering cactus and sat with the raven's feather I'd brought. Again, I was moved by the absolute beauty surrounding me. Gratitude flooded my entire being, and I rose to greet the sky with arms outstretched. Sounds came out of my mouth that I'd never heard before, and I raised the feather in salute to the Gods that be, swaying and dancing in a circle. I was full and empty at the same time, and after I'd bowed to the Four Corners, I sat quietly with no thought or noise to distract my sense of unity.

Gradually, we gathered by the foot of the Grandmother tree, and after saying a few more words of thanks, walked back to the utility vehicle. Everyone was quiet as we made our way down the mountain, reflecting on what we'd seen and felt.

We had spent only three hours on the mountain, but it was an experience I would carry with me forever... the picture of serenity juxtaposed with the image of destruction.

Roland suggested that we have a late lunch at a local spot where the food was wonderful. The River Deli was an old style roadside café, complete with swinging door and wooden porch. Inside, the smell of home cooking beckoned. Several in our group ordered grilled cheese sandwiches, made with a combination of cheddar, swiss and grilled onions on delicious homemade bread. One of us had a patty melt and said it was the best he'd ever tasted, and I opted for a hamburger on a homemade bun with french fries, in spite of knowing better. It was absolutely delicious and I enjoyed every morsel!

Mark looked over at me, a twinkle in his eye. "You sure enjoy your food, don't you?" My mouth full, I was immediately self-conscious, and felt my stomach muscles contract. I refused to get hooked into this and remembered the admonition I'd received at the

Labyrinth to not exclude humor or take myself too seriously, so I puffed out my cheeks with glee and instead of defending my love of food, nodded my head vigorously. "Mm-hum. I sure do!" Everyone laughed and a tense moment passed.

Everything is perception, I thought. How often our feelings are hurt by an inconsequential comment someone makes thoughtlessly. Yet, we blow it out of proportion and allow it to fester inside. How important to stay present in every moment and keep things clear. Had I been alone with Mark, I might have told him that his comment hurt my feelings. There didn't seem any need to do this in the group.

It was three-thirty in the afternoon, and Roland suggested that we go back to the house. We'd have time for the river later in the week, but for now, he wanted to go over a few things with each of us individually before we broke for late supper. We paid the bill, and were off again to our next session.

As we climbed out of the valley, the sun became brighter. I was aware of how little daylight there was in a canyon, and thought that I much preferred being near the top of the mountain. In fact, I thought Roland Ivory's house was located in an almost perfect setting.

At the house, Roland suggested that everyone take a half-hour to themselves and then we could gather in the workshop area. I made my way to the little bungalow that was home away from home and pulled out my sketchpad and notebook. I wanted to draw everything I'd witnessed earlier. Putting my perception into words that would remind me of the experience was important, but I wanted to capture the visual feel as well.

At the appointed hour, I meandered over to the

workshop area. Roland was in discussion with Lillian, and I moved to the verandah. Mark was also there. He looked over at me sheepishly. "I'm sorry if I upset you earlier. I really didn't mean to embarrass you. You just looked so enthusiastic about eating that the words tumbled out of my mouth."

I appreciated his sensitivity. "Thank you. I was a little offended, but it gave me a good opportunity to use a little humor. That's one of the things I'm supposed to remember so that I don't get too serious."

He responded in kind. "I know what you mean. I've got the need to lighten up, too. This journey can get pretty intense at times, and it's hard to keep things in perspective without taking it all to heart."

We talked more about our respective work, and he expressed some of his concerns to me about his abilities. He had an uncanny knack of seeing into people... beyond their defenses. He was able to pierce a shield and read what was possible for them, but he didn't know how much he should reveal. Sometimes he felt the information could be overwhelming.

I understood his dilemma, and said I felt if they gave their consent to be read, he ought to tell them what he saw. "Further," I added, "I think sometimes we're used as instruments to bring information to others. We have to overcome our own egos and just do it without blocking the message. I know for myself that I judge constantly and have avoided telling people some things that would have been very helpful to them. But I couldn't get out of the way."

I recalled several times when that had occurred.

He looked at me oddly. "Would you want to know if someone saw something for you?"

I looked up abruptly because I sensed he felt something about me that he wanted to communicate. "Well, yes. But I'd want to know the caliber of the person giving the information, because I think a lot of times people can be read incorrectly by someone whose own lens is fuzzy. I always find out about the people I work with who are going to "read" me so that I know where they are coming from. In fact, I haven't had a reading from anyone in years. I prefer to pay attention to my own counsel."

"Well, when I'm on, I'm on, and when I'm off, I'm way off," he said. We both laughed. "But seriously, I do see something I think you ought to know."

I felt a little anxious internally. What would Mark have to tell me that I didn't want to know? I looked at him and tried to "tune in" to his motivation. It seemed clear, and I gathered that his reason for wanting to tell me was altruistic.

"Okay. If we're all on this Grail quest together, why not? Go ahead, but be kind." I tried to lighten the mood.

"Can I touch you?" he asked.

"Sure."

He then took both my hands in his and continued. "What I feel is that you are an incredibly powerful person who has come with a very important mission in service to humanity. I see you as needing to write something that will help wake people up. You are a healer and a teacher, and frequency is going to be very important in your work as the years unfold.

"You need to clean up your act around food...this is a problem because you're eating things that are too rich for you. Your system is seeking to be nourished by finer vibrations, and some of what you eat is way too heavy. Sorry about that!" He smiled. "So I get that I'm supposed to tell you that you will have all the help you need, and that Roland is going to play an important part in your life."

He stopped. "That's enough for now. Hope it helps."

We had been sitting on two of the lounge chairs, and I could feel the heat that was generated as he gave me the reading. Mark's assessment was accurate. My body resonated and I tingled from head to foot after he finished his statements.

"Thank you. That was right on. I already have a sense of the food thing, and I've been told by everyone who ever read me that I have something to write." I shook my head. "It feels burdensome, but I'll find my way to it." I looked at him, stripping away all pretension. "You know, Mark, I made a vow to God that I would take whatever path He chose for me. I've done a lot of changing in my life, and I'm willing to continue in whatever way He wants."

Mark looked at me wryly. "Well," he said, "I think She wants you to pay attention and get ready." He laughed. "You haven't got a clue of how big this can be." He paused and then continued. "I also get that it's very important for you to recognize that you don't have to do this alone. There is a soul group for you to work with. I might be one of them... but you'll know as the time is right. There will be an inner group and an outer group. This has nothing to do with hierarchy. It's about the work that is close to your soul's purpose, and then the work that you do with those for whom you have a different type of affection. You will absolutely know the difference."

"Thank you, Mark."

"Yeah, thank you. I'm really glad I know you." He radiated tremendous warmth and I felt good in his presence.

Roland stuck his head out the door. "Mark, I'd like to talk with you now, if you're ready." Mark and I looked at each other, a veil lifted between us, and before he left, we gave each other a heartfelt embrace.

"Thanks again," I murmured. He squeezed my arm and left.

What had he told me that I didn't already know? Well, it wasn't that I didn't know. It was that the knowing was dormant. As he spoke what felt like truth, a center inside of me came to attention, like a light going on. There was a tone associated with it as well. I felt if I were sharp enough, I'd recognize a color, too.

I knew we had energy centers in our body. From the Hindu perspective, where much of the work had been done on these centers, they were called *Chakras*. Some teachers said we had seven, while others said we had nine, or twelve. Now, another one was supposedly becoming active. I didn't much care, because it was more important to me to pay attention to what I felt internally.

In the western tradition, the chakras lined up along the spine, and this was called the 'rod' or 'staff' in our esoteric literature. So, when the Bible referred to the rod and the staff, it was referring esoterically to the spinal column in the human being, and the chakras were the points of light along that line.

Each center reflected a power point, and when we

were perfectly aligned, it was as though the entire column hummed and vibrated with a liquid light. The
light was made of different colors that corresponded
to the area in question. When we were out of sorts
with ourselves, whatever center was affected would
become dim. This influenced what was called our
aura, the energy field around our body. All of these
esoteric terms really only mapped out parts of the
human energy system that were basic to life, and we
were doing the breathing, sound, and color exercises
to make sure we remained in harmony so we could
complete our life's purpose.

What Mark said made sense. I knew that I had to
address my relationship to food. As I was getting
older and going through hormonal changes in my
body, the food requirements were also changing. I
didn't need to eat as much, and I needed to be more
selective about what I ate. This tied in perfectly to
what my friends and I received at the Labyrinth a couple of weeks ago, but it wasn't easy to implement the
changes.

As far as writing, I knew I had to wait until it was
'time.' To write for the sake of writing appeased the
ego, but did nothing to further knowledge. I sensed
that when it was right, I would know. I also sensed
that the writing referred to was not my newsletter.
That was my apprenticeship. As my good friend John
always said, 'If you hang around long enough, everything will be revealed to you."

The night sky was rising, and the stars fairly
popped out in the heavens. There was so much depth
and space to this piece of land called New Mexico. I
was truly impressed by its primal beauty.

"Are you ready?" Roland was at the door, looking at me with the intensity of a scientist ready to dissect a butterfly. I nodded, and he motioned me to walk with him in the garden of the inner courtyard. I felt tension welling up inside and consciously brought remembrance back to my breath. Breathing rhythmically, I was soothed, and reminded myself that I did not have to be afraid of anything he would say to me.

"You really zeroed right in to Grandmother Tree." He looked at me questioningly. "You have a very refined sense of perception. Have you noticed that before?"

I thought for a moment and then nodded. "Yes. I do know that about myself now. When I went to Europe in 1992, we were flying into London. As we came in for our landing, I could see World War II bombers flying beside us. It was uncanny! They were like filaments. Then, when we went to Germany we were seated at an outdoor café in Dresden, and the sirens of a police car or fire engine sounded. Suddenly, everything around was burning and I could see people running. This wasn't actually happening at that moment, but it *was happening.* I began to cry. After that, we drove through Germany on the Autobahn and I could see the tanks rolling alongside us. The dimensions were interpenetrating and, in that moment, I realized there is no time or space. *Everything happens simultaneously.* It was an amazing coinciding of events, and I recognized that Europe, and Germany in particular, is going to take a long time to heal from the scars of that war. It is psychically impaled."

Just relating the events brought me back to them.

He looked at me knowingly, and paused before speaking. "I'll bet you always wondered why you were born where you were?"

I smiled. "Yes, I did. How did you know that? I always questioned it... Why San Francisco and not in another country, or another state?"

"You were born in California because it's one of the least psychically impacted areas within the country. Its history is fairly benign, relatively speaking. Of course, if you go down the coast to the missions, you'll feel the anguish, and there are pockets of exploitation and horror related to the treatment of Chinese and Japanese, but San Francisco does not have a lot of psychic residue. It's one of the more inclusive areas within this country. With your love of freedom and spirit of inquiry, you needed diversity to allow you to flourish and expand. San Francisco was the perfect soil for who you are."

Then he continued. "We all find ourselves where we need to be, and those who are born in one area and migrate elsewhere need to make peace with the location and details of their birth, their family, and upbringing. Nothing is without purpose, and once we come to terms with the intention, the soul is free to soar. Until then, there is always a blockage to movement forward."

This man had uncommon wisdom, and my respect for his insights was growing.

"How did you come to be who you are?" I asked.

"The same way you came to be you," he laughed.

Roland told me a little about himself as I gently prodded. He had come from a background of French, Irish, German and Native American ancestry. How all of those groups got together amazed me. At any rate, he had a wonderful great-grandfather from the Hopi tribe who was still versed in the Hopi ways. His young charge was a willing and eager student, knowing from early age that he was here to do something worthwhile with his life.

He had gone on many vision quests before the white man had made them fashionable, and was accepted into training by the elders when he was nine. They believed he had been given a special gift that needed nourishment before he would be plucked out of the natural environment of New Mexico, and did everything possible to encourage his full participation and understanding.

His father died shortly after his birth. When he was 14, his mother was killed in an automobile accident, and he was entrusted to the care of European relatives, spending six years in France, where he learned to read and speak fluent French as well as Greek and Latin. He had a facility for languages based on tonal nuances, and went on to get a degree in linguistics.

He spent two years in Vietnam, and after being released from the army, he earned a Masters degree in archaeology. He was sent to Egypt to work on digs near the tombs of the pharaohs and made the acquaintance of several rebel archaeologists who had different theories about the origin and purposes of the sphinx and pyramids. He was then sent to sites near Jerusalem where he delved into the roots of Christian, Muslim and Jewish religions.

Roland certainly qualified as one who took a road less traveled. He was unassuming and assured. He had been tested in the fire, and came forth stronger and more certain of what was important for him. His journeys in lands of antiquity gave him exposure to the beginning of biblical time. The training with elders in his youth gave him the ability to pierce appearances and extract insight. What he had learned to do for himself, he was now able to impart to others.

We had stopped walking, and Roland was looking at me. However, this time it was not the look of one who was ready to dissect. He seemed more vulnerable, his shield down. There was a sense of weariness that came from him, too.

"I hope you understand how important this journey is. It isn't just a matter of finding an object and then going on to something else. This is a lifelong process." He looked at me intently. "Are you willing to make the commitment it requires?" I was. Everything had come into focus.

"Roland, I've never been more aware of the importance of anything in my life. I know we were created for a purpose, and I have yearned to find it forever. We aren't here to live petty lives, we are here to reclaim the sacred element of our being."

I felt these statements passionately, from the deepest space in myself, and started to cry. "I don't want anything else. The way I felt today on the mountain, the total connection to everything, nothing has meaning for me without that!"

I wiped the tears from my eyes, and he took my hand in his and squeezed it. He nodded his head and gave me a knowing smile.

"Good," he said. "Now we can get to work."

Chapter 7
❧ *All That Glitters* ❧

I arrived at the workshop area quite a bit earlier than usual. Lillian was already there and asked how I'd done in the evening discussion with Roland. I told her he made me realize how important this journey was in my life, and then she and I began talking about our experiences since being at his home. She told me she was sorry I'd missed going to the springs with them, and when I asked how it was, she was animated.

"It was marvelous! The water was hot, the wind was warm, and the night was spectacular. I wanted to grab my paints and capture the Lady of the Night!" Lillian was enraptured!

"Who's the Lady of the Night?" I asked.

"She's the light that comes from the combination of colors when the weather conditions are just right. There's an old tale that when the religions of Europe came, they swept all vestiges of Mother's reign on earth aside. They called this takeover the Patriarchy, and it was especially jealous of her colorful creations, so it banned beauty. Everything became drab, color-less, and non-sexual.

"To make her presence known to her children so they wouldn't forget her, Mother used her colors to paint the sky, especially in the southwest, because the patriarchy had not yet found the means to control the heavens. In this way, the people of earth could look up to beauty, since they were not allowed to have it on earth, and there's nothing like the sunsets of New Mexico. They are magical."

I smiled. "What a lovely story, Lillian. I'll bet you are a wonderful artist. You are so impassioned by what you see, and you are so lyrical in your presentation! It must be terrific to always have had this gift."

Lillian shook her head. "I didn't always have this gift," she said. "I had to earn it."

I was surprised. "Haven't you always been an artist? I had the impression that you've lived in Taos for years and have a wonderful life in the artist colony there."

She tilted her head back and laughed. Speaking in her husky voice, she said, "Oh, good God, no! I used to live in the Bay Area, like you. This is my third incarnation!"

My curiosity was piqued. "Do you mind if I ask what happened?"

Again, she shook her head. "No, I don't mind. We've got a little time before the group arrives, so let's sit down, and I'll tell you."

Lillian was remarkably candid. She had married while in college and quit school, working at odd jobs to help her husband finish his degree. He went on to get a Master's Degree so he could teach at the university level, and she again deferred her own education for his. Meanwhile, the Korean War broke out, and the young men were being drafted. When her husband realized he would be called up, he insisted that they have children so he wouldn't have to go. She had wanted to complete her education in art before starting a family, but he convinced her to wait.

As the years went by, she had three children, and her inclination to go back to school was replaced by concerns around the children and her desire to help her husband. He had finished his degree, started teaching, and began writing books that were considered brilliant in the field of economics. As his notoriety grew, he began to lecture throughout the country and the world. Lillian was left home to care for the children, and always wondered when there would be time for them to be a family. He was on a fast track with his career, and that seemed to consume him.

As his position and stature grew within the world, his need for more and bigger also grew. First, he wanted a more prestigious house. Next, he wanted the Porsche, the Mercedes, the van, then the boat and yacht club, the children in private school, the country club. With each acquisition, Lillian kept thinking this would be the one that would make him happy, and they could finally enjoy what they had. It took 18 years for her to realize that this was never going to happen.

He went back to school to get more degrees, to make more money, and began investing in real estate. Lillian said that as time went by, he was barely able to sit still, and one day she looked out the bay window of her twelve-room house and asked if this was all there was. It was at that moment that she knew if she stayed within the marriage she would die.

She had suggested simplification. He wanted more. She said they'd needed counseling. He said everything was fine. She asked for a little of his time. He said he was busy, and so it went until the lifeblood was squeezed out of the marriage, and she knew she would have to leave.

"How did you do that?" I asked, thinking about my own failed marriage.

"Not very graciously. I found a lover. I was so desperate for someone who would show interest in the things that were important to me, who would want to spend time with me, that I wasn't terribly discreet. It was a very messy divorce!"

Lillian said that the children had been devastated, as had their entire community of friends and associates. Everyone thought she and her husband had the perfect marriage and were the epitome of the perfect couple.

"It was like all those programs on television... *Ozzie and Harriet, Father Knows Best, Leave It to Beaver.* Everything looked just great, but in the end, they all got canceled, and so did we." She looked off into the distance, and I could tell these were powerful memories that haunted her.

"You know, the saddest thing about it was that we were both decent people. But our reasons for marrying in those days were so distorted. We never considered the consequences of our choices, and he and I were as philosophically opposed as any two people could be. I mean, how do you reconcile art and economics? This was pre-80's, for God's sake!"

She laughed, and I joined her. Looking back at my own short-lived marriage, what she said hit home. Our reasons for marrying were very shallow. Lillian was a good 15 or 20 years older than I, but we in the baby boom years had no concept of relationship reality. I remember a friend of mine who confessed that the reason she married her husband was because he wanted her to go to Europe with him. This was in the transition time before "free love," and most men and women didn't go off together without benefit of marriage. The problem, she said, was that she hadn't counted on the fact that after Europe she'd have to live with him!

When I thought about the movies that exemplified our age group: Gidget, Tammy, *Where The Boys Are,* etc., not to mention the television shows Lillian talked about, we were living in a bubble of naïveté, and when it burst, we had no concept of the fallout, and the number of people who would be hurt, especially the children.

Lillian said that after the divorce, she drifted away from her lover, and began to find out who she was. She had lost herself in her concern for everyone else and forgot that she was an important factor in the quotient. Her years as a homemaker had been taken for granted, and she used to quip to her husband, "The one thing we have in common is our interest in you." We both laughed.

Lillian was encouraged to go back to school. She worked part-time and managed to go to the San Francisco Academy of Art where her capabilities were appreciated and flourished. She moved into a phase that completely revitalized her life, befriended by poets and writers, sculptors and political activists. This was the heyday of the self-improvement 70s, and she found herself, her passion, and a purpose for living. She moved to Taos with a group of fellow artisans and lived there ever since – traveling, exploring inner realms, and contributing her talent to the world.

I asked about the children and the aftermath of the

breakup as it affected them. "You know, if I had only known earlier what I knew later, I would have packed them up and taken them with me into this life much sooner. One of my reasons for staying in the marriage was because I was concerned I couldn't offer them the economic privileges that they had while he and I were married. It never occurred to me that I could make very much money painting, but I had not counted on the fact that the life we lived offered them a lot of perks, but little substance.

"I think they would have gained so much more character being exposed to the life I lead now. As it was, their father didn't have time for them any more than he had for me. When I finally left him, they were pretty much grown. All that money did nothing to add dimension to their lives. They were poor little rich kids, and I'll regret that for my entire life. Now their children come to be with me, and my eldest daughter has followed a passion for sculpting."

That was quite a story, and as she finished, I wondered how many men and women were in marriages or jobs that stifled their true essence and diminished their being. How many stayed with the status quo because of fear? This was one thing our group had in common. We were not afraid to risk living, because each one of us knew first hand that doing anything else was slow death.

Mark walked into the workshop area and sat down. "Roland had to leave for the day. An emergency came up, and he asked me to take over and share part of my work with you.

I was disappointed that Roland wasn't going to be there, but curious about what Mark would do. There was an easy comfort between Mark and the group. I was aware that by not going to the sulfur springs I had missed a special ingredient in the bonding process to the others.

He led us through the breathing, sound and color exercise, and it was easier to do than the day before. When we were finished, I felt peaceful, waves of light passing through me. As we gently came back to reality, Mark was looking intently at each one of us, Roland the Second.

"Okay. So, I've got to level with you. I have certain abilities that allow me to see into another person's energy patterns, and I can see where the blocks are. I don't have the same gift of finesse, as does our host, so sometimes what I say might appear to be blunt, but I've found that I'm guided to give out what each person needs to hear.

"Before we continue, I need to know if any of you has a problem with me bringing something forward about you in the group?"

Nathan smiled. "As far as I'm concerned, go for it!"

Lillian and Fiona indicated that neither one of them minded. I felt a sense of discomfort and contraction in my stomach muscles, but decided I had to go along, so nodded that it was all right with me.

"Okay. I want you to understand the purpose for me bringing these things to the surface. First, they're getting in the way of each of you being all that you can be. Sounds like a commercial, but it's the truth. And second, we cannot operate as an effective body of energy if there are glitches that keep us from full participation. We have to be energetically present and open for the exercises we're doing this week.

"The major thing that keeps us from being whole is fear. We are afraid of opening areas within ourselves that are uncomfortable or unsafe. We are afraid of the judgment of others. We are afraid that we'll be discounted, abandoned or betrayed, and one of the major stumbling blocks is that we're afraid to be out of control. If we give up control, we might be annihilated, and that's pretty scary. We're afraid to bring our voice forward because we might be misunderstood, misquoted, or ripped off.

"The problem with all of these fears is that they keep us locked up in containers that are too small for us. They keep us from becoming our potential. Self-protection stems from self-consciousness, and our task is to overcome the things that separate us from one another. Any questions so far?"

I was squirming, and spoke up. "But it's important to protect ourselves. If we don't, we're vulnerable to attack. For instance, I cannot look at people in crowds because I'm impacted by their pain. It moves into me and I take it on."

Mark looked at me steadily. "Why? What do you gain from taking on their pain?"

I could feel anger welling up inside. "Come on, Mark, don't psychoanalyze me. This isn't an encounter group. I don't gain anything from it, it just happens."

"No. I disagree. There's a payoff for you at a psychic level. You need to go into that. You don't have to do that now, and I'm not judging you. Get that. None of this is about judgment. It's about removing the layers that we've piled on that keep us from our authentic selves. If we can strip away the layers and over-come our defenses, we're going to find that at the bot-tom of it all is a huge core of love.

"A lot of the things we do are self-protective as a result of our own experiences. But a lot of things we do to protect ourselves stem from the collective unconscious. Hatred between groups, whether reli-gious, racial, ethnic, gender, or any other combination that comes up, is from a collective pool of fear.

"If you put a group of very small children, I mean before the imprint of their separateness is stamped on them, maybe age one, you'd have kids of every color and religious view, conservative and liberal – you name it – being curious about one another. They'd want to touch each other. They aren't separated yet by artificial divisions, based on perceptions of fear. They still have the spark of remembrance of where they came from, which was the same place, the same genet-ic pool – and they, and we, are all going to return to it when we're done here.

"So, we have to get out of trying to protect our-selves from life. None of us came here to 'be safe.' We came to grow and to unfold to everything that's pos-sible for us. We were given a birth assignment, and then we proceeded to forget."

Fiona chimed in. "You know, Mark. In esoteric tra-dition, there is a story about the Grail and its twin. One is the cup of remembrance, and the other of for-getfulness. We come down into earth with the draught of remembrance, and once we arrive, we drink from the other, and forget who we are. Our task is to find that original cup, and reunite. This is partially what the yearning for the Grail is all about. We want to overcome our separation."

"Yup. That's right." Mark paused. He looked at me.

"Are you alright with this now?"

I nodded that I was.

"Okay, then let's go on." He closed his eyes for a moment and then looked at each person individually, much the same as Roland had done.

"What I want to say to each of you is that as I look at your energy bodies, I can see where you're fully connecting and where you are missing elements that would allow you to flow more harmoniously within your energy fields. You might want to call these the chakras, which relate to the magnetic fields of your body, but also I'm looking at the electrical grid points of your body, which are represented by Acupuncture points. The combination of the electric and magnetic fields contribute to the quality of your Aura, which you know as the light that surrounds your body. I know you already know this stuff, but I want you to understand where I'm coming from...what my frame of reference is."

"What information are you getting when you look at us?" I asked.

"I'm talking non-verbally to your body when I do that. The body will not lie. You can rationalize with your mind, and you can schmooze through emotions, but the body will always tell the truth. In fact, this is an area that is not given nearly the attention it requires. It's real important to involve ourselves in bodywork that bypasses the mental process. You can reach issues through the dynamics of working with the body that you can't get through the psychological process. When I've sent clients to body movement specialists, their therapy process has been cut by at least half. So, your body is telling me what it wants you to know."

He turned first to Nathan and told him that he saw a highly developed intellect with good sexual grounding, but the need to open to heart and spirit more fully.

He then turned to Lillian and told her that her energy level was so dynamic and turned on that she radiated passion for life in all areas. He felt there were vestiges of guilt that held her back, which could be worked on.

For Fiona, he saw beautiful nurturing energy, with good heart, intellect and spiritual compassion. However, he saw a deep wound of sorrow that held her in a space that would not allow her to move fully into her potential. As he described this to her, she cried softly, and then sobbed. Mark and the others gathered to comfort her. I felt empathy, but was unable to move. As her discomfort lessened, each took their places and the focus was turned to me.

My level of self-consciousness had brimmed again to the surface, and I couldn't stand the thought of what I would hear, so I blurted out that I didn't feel well, and needed to leave. I mumbled apologies, but could not get out of the room fast enough.

As I headed for my bungalow, I was enraged. Why did I react this way? The constriction around me was so tight that I could hardly breathe or swallow. All I wanted to do was escape. It was a similar act of defensiveness that I'd experienced with Roland. I was always ready to protect myself, but how much of life was I missing through this need to be in control?

Once back in my room, I sat down and practiced breathing, returning to harmony. As I did this, tension eased, and the constriction in my body lessened.

What was I afraid of, and why was I sabotaging myself? This behavior reminded me of encounter groups where I'd learned a lot, but was uncomfortable with the process. Delving into realms of Spirit seemed far more liberating, and much less confrontational.

I felt foolish recognizing I'd allowed fear to overcome possibility. I decided it would be inappropriate to go back in the middle of the session, so instead I decided to take a walk. My mind wandered to other things; wondering what had forced Roland to leave, thinking about my friends, and questioning if I'd make it through the rest of this week without completely short-circuiting the process. As long as things stayed impersonal, I was fine. However, I did not like when the lens of inquiry was focused on me.

Walking up the mountain trail beyond the house, I came to two forks in the road, and took the path that led toward a wooded area, as it was going to be a hot day. The smell of piñon trees was wonderful. They had gnarled branches and often their shapes looked like frozen images of people or animals. As I reflected on their beauty, I heard rustling in the bushes. Thinking it might be a mountain lion, I turned very slowly, only to see a bearded man with a large potato sack partially filled with branches of the piñon.

Coincidence! I made a sound so as to let him know I was there. He turned, and a most intriguing face greeted me with a wonderful smile and merry blue eyes that signaled mischief. I liked him immediately.

"Hello!" I introduced myself and he walked over,

setting down his bag, reaching out to shake my hand.

"Earl Nightrider at your service!"

He swooped off an imaginary cap and bowed in a low, graceful movement.

"...Transplanted lover of life, corrupter of the arts, and strolling lunatic!" he continued.

He made me giggle. I asked him what he meant by his cryptic introduction, and after looking me over to see if I was worth relating it to, he motioned me to sit on the stump of a downed tree, where he proceeded to tell me the story of his life.

As a young boy he had been fascinated with wood and had grown up in a family of cabinetmakers. He spent most of his life keeping two steps ahead of civilization, as he told it. "I could smell 'em coming from a hundred miles downwind. When they got that close, it was time to move on."

He found a good woman and they lived a life on the fringe of society. He built cabinets for others and took to sculpting and carving figures from the downed piñon branches that were plentiful in the southwest. In recent years he added touches of mythology to his pieces, and they had become unbearably popular, to the point that it was difficult for him to remain anonymous. He determined that living in Sulfur Springs was an acceptable compromise, and spent his time following the joy of liberating the wood, as he cuttingly referred to his craft, and philosophizing to the trees and to anyone else who would listen.

I appreciated his humorous account, for it relieved me of my self-imposed seriousness. He turned and watched me as he finished his narrative. "So, little lady, what about you? What brings you to these woods?"

It sounded like the lead in for a fairy tale like Little Red Riding Hood, and I couldn't resist the temptation.

"Well," I squeaked in a high voice, "My grandmother sent me into the forest to look for berries."

He roared with laughter. "Good answer! You've got a sense of humor."

I laughed, too. "Sometimes yes, sometimes no. I'm afraid when I get self-conscious I tend to get overly serious."

"Oh, well, welcome to the human race. We all do. Trick is to catch yourself before you let it go too far. It's like sculpting. You start out with an idea, move into it, and then get self-conscious. Is it going to turn out the way it 'should?' All of a sudden the self-consciousness takes over and there is no sculpting. The fingers and the knife won't move because the mind has clamped down. It has to look, be, feel *this* way... *my* way."

"So what do you do when that happens?" I asked.

"Nothing. You just have to stop the process and go for a walk. Let it shake itself out. When your head gets tired, it'll let the muse take over again. Then you find your way back in. Only trouble is, you've lost your innocence. Now the piece is someone you know intimately, and intimacy means carving away the illusions. You have to grapple with the issues, and you have to make adjustments and compromises. There are moments of struggle, moments of promise, of disillusionment, and triumph. No doubt, though. No two pieces ever look the same, and no piece ever looks the way you thought it would. Whatever your medium, art is one heck of a teacher."

"Well Earl, I write and I do consultant work. So it isn't quite the same."

"Of course it is! Whatever you are involved with becomes the teacher. The art of living isn't relegated to those of us who work in the field of paints, clay or wood. It is the same thing with anyone or anything you involve yourself in. You have an idea; you get enthusiastic; you jump in, and then you find that it isn't going the way you thought it should. You get frustrated, you want to quit. And, here is the juncture. Which fork in the road do you take? You either shake out the cobwebs and march right back in there, or you leave it and it becomes one big dangling participle. It wreaks havoc on your psyche when you don't complete the process, regardless of the outcome. Can you relate to that?"

I looked at him, a grin on my face. "You've just named a major issue in my life. Thank you!"

He got up and helped me to my feet. "Well, Little Red Riding Hood, it was nice meeting you. Stay away from the big bad wolf, and good luck to you!"

He collected his sack of wood and went off whistling amidst the trees.

I stood for a few minutes reflecting on the coincidence of meeting him here at this moment in time.

"Oh, God" I said, looking up at the sky, "You are so awesome!" If only I could stay tuned and remember.

It was time for me to go back now and face the music.

Chapter 8
♣ Need and Greed ♣

I went back to the house after stopping momentarily at my bungalow. Everyone had disappeared, and I assumed they went to town for lunch. As I walked past the main kitchen, I saw Doreen, the woman who was angry about the coin. I decided to take care of this issue so it wouldn't be, as Earl Nightrider had put it, 'a dangling participle.'

I walked in as she was peeling a pot full of potatoes. "Hello?" She looked up at me and nodded, and I asked if I could talk with her for a moment. She shrugged her shoulders, not particularly delighted by the prospect, but motioned me over to a stool near where she was working.

"May I help?" I was sincere in an attempt to give a hand.

"Not necessary," she said quickly.

"I'd like to tell you a little about what happened before I found the coin the other night, and why I wanted to keep it." I told her about the meditation that prompted this search for the Grail, the powerful dreams I'd had, and how all the events led me to meet Roland and come to New Mexico.

When I was done, I took the coin out of my pocket, where I'd kept it, and handed it to her.

"I didn't understand how much pain this coin represented from the past or how much trouble it could bring today. My reason for wanting to keep it was because of what I told you. I have no interest in finding gold or exploiting anybody. So, I'd like you to take the coin and do what you want with it."

She looked at me differently, and the veil of protection lifted from her eyes. She smiled wholeheartedly, and we reached out to one another, as women will do, and embraced. I had tears in my eyes, and mumbled an apology.

"I am so sorry for what my ancestors did to yours. Please forgive us." The psychic wounds went deep, and although it may have seemed unnecessary to an onlooker, the apology was important for both of us.

We each pulled tissues from our pockets to dab wet eyes, and what had been an uncomfortable situation turned into a new friendship. Doreen reached into a drawer, handed me another peeler, and we sat chatting contentedly. The potatoes glistened as they were separated from their coarse skins, the metaphor of our interaction.

At 4 o'clock the group returned, and I apologized for having left. Rather than pull away from me, they each hugged me in turn. I realized that sometimes what appears to be a negative opens us to something better. My departure and the subsequent gifts of insight I'd received were priceless. Without acting on my feelings of isolation, I would not have met Earl Nightrider, nor come to this greater recognition of connection.

Mark walked up behind me as we moved toward the workshop area. "I'd like to have a few minutes to talk with you." The others were going to spend the rest of the afternoon in informal conversation.

"Listen," Nathan said with a twinkle in his eye,

"We're all going dancing tonight in Santa Fe, and you don't get off without joining us this time!"

I laughed, and agreed to go.

"Good," he said. "We're leaving at 6:30."

Mark and I walked to the verandah, and he motioned me to sit down. He pulled his chair directly across from mine, and took both my hands in his. He got a smirky little smile on his face and looked me over, head to toe.

"What did you think I'd tell you, that you were an ax murderer?"

"No." I laughed. "I didn't know what you'd say, but I didn't want to hear it. I got defensive and just wanted to get away."

"Well, I'm glad you came back." He squeezed my hands and let go. "Can I tell you what I see now?"

I nodded, and he closed his eyes for a minute, gathering his insights. Then he told me that I radiated a high level of spirituality, but that I only brought my breath down to the solar plexus area of my body.

"Anything below your waist is a 'no-no' to you. You're keeping yourself top heavy. You have no problem with height, in fact, you'd go out of the stratosphere, and you're willing to move sideways, but you won't ground it."

"What do I need to do?" I asked.

"Abandonment. You need to allow yourself to act with abandon and the issue relates to being abandoned. How's that for a paradox?"

I looked at him closely. "I never thought of it that way, Mark, but it's true. I felt abandoned by my father when he died. I was nine years old, and made a decision never to be emotionally abandoned again, either literally or figuratively. So how do I overcome this?"

"Well," he responded. "First of all, the way you breathe tells the story. The fear is of losing control, so you confine your breath to the upper portion of your body. The sexual area is much more complex for you, and you aren't willing to bring life all the way down to the root of your pelvic area. What happens is that you restrict the vibrancy of the chakras by doing this. They need oxygen as a stimulant, and the first three chakras are not getting a lot of nourishment. This makes the other centers over-compensate, and the entire system is stressed as a result.

"When you understand what's happening and see the effect breath can have on the body, you'll be able to work with it to bring about a non-verbal agreement between you and the body memory of abandonment."

"What do you mean by that?" I asked.

"Okay. You missed this when you left." He paused a moment, gathering his thoughts. "For you, the memory of abandonment has created something that can be thought of as a firewall. You won't go deeper, because you don't want to feel the pain of that original loss. One of the ways to work with fear is to breathe into it. What I told the group is that there are several different ways to breathe. You have no problem with air going to the upper portions of your body... you draw it in and let oxygen go way up into your brain cavity... but you stop it here at the solar plexus.

"So now what I want you to do is a reverse breathing technique. Exhale when you would normally inhale, and inhale as you extend your stomach forward. Then I want you to feel where the air is going in your body."

I pulled the air in and felt how easily it stayed in my chest and head area, swirling around there, but as I paid attention to the lower portion of my body, it was as though there was a gate that was locked shut, with a sign reading, 'Air not welcome here!' Mark placed his hands on the part of my body that he wanted me to bring breath to, and I concentrated on extending the level further and further down. It wasn't easy at first. He told me not to force the air, and explained more about how the process worked.

"When you want more breadth and width in your life, you expand the chest cavity with air. You feel it going sideways and front and back, beyond your skin, extending out toward the wall of the room, and then visualize it going out into the surroundings and eventually linking up with everything in the world. You do the same thing with height. You visualize your breath going beyond you to an unlimited space in the cosmos. And then you have to anchor it all by feeling the air going down as far as it can reach. See it move into the ground, penetrating the earth's core until it goes to the center. You breathe the earth, and the earth breathes you.

"When you put them all together, you have powerful resonance in the body. It begins to affect the cells, and cellular memory. You can expand, and alter perception non-verbally. You are also able to affect physical health through this process, so the quality of your breath really does impact the quality of your life."

He went on to tell me that doing this for four minutes every morning before getting up, and four minutes in the evening before going to sleep would begin to make a gradual change in my body and psyche.

"You see, you've already done an incredible amount of work on yourself. You've done the psychological work and been willing to dredge up the ghosts. But this is residue stuff. It is very subtle, and it gets in the way. We're all trying to clear up our own glitches in order that we can come together to do the more advanced techniques that are going to allow us to be highly effective as individuals and as a group."

I wished I'd been there for his presentation. "I'm sorry I missed what you did with the others. I guess this is an opportunity for me to be aware of how my fear level short-circuits me at times."

Mark smiled. "We all have trigger points. They're different for everyone, but life makes sure we each get our fair share of reminders." We both laughed, and he continued. "Another technique I've seen used which is very effective is one where we breathe and then listen to different sounds. It's a variation on what Sarasvati taught us. There are some tones that will bring you to tears, and others that agitate you, excite you, or cause you to feel incredibly connected. The idea is to find a place of focus through breath that doesn't get hooked by any of those sounds, so that you can experience pain and pleasure without becoming them. This is going to be very important in the coming years as we may be bombarded by new frequencies. We have to maintain equilibrium internally when it's not available in the outside world."

"Does this have anything to do with high frequency tests being done by the government?" I asked.

"That's part of it. The earth has got something going on now with the magnetic fields dropping that is allowing more frequency to penetrate us from the rest of the universe, so there are a lot of factors. Some of this stuff was prophesied by many different cultures as all happening around the End Times."

"You think that's real?" I wasn't sure.

"Yup. I do. A few years ago, we were approaching the threshold, but now we're in it for sure. We're not in Kansas anymore, Toto. That's why Roland has us doing these exercises that our Indian friend taught us the other day."

The door opened and Roland appeared. It was good to see him back, but I was glad Mark led us in the exploration during the day, because the focus was on the knowledge rather than on the person presenting the insights. I realized I'd been feeling a sort of hero worship for Roland that was based partially on my deep desire to find someone who represented perfection. Now he could be one voice among many, and I could react more appropriately to whomever that meant he was.

After dinner was over we piled into Nathan's rented Buick Park Avenue. We drove through the mountain range toward Santa Fe, passing a huge caldera, where an extinct volcano had erupted thousands of years before. It was said that parts of the eruption had been found as far away as fields in Kansas.

Nathan had a collection of tapes he'd brought, and the music of Carlos Nakai's *Emergence* was perfect for our ride through the gorgeous mountain scenery. We passed through Los Alamos, and I was struck by the natural beauty of the town where death had been manufactured in the form of an Atomic bomb. Again, here was evidence of the sacred and profane coinciding. If we looked, we could find examples of paradox everywhere in life.

We turned onto a highway that passed a particularly spectacular mountain range, and I felt myself pulled in by their beauty and poise. They were truly awesome, and I could understand why so much art came out of New Mexico. The natural setting was an artist's incubator, and the steadiness of the earth fostered unhindered creativity.

Moving down from the mountain range, we came to a long stretch of straight highway that would take us into Santa Fe. We passed an Indian Casino on the left, and Roland made a comment that it was the best place to gamble in the area.

Fiona commented that she felt gambling was immoral, and Nathan laughed.

"Do you invest in stocks, Fiona?"

"Well yes, some. Doesn't everyone?"

Nathan looked over his shoulder at her. "The largest gambling casino in the world is the New York Stock Exchange!"

Mark laughed. "That's an interesting take on it."

Lillian spoke up. "Did you know that gambling can be a modern form of Samurai training?"

We all laughed. Her remark came straight out of left field.

"No, I'm serious. There are schools that train people how to gamble. It has very little to do with luck, and everything to do with your state of concentration, your ability to remain detached in the face of winning and losing. There are people who make good livings as gamblers. They come to it as a discipline, and they do not violate their code of ethics while playing.

She was serious! "They know when to place a bet, how much to spend, and when to stop. They have a quota, and they have to be aware of their state of consciousness when they play. It can never become emotional or personal, and if it does, they have to walk away. Gambling from a professional perspective is not about winning the highest stakes. Everything is gauged by a formula."

"Good Lord," said Fiona. "Being with this group means you never stop learning, not even on the way to go dancing!"

"How do you know about this, Lillian?" asked Mark.

She arched one eyebrow and with an enigmatic smile replied, "I've lived with one of them."

Again, we laughed, and the rest of the trip was filled with lighter conversation.

As we came to the outskirts of Santa Fe, I was struck by the architecture. Everything blended into the scenery. The houses were adobe; some simple and others very lavish. Nothing detracted from the natural setting, and these dwellings were placed in such a way that they did not intrude.

The importance of harmony in relation to the natural setting was very apparent as we drove through the outskirts of town. I could see why the real estate and aesthetic value of places with strict building codes remained consistently high. Enlightened planning integrated place, space and human interaction. It required long-range objectives, and willingness to go against the obvious monetary pressures. The result was an elevation of the soul!

Arriving at dusk, we were treated to an awesome

sky with strands of purple, gold and red entwined. There was so much richness of color in the skies of New Mexico; it took my breath away. After we'd parked the car, I lingered outside as long as possible so as not to lose the memory of this beauty.

Roland and Lillian pointed out a favorite gallery of theirs, and we stopped to see the sculptures and paintings. As we walked in, I was aware of a distinctive looking man staring at Lillian. He walked over to her, and as she turned, they smiled at one another.

"Russell Stolitz, you son of a gun!" Lillian chuckled a husky greeting.

He grabbed her in his arms and gave her a bear hug. She introduced us to him, and as we met, I had the vague impression I'd seen him somewhere before.

"Russell was an advisor to the President. He's a business wizard, and one terrific advocate for getting America into other economic markets. We've known each other forever!"

Suddenly it dawned on me where I'd seen him before. He was the man in my dreams several weeks ago! I almost gasped aloud, because the name was almost the same as it had been when I dreamt about him. But he had been in an adversarial position then until I'd recognized him for who he truly was. I wondered about the real person, and why I dreamt about him.

Lillian invited him to come dancing with us, and he was more than happy to tag along. They fell into animated conversation, and she told him about our meeting as a group. He seemed quite interested and talked with Roland and Mark at length about the breathing exercises for clearing.

The sky was still gorgeous, the air dry and warm, with twinkling stars beginning to peer through the red and purple mantle. I walked ahead with Nathan and Fiona and we stopped in at a store that had some interesting things in the window. Fiona headed immediately for a counter where they sold unusual objects, and I found a sculpted tin feather in turquoise that had a small bird feather attached.

We paid for our purchases and joined the others. People stopped Lillian periodically to remark about her paintings. She was well known in New Mexico, and seemed very comfortable with the attention she received.

Once at the hotel, we were told that there would be no dancing because the group had to cancel at the last minute. Disappointed, Fiona feigned a tantrum, and the manager asked us all to be his guests for cocktails. I could see that the two of them knew each other and that he was attracted to her.

The hotel had a comfortable lobby, similar to the Empress Hotel in Victoria, British Colombia, with grand, overstuffed chairs and couches, area rugs, and dark wood tables, complimented by an extraordinary fireplace, and quality paintings.

We found an area where the seven of us could sit, and Roland asked Russell about himself.

"Well, I went to the Wharton School of Business, served in Vietnam, and came back to work for my dad. My father was a very shrewd investor, and had a real feel for where the country was going. I expanded on his vision, and in my early years was only intent on increasing our bottom line without thinking about the people whom we employed in the process.

"One of our competitors had a major fire in his factory, and my father was delighted that the guy was going out of business. He didn't have much respect for the man, because he was "soft" on his workers.

"I was to go out and pick up some of this man's contracts since he wasn't going to be able to honor them, and an amazing thing happened in the process. I found customers who had total loyalty to the man who was their supplier. They were offering to help him find space in the interim before the rebuilding of his plant was finished and supplying loans to make sure he got back on his feet.

"On top of it, this competitor of my father's was paying his employees their regular salaries while the buildings were under construction. That's unheard of in the industry. Rather than take the insurance money for himself, he poured everything, including his own money, back into the community to keep it going, because he knew that without his help two small towns would die.

"That experience changed me. When I went out and talked to his employees, they spoke of this man as though he were a hero, and they pitched in to make sure that everything was done to resume work as quickly as possible to supply their contracts so the business would stay afloat. It was a real lesson for me in the spirit of doing business. We never learned that at business school!" He laughed.

"What ever happened to that guy and his business?" Mark asked.

Russell chuckled. "In the midst of everything, he'd been working on a new process that revolutionized materials being used, and increased revenues within six months after the fire. He was able to hire back almost all the workers during that time, and once the plant was rebuilt, they tripled their profits. It caused a few of us to rethink the way we looked at employees."

"So how did you get involved with the government?" Nathan asked.

"Well, I made inroads in expanding foreign markets for our company when we couldn't get the labor we need here. The opportunities have been good for everyone, and our results indicate long-term growth. That's how I came to the attention of the President. We needed to strengthen our existing economic ties worldwide and broaden into new arenas. There's a lot of competition now that there's more equal footing amongst the developed nations."

Fiona asked him about his view of technology in the future, and he felt we were making gigantic leaps that would make what was cutting edge in the present seem archaic very soon.

"What we're doing is developing a technology that will practically be able to advance itself. We've set things in motion that are going to outdistance our ability to stay abreast unless we do some fast shuffling. We have to improve education in this country because we're already unable to find the people we need for the technological jobs we have, so we have to get them elsewhere. It's an interesting phenomenon. The United States has produced the most advanced technology in the world, and is unable to draw upon its own work force for the needs that we've created.

"When I went into the advisory position, I was pretty idealistic, but I became disillusioned fairly soon after I saw how little long-range planning was going on. Our political system has forged a quick-fix mentality in order to get votes and cater to special interest groups. It is pathetic how many lobbyists have the upper hand in Washington. If you really knew who was running the country, you would be appalled!"

"Well," Nathan interjected, "that's the same thing that's happening on Wall Street with stocks. Everybody is doing what's going to work in the moment to get new shareholders, without concern for the long-range effects on a company. Hey, we're hiring people at the CEO and CFO levels at about 500 percent above past salary ratios between top management and the rest of the work force. It really ticks me off! We're compromising integrity by giving stock options that are ludicrous to decision makers who have a vested interest in making the stock soar in order to exercise their options."

Russell nodded. "I can't argue with you on that point. I can tell you, though, that there are lots of good companies like the one I told you about operating on solid ethical business practices. It's the dramatic examples that hit the news. No doubt, though, we are not looking forward in our decisions toward the future."

"So," Lillian said somewhat sarcastically, "There are times when living in the moment is not the appropriate response!"

"Very true." Russell shook his head, and our drinks arrived. We toasted one another and our country, hoping for better decisions to insure a vital future for the nation that we all loved.

From out of nowhere, a burly man appeared, swearing, calling Russell a 'stooge of the third world,' and yelling that he had no chance in hell of going to heaven; that he was a rich S.O.B. with no soul, who was selling the country down the river.

Here was the aggression from my dream, but not in the way it had been portrayed. Roland and Russell rose from their seats simultaneously, and Roland invoked a tone that caused the man to stop his attack. The manager rushed over and apologized profusely as two of his employees ushered the man out of the hotel.

"This kind of thing is going to happen more and more," Russell said. "People don't realize what's going on. We're exporting jobs because we can't hire cheap labor in our own country, and we have to import high-priced labor because we don't have the trained manpower to fill the high tech jobs we do have. What's wrong with this picture?"

"Well," said Nathan. "Nobody wants to pass the bonds necessary to increase aid to education, because there's no immediate return. As you said, we tend to be shortsighted about most things that involve long range planning."

Russell nodded. "It's even more fundamental than that. Throwing money at education doesn't necessarily guarantee results. We have to revamp the system to reflect the dramatic changes we've experienced as a society and teach children in ways that will make sense to them. Our present concept is pretty archaic."

Lillian asked Russell if he thought that was part of the reason why people did not want to pass bonds, or if they just didn't want to pay out any more money on something that wouldn't give them a return.

Russell smiled. "Well, that may be a small part of

the reason, but you can see the ostrich approach to planning on a lot of fronts. For instance, a very small percentage of Americans have adequate savings plans, which is pretty troubling, since we are not a socialist country. People do not understand that other than their own planning, there really is no effective safety net.

"We complain about social security, but it was never intended as a retirement plan. It was supplementary, and when it was instituted, the idea was that the individual might live five or ten years from the time they started collecting. Now, we're living well into old age, and we are asking that system to do something it was never intended to do. We are a nation of debtors, and our European and Asian allies cringe at our lack of foresight, because they are much more oriented to the long range financial effect of their actions, individually and collectively."

"Exactly!" Nathan nodded in agreement. "This is our problem. You have a general public who doesn't want to save money, who will not make decisions to invest in the long term... you have special interest groups who want to deplete our reserves now in order to make an immediate profit...and the result is a compromised future."

Fiona was concerned about this. "Why do you think Americans feel this way?" she asked.

Russell looked thoughtful. "Well, it's a complex issue, and there are a lot of reasons, but number one, this has been a country that has always had plenty of renewable resources. Waste was never an issue, because there was more and bigger. During a great portion of our history as a country, we were in a dynamic trade position with other nations who did not have the amount of raw energy or goods to trade. It's also a nation of resilient, adolescent energy. So there's never been a feeling that anything couldn't be done, almost an arrogance that you'd see in teenagers. But we've been able to pull it off.

"The problem now is that the rest of the world is catching up, or has caught up, and they have drawn their growth from a long history that we don't share. We are the young ones in terms of vantage point. They are not. This works to our advantage in many cases, because we believe in possibilities. But we don't have a long attention span, and we tend to look for quick solutions. This isn't new. When the World War II broke out, we were abysmally unprepared. Howard Hughes bailed this country out in a big way then, and we had the enthusiasm, energy, and resources to mobilize very quickly, getting things done that countries more entrenched in conservative thinking would not have been able to do. So again, the issues that face us are complex and double edged many times."

"Russell, what do you think the solution is?" asked Fiona.

Russell warmed to the question. "Well, one of my major concerns right now is our educational demise. We've already lost at least one generation, and given the present political climate, it's going to boil down to companies becoming involved in education. If we want a competent work force from our own country, that will be the only way it's going to happen. The question is whether companies will be willing to educate the whole person, or concentrate solely on the area that affects their economic investment. We have a lot of thorny questions to answer. It's not going to be easy, no matter what we decide to do, because we have let this problem get out of hand."

Roland, who had been quiet throughout the discussion, spoke. "And in educating, to make that education compatible with the future. Our whole methodology is geared to the past, and we are educating a group of individuals whose frame of reference is light years beyond the industrial revolution... which was the model for our present system. We have to make the necessary shifts to insure that our children will be prepared to cope with the new paradigms that are being put in place.

"Everything you brought up throughout this discussion is an example on a daily level of what's happening at an energetic level on our planet. We are struggling between an electric, forward moving action and a magnetic, binding reaction. We are not aware of the cost ecologically when we cut down rain forests, or tamper with technology we're not capable of controlling, because we're not looking at the long-range consequences of our actions. We are only focused on the momentary gain, and the familiarity and workability of our past course of action.

"So we cause major disruption to the system in which we live and feel justified in doing so because we're operating from a belief system that is no longer adequate. There are people who are awake and aware, like the man whose factory burned down. They are progressive realists who understand how the whole system is tied together, that if one part falls, it all falls. These people make a positive difference, but they don't get the press because our media reflects the consciousness of this time period, which is steeped in fear, and their reporting becomes a litany of the latest murder, rape and explosion.

"It's as though only the negative elements qualify as news. But in a world of over seven billion people, how is it that what happens to maybe 10,000 is considered newsworthy? Our news feeds fear, and we create a self-fulfilling prophecy."

Russell nodded. "You're right, Roland. You've really found an area where you can put your effort into helping people wake up. Each of us has to pick our fight, and although I'm not cut out to be a politician, I am willing to gather for discussion with others who have concern and want to see something happen to get us moving in a healthy direction again.

"As you can tell, I have a real interest in education. Fiona, I think that you, as a filmmaker, can do a lot to make a contribution. We need people to bring a collective vision forward that makes sense to the nation. Americans are not stupid. We're a little stubborn, but that goes back to our pioneer heritage, and as the adage from our friends in Missouri says, 'Show me!' "

Lillian had been listening intently and shook her head. "And don't forget in this picture you're painting to remember the arts. All of these logical ingredients are fine, but if the soul isn't inspired, we lose our connection to the driving force behind life."

Everyone nodded, and we sat quietly in reflection for a time. Lillian looked over at Russell and broke the silence.

"Well, my friend, you certainly don't seem to be a raging capitalist selling the country down the river as the intruder suggested, so I don't necessarily think you'll be going to hell anytime soon."

He chuckled. "Well, isn't it easier for a camel to go through the eye of a needle?"

I perked up, and told him the Aramaic translation about a rope going through the eye of the needle, not a camel.

He thought for a moment. "Good! I like that. The rope is important because it can lift a heavier load, whereas a strand would snap under the weight. The trick is to know when to be the rope and when to simplify and become the strand. So, that's a much more hopeful prognosis, and if I get it right, I might be able to join you good people in the great beyond after all!"

It was getting late, and Lillian and Russell went off by themselves for a few moments as the rest of us chatted amongst ourselves. Mark commented that we needed more people like Russell serving in office.

Roland laughed and shook his head. "Not just politics, my friend. We need more people like him showing up to serve life!"

Everyone nodded in agreement, and it was time to go home. On our way back to Sulfur Springs, we listened to a tape of the Gypsy Kings, sang songs, and shared ideas. It was a thoroughly wonderful end to what began as a difficult day.

Chapter 9
❧ On Life and Creation ❧

Wed become closer through the events of
the week, and as we collected next morning
in the workroom, everyone greeted each
other warmly. It was a true group of peers, with
Roland acting as our facilitator. I had fully overcome
my hero worship, and found he was an interesting
and very complex person. His emergency involved
horses he owned having to be moved from one locale
to another in the high country up north. He had a
deadline to get them out of one location, and the people who were supposed to handle the move had
backed out.

We were ready for our morning exercises, and took
our places in the same seats we'd occupied from the
first day, little creatures of habit that we were.

Roland intoned the sound, and gradually thought
filtered out. There was only the rhythm of breath,
tone, and color – a play of energy merging us into a
harmonious unit. I was beyond space and time, feeling the connection to the others through strands of
light that grew stronger as our bonds to one another
developed. I could feel our heartbeats converging,
everything pulsing to the vibration of love.

I had never experienced anything like this before
in my life, and was overjoyed to have found it,
because it showed me that in truth, we really are all
part of one system of energy. When the process rolled

to conclusion, I didn't want to come back into the room. The gentle sound of a bell called me forth, and I opened my eyes. Looking around, I could see connecting lights between each of us. They were of a similar pattern and hue, becoming more vibrant and physically visible with each day.

Roland suggested the night before that we should see the historical sites of the area, including a museum dedicated to the Native Americans living in the area. It included the ruins of a catholic church that was burned out during the rebellion in the 1600s by the natives who had formed the community atop the mountain we had visited earlier in the week. After our morning session and lunch, we piled into the Ford Explorer for our trip to town.

The layout of the museum and the church ruins was well done. First, we went through a small building that housed the memorabilia of the early tribe, and we read the history of the events that unfolded. As the Spaniards encroached on the southwest, they enslaved the natives and forced them into torturous labor. Often, workers would die because the heat and conditions were so oppressive to them. They were forced to abandon their culture and their ceremonies, the lifeblood of their society. In addition, Europeans brought strange diseases for which the natives had no immunity, and many succumbed to these illnesses as well.

Walking through the museum was an education, and I felt tears welling inside. Something about the culture of these people in their closeness to God, whom they knew as Great Spirit, caused me anguish. They had been overrun by invaders in the name of what was termed God, but really represented the machinations of power, greed, and acquisition. To view the remnants of a civilization that lived close to the source of life in simplicity, with respect for all, was moving. To see what deposed it broke my heart. There was no light, no love, and no mercy. This was another example of the arrogance we humans displayed throughout history.

When we walked out of the museum to the ruins of the church, we passed a kiva, which had been the spiritual center for the tribe. It was a deep hole in the ground, and as I looked at it, I realized this was their form of a Holy Grail. When the Spaniards took over, use of it was forbidden, and it became a depository for the beaten, mutilated, and tortured souls who were left to die as punishment for transgressions against their oppressors.

As much as I had been impacted by the psychic connections to World War II in Europe, this affected me more, because it represented the rape of innocence. Europe's innocence had vanished centuries before. I looked at the kiva, and asked forgiveness for my part in their pain. I came from a European background; I was part of the white race. My need to atone was not logical; it sprang from my soul.

Walking through the destroyed church, I could feel the exclusivity and constriction of the Spaniards. I found myself cheering the natives who had finally rebelled and burned everything. They were able to rid themselves of their oppressors for a time. However, as I continued walking along the entire circumference of the site, I felt the pain of the priests, as well. What punishment did this assignment in the New World represent for them? They had often been exiled because of politics or because they had offended an aspect of the prescribed doctrine. So here were two groups, brought together in a moment of destiny that shattered innocence and dealt retribution. Again, the paradox of life played itself out.

By the time I finished walking the site, I had come full circle in my prayer for the victim and victimizer. They were all caught in a web of someone else's creation.

When we gathered at one of the picnic tables on the perimeter, I was very quiet. Roland watched me closely. I needed to be alone, so excused myself to walk through my feelings. As I moved away, experiencing the pain that had occurred at this site, Roland came up to me.

"Are you all right?"

I nodded my head. "I'm just overwhelmed by the sense of injustice. It wasn't just the natives. It was also the priests, and the troops. They were all caught in a vice of time and politics." I looked up at him with so much feeling, that I could see he was touched.

"You have such incredible sensitivity," he said softly. He took my hand and held it tightly in his.

He spoke as we walked. "Injustice happens. We have an idealistic notion that if you do everything right, you'll be fine. We look for the just to be rewarded and the unjust to be punished immediately, but life doesn't work that way. The sun shines on everybody without distinction. And, as the Good Book says, the wheels of justice grind slowly, but they don't grind coffee." He looked at me humorously.

"What?" I couldn't believe he said that. "I think

the saying is, 'They grind exceedingly fine,'" I inter-jected.

"No, really?" He was teasing me.

It was just what I needed at that moment. Since coming to New Mexico, I was very easily touched emotionally by things that I saw, whereas at home, I was much more matter-of-fact. Perhaps this was why I'd been born and lived in the San Francisco area, as Roland had suggested. I was too vulnerable to ghosts of the past.

Roland was a surprising mixture to me, a combination of wisdom and earthiness. He was a man with a keen ability to distill experience, yet had no need to flaunt it, or be the center of attention. He seemed to live a full life, filled with passion and humor. However, there was something about him that was isolated. We walked along quietly, without speaking, and it felt very comfortable to be alone with him.

"I'm going to have to go back to the Bay Area after our retreat. I'd like to get together with you while I'm there," Roland said.

"I'd be delighted. Are you going to give another series of lectures about the book?" I looked at him questioningly.

"I'll be doing a book tour in the Midwest, and then at the end of the month in Oregon, but this is for follow up tests I have to take at Stanford Hospital."

I looked at him, surprised and alarmed. "Roland, are you all right?"

"No, not really." He paused. "I was involved in a direct hit during my stint in Vietnam. My platoon was in a target zone when our boys dropped Agent Orange. We got the brunt of it, and I'm one of three remaining members of a twelve man outfit."

He looked at me, waiting for a response. I said nothing.

"I've been very lucky. Through my own knowledge of healing techniques, I've been able to forestall the effects of the chemicals. However, the long-range toll on the liver is pretty unforgiving. Agent Orange was a very effective weapon that fulfilled its intention."

There was nothing I could say. My mind was drawn to the early death of my father, and my subsequent expectation that when I loved, I would lose. Here was a man I felt I could care about, because he touched me at a level I always yearned for. He was rich in qualities that were important to me, as my father had been. The old wound opened, and my fear of loss was ignited once again.

"What does this mean for you?" I asked, a lump in my throat.

"They have a new drug that's been very successful in retarding liver deterioration, so I'll be going back after we're done to start the program."

The implication of his illness was troubling. "Why you?" My question was more a comment. It seemed so disillusioning that the good were often affected by tragedy.

"Why not me? We go back to the wheels of justice. Our government developed a powerful chemical weapon to defoliate the area, and it had devastating effects on humans as well. When you unleash something like that, it affects everything in the system. Chemicals don't play favorites."

I nodded. "I know. But it seems so unfair."

"It seemed very unfair to the Vietnamese, too. I went back years later and met with a group of our former enemies. There was a North Vietnamese colonel who had been caught in the same bombardment I was in. He was dying, and when I visited him in the hospital on his deathbed, he greeted me like a brother. I was so shaken by the feeling of friendship he offered, that I asked him how he could accept me, having been part of the forces that now caused his imminent death. Do you know what he said?"

I shook my head.

"He said, 'Living, dying, it's all the same. No blame.' He had the sweetest expression on his face. I spent some remarkable time with his family, and his Buddhist philosophy brought me back to the wisdom of my great-grandfather and the others who taught me when I was young. I vowed that when I finished my contract in the middle east, I'd return to New Mexico as soon as I could. I never wanted to lose the link with truth, or the earth again."

It was evident that the experience touched him deeply. Again, we walked in silence, and this time it was I who took his hand and squeezed it.

He spoke quietly again. "We're all part of the same system. It's one big unit that is tied together, and Agent Orange is child's play in comparison to some of the chemical weapons that are being developed all over the world right now."

As we turned to go back toward the group, I stopped.

"Is there anything I can do for you?"

"Yes, just be yourself and don't give up on me... I'm not dead yet!" He laughed aloud, and we rejoined the others, who were still deep in conversation.

We talked about our individual experiences at the ruins and then got into the car to go over to the river. Roland had a special place where he wanted us to meditate.

As we drove down the road, I was riveted by the beauty of the landscape. I'd never seen cottonwood trees before this trip, and they were lovely and gracious, providing shelter from the hot sun. Roland chose one of the sites amongst many, and after parking, we found our way to the water's edge.

The river was approximately 30 feet across, with a backdrop of huge mountains. Roland wanted us to find places along the riverbank where we could sit comfortably in meditation. Boulders dotted the area, and I decided to find one that would give me shade and keep me off the ground. He felt we had absorbed a lot in the last few days, and that it was important to ask in meditation for our purpose as a group. He commented about the ties that we had with one another, emphasizing the need for a clear group vision in order to move forward in a meaningful way.

I had a hard time settling down, wanting to choose the perfect rock to sit on, but went from one to another until finally, I reclaimed my first choice. The sound of water splashing over a log that had fallen across the river challenged silence, and I marveled that the others seemed to move easily into meditation. I wasn't able to because I was full of my encounter with Roland.

I looked at the scenery, recognizing again the peace and solidity that I felt in New Mexico, and then glanced over at the mountains. Gradually, my restlessness gave way to interest. The mountains seemed to beckon me and spoke through their repose. I found myself staring at the sleek sheer walls jutting out from the normal rounded mountain, like landscapes from another planet. They were dramatic statements, but they were also dignity and strength, modeled by the etchings of time that defined them, and I was aware of their serenity of being. They did not bow, nor make apology for their grandeur. I thought of us as humans, constantly trying to justify our existence. They just were.

As I stared at them, I was reminded of Nelson Mandela's Inaugural Address in 1994, where he posed the following eloquent possibility to the people of South Africa:

"Our deepest fear is not that we are inadequate.

Our deepest fear is that we are powerful beyond measure.

It is our light, not our darkness, that most frightens us.

We ask ourselves, who am I to be brilliant, gorgeous, talented, fabulous? Actually, who are you not to be?

You are a child of God. Your playing small doesn't serve the world.

There is nothing enlightened about shrinking so that other people won't feel insecure around you.

We were born to make manifest the glory of God that is within us.

It is not just in some of us; it is in everyone.

And as we let our own light shine we unconsciously give other people the permission to do the same.

As we are liberated from our own fear, our presence automatically liberates others."

I had memorized that speech and was elevated every time I thought of it. I had the same response to the mountains. The depth of connection I felt to them was awesome.

As I eased into meditation, I felt their presence, alive and vital. I moved into them and they received me with welcome. As I felt the connection grow, I could see how ignorant we as humans were. We thought mountains were rooted in one place, yet these were not stationary objects, they were living outcroppings of the Earth, receptors of the cosmos, and eloquent statements jotted on the landscape.

My meditation deepened, and I was moved back in time to the origin of the planet. I saw huge forces spewing gasses, fire, and mass in an incredible burst of energy. This was creation, and I was there. I came as part of the birth process, formed as a mountain, and then was wrenched away, banished to the human kingdom.

I opened my eyes to view these majestic giants across the river. Only a few moments had passed, but for me, it was a timeless event. Here were incredible structures that had endured time and travail. They looked like elders to me, robed in earth. They were open to scrutiny, showing the granite, the shoal, the soft, the defensible, and the impenetrable. They were majestic, a revelation in layers.

We could learn from them. We didn't have to hide from our experience. It shaped us. We didn't have to apologize for the lines on our faces, for they were the markings of our passage. Through adversity, we were strengthened, tempered and refined. Insight was born of a willing heart, and life was the great teacher.

These mountains were the old ones, and I recognized in relation to our group that we were to be as they were. Time would bring change, and we would live and we would die, yet we were to support one another in a vision of the Grail, to help each remain true to that purpose, and at some point, to share the insights with others.

The mountains were guardians of the Earth, as were the trees. Humans would come and go, but the mountains would remain. The indigenous people knew, but the white man was so far removed from his origin that he could not see. I perceived how small we were in relation to the consciousness of Earth. Earth was the child of the Cosmos, and we were a sub-species.

Returning to the present, I sat quietly. There was so much to digest. I had met myself in a different form that gave me a sense of belonging to a larger reality. It was such a vast, expansive feeling to be part of the mountains. To be only human seemed isolating and restrictive.

Roland suggested that we share our insights when we got back to the house, so we climbed into the car once again. On our way home Fiona wanted to stop at an intriguing little gallery on the side of the road.

The Lost World Gallery was housed in a magnificent adobe structure with curved walls and meandering desert gardens. Once inside, the Belgian owners introduced the uninitiated into a festival of delightful art and jewelry. According to Lillian, the prices were much more reason-able than in Taos or Santa Fe, and the selection was quite fine.

Browsing through the round shaped building, I

found unique jewelry and purchased a stunning bronze necklace for myself, and earrings for friends. Roland was engaged in conversation with the owners, a warm rapport between them. As I watched him, I thought that he didn't look unhealthy. He seemed the picture of well-being. I hoped that the prognosis at Stanford would be better after the next round of tests, and that the new drug he was going to take did its job.

We had become a soul family. The mountains and these people meant a great deal to me, and I didn't want to lose any one of them.

Chapter 10
❧ *Revelation* ❧

Roland shared his medical news with the others at breakfast, and everyone was genuinely concerned. Fiona went up to him and held him in a tight embrace.

"Roland Ivory, you can't be ill. We need you!"

He chuckled. "Well, I need me, too, so I'm doing my best to make sure that whatever can be done will be done."

Mark looked at him seriously. "Roland, I know of a very good healer in Oregon who I'd like you to see. He's had a remarkable track record with a lot of people. In fact, they are using him for inoperable diseases up at some of our hospitals in Portland, and he's able to actually cause cells to regenerate. I'll call him the minute I get back and put you two in touch."

"Thanks, Mark. I appreciate that. I'm using conventional and unconventional methods to treat this disease. So far, I've been able to hold my own. It's just apparently moved into another more critical stage, and I want to make sure I stabilize things before they get out of hand."

Nathan mentioned machines that were doing incredible things, although the American Medical Association was trying to keep them under wraps. Lillian knew someone in Taos, and Fiona had the names of several alternative healers in the United Kingdom. As for me, I thought of Bob Sherman, another of the many priests I knew who had branched beyond the church.

Bob was given an extraordinary gift at birth. It was the power of vision and prayer, and he used the combination effectively throughout his 20 years as a priest. However, he found the need to make his gifts available to more people, as the numbers of non-Catholics kept pouring into his parish. They wanted him, not the teachings, and this did not sit well with the Church. So, Bob made a decision that his calling was healing, not orthodoxy.

He set up a foundation dedicated to the work of prayer, and had remarkable results with people of strong faith and those who had none. He would invoke what he called the "Holy Spirit," and a force would enter the room that often knocked over the individual being prayed for. Bob kept his requested fees very nominal, so that no one would be turned away from healing sessions with him, and his lack of greed made a major impact on others. Here was a man who truly followed a calling of healing, and did not do it to become wealthy.

Bob always said that the gift he'd been given was just that, a gift, and he knew that it was to be given to others without penalty for their financial status. Those who could, gave more. Those who couldn't, gave little. 'It all works out in the wash,' he would say. And it did. He was slowly becoming known throughout the nation, and had the kind of integrity that is a guideline to ethical consideration and respect for ourselves and one another. I felt that Roland could be helped by Bob, so I told him that when he came to the Bay Area, I'd call and try to set something up.

After we finished talking about the process Roland was engaged in, we sat down. "You see," he said, "life still continues. We don't get out of the details, we just try to make them finer points."

As part of the agenda for the week, Roland had each of us share aspects of our work, and Nathan told us about the life of a mathematical equation, called a fractal. He showed a beautiful video that chronicled its life in gorgeous colors, like the surrealistic dance of a kaleidoscope. He said that during the life of the equation there would be continuous stimulus that appeared chaotic, but caused reactions that would eventually lead to one point where balance was achieved.

In that instant, the patterns changed, and new stimulus was presented until the equation's death, when equilibrium was achieved for one last time. Nathan said that the life of the equation mimicked all life from chaos to order, and the return to chaos again... in other words, creation, life, and death.

"Wow, that's really a trip!" exclaimed Mark. "How do you equate it to us?"

"Well," said Nathan, "as we work with more complex forms to see patterns emerge, and then manipulate them to create different reactions, we're able to understand the mechanism of life from a mathematical perspective. We can translate that knowledge to other branches of science, which includes our understanding of the patterns of genetics and DNA. From where I stand, life is a gigantic mathematical equation, and I want to figure it out."

Roland added a comment. "We've shared our unique work with one another, and we've seen the value of other perspectives that can contribute to our own picture as we keep an open mind. Respecting our differences rather than trying to convince each other that our particular view is the only one, or the right one is very important. In this complex time period we need to cooperate more than ever, and that's why it's essential to gain clarity about ourselves so we don't let our singular viewpoints and issues intrude on the larger reality."

Fiona spoke up. "That reminds me of a story about people who had never seen an elephant because they were blind. They were asked to describe what it looked like based on their perception from touching different parts of the elephant. The one who had the tail said that the elephant was like a rope. The one holding the trunk was sure the elephant was similar to a long tube. The one feeling a leg said that the elephant was the same as a tall tree, and on and on.

"They could not see anything other than their portion, and had difficulty envisioning what the others perceived as the elephant because they had not experienced it. And that is an example to me of how we all have trouble allowing for something more than what we have been taught is the way. We seem to be threatened by other viewpoints."

"So what's the message in that?" Roland asked.

After a couple of moments, Mark spoke. "When people are so concerned about being right, they're coming from fear, because at a deeper level, they know they don't have the whole truth, and somehow that knowledge causes them to feel diminished and out of control. We need to recognize it isn't possible for any one of us to have it all. We're meant to join forces and share our stories and pictures of reality because that's the only way we're going to grow and the only way we'll get the whole elephant."

Nathan felt it was important to take a scientific approach to all information. He said we should analyze and investigate different data and then bring it together. In the case of the elephant, he felt that by combining the perspectives in spatial relationship to one another, a logical finished product could be constructed.

Lillian added her own spin to the concept. "The beauty of painting is that you play with reality and find different ways to express it, so I would engage the artistic spirit. Have one person paint what each of the others perceives, and you'll either come up with a complete elephant, or a fantastic surrealistic version of one!"

We laughed, and Roland continued.

"This is the purpose for the processes we're going through. If we can clear up our own misconceptions and bring something greater to light as a group, we're creating a template for that experience in others. We've been so polarized as a species to limit ourselves... and don't get me wrong, as a species we're doing well, because we're still very young. But the potential of humans to extract ourselves from the cycle of repetition is tremendous. We've put blinders on, and now it's time to open to the possibility of a larger, world view, to a greater cosmic vision.

"We're not the only ones gathering in this process. There are others who are spontaneously feeling the call as well. Each of us is part of a vanguard that has to move perceptually from fear to love, moving out of the root into the heart chakra. Everything is speeding up. Nathan can explain more about that."

Nathan nodded, and expressed how the earth's electrical frequency is increasing while the magnetic field is dropping, which makes things much more intense. He said that the magnetic field represents the past, while the electrical frequency represents the future. Therefore, the electromagnetic field is present time.

"This is affecting all of us, and the end result is that time is speeding up. There is much more dynamic tension between earth and other planets within our solar system. We can look at planets like Jupiter and the Sun and see that all kinds of anomalies are taking place. We're discovering new star systems, and our horizons are widening as technology is advancing. The problem is that technology has outdistanced our humanity, and now we have to catch up."

Roland nodded in agreement. "So, we are given a very important piece of information here that helps explain what is going on in our lives at this moment. If the magnetic fields which hold the past are dropping, and the electrical frequency representing the future is increasing, the electromagnetic field of the present is being skewed away from what has been familiar, and forcing us to open to new data.

"That explains why everything is more intense now. We are all being required to change frequency. We are going through an attunement process, and a new Grail is being formed. But we cannot experience it until we release the things that hold us back from hearing the new tone.

"Every vestige of history that we carry holds us

back. Each unresolved relationship in our lives does the same. Everything we put into our body that restricts the flow of light is retarding our progress, and it is essential to get ourselves ready to absorb subtle energy, because we are in a time frame of major change."

We were all quiet. The information was slightly overwhelming, and I wondered if I was up to the task. Fiona broke the silence.

"Roland, you make this sound like there is a time-line. I'm feeling a little concerned that I might not be able to meet the requirements in the allotted time."

Roland nodded. "That's understandable. It seems like a lot on our plates at one time. But that's just it. We've already been experiencing the stress, the coincidences. We've each found our sleep patterns altering. There is more tension, and often a feeling of exhaustion even when we've had the required amount of sleep. We are being forced to face every one of our past fears, or our judgments. It's getting harder and harder to keep blaming somebody else for things not working in our lives.

"We are part of something much bigger than ourselves. This is a timeline set in motion eons ago, and we just happen to be here at its culminating point. We'll be able to get where we need to be if we start following a program that helps in the awakening. Otherwise, this period can be pretty stressful."

It was time to break for the afternoon. We'd taken in a lot of information, and I needed to do something more light hearted to balance things out.

On my way back to the bungalow, I passed the kitchen. Doreen waved to me, and I stopped to talk with her.

"How would you like to visit with a friend of mine from the village who is a medicine woman?" Doreen was inviting me on an adventure, and I was delighted that she thought enough of me to ask. I told her I'd thoroughly enjoy the opportunity.

Doreen had everything ready to put in the oven for dinner, and removed her apron. She hung it on the wall, and took my hand as though leading me to a secret hiding place. We got into her compact car and headed for the village. As we drove onto the reservation, I noticed that some of the houses were rundown, and many of the adobe buildings had kilns in front of them. There were dogs running free and children playing on the roadways. People moved unhurriedly, and although the area was poor, the spirit was not.

We turned up a dirt road and wove between several houses until we came to an adobe settled back against the hills. We parked the car and as we approached the entrance, an elderly woman, who had an unworldly look in her eyes, opened the heavy wooden door. Doreen brought an armful of vegetables and walked into the house, beckoning me to follow.

Inside, the room was a perfect temperature. There was a cool feeling from the adobe and the roof was low with rough wooden beams over a mixture of straw and clay. The furnishings were simple, but comfortable. Doreen spoke to the older woman in a language I didn't understand, and then took me by the hand and brought me in front of her. As I got closer, I realized that the woman was blind.

Tia Minnie, as Doreen referred to her, had experienced a lot through the years. She had a beautiful round face, weathered by the sun, and reminded me of the wonderful earthy women I had seen in Eastern Europe. Her countenance was warm and inviting, and she held my hands in hers and then put her hands on my face, tracing its outline with her nimble fingers. She murmured something to Doreen and we sat down.

Doreen told me that Tia Minnie had developed a special blend of herbs, mineral oils, and gems that were powerful medicine, and that people came from all over the country to see her. Since she lost her sight as a child, she developed other faculties, and had a keen awareness of unseen realities. She became known within her tribe as a powerful medicine woman, respected by all. Although she was blind, she had a feeling for color. She developed beautiful shades for the bottles that housed the mixtures she created, recognizing the hues by some means that was inexplicable to the rest of us.

Doreen asked Tia Minnie if she could show the bottles to me, and when the older woman smiled and nodded, Doreen took me to the next room where every color and shade of the rainbow lined shelves on the walls. It was quite an extraordinary sight, and I asked Doreen if her friend had arranged the bottles herself, or had a sighted person do it.

"No, she does everything herself. She 'feels' the colors and arranges them together by the heat they give off. She has everything in its right place because the colors speak to her. She plays a flute and says the sounds of the music also have color, and when she plays, the bottles get brighter."

I was amazed at the array in front of me, and

Doreen asked if I'd like to hear Tia Minnie play.

"Oh, I'd love to, but I don't want to disturb her."

Doreen smiled. "She enjoys doing it for people she likes. She told me she likes you."

Doreen asked Tia Minnie to play, and the older woman shuffled over with her flute to a seat in the room of colored bottles. She began playing a haunting refrain, and I felt myself close to tears at some points. When the music was sad, the blue bottles seemed to be sharper in color. When she played sounds that were warm, the red and yellow tones radiated vibrantly. As she continued, I noticed how the colors of the bottles were also 'playing' her song. I was fascinated, as I'd never seen anything like that before.

When she finished, she said something to Doreen, who turned to me and said that Tia Minnie wanted me to choose three bottles that I found attractive. I was quite touched, and looking around the room, a vibrant red bottle, a purple one, and a deep indigo blue seemed to leap out at me, so I chose the trio. When I did, Tia Minnie took them from me and held them to her chest. She smiled, and murmured, "Good!" Then she opened the red bottle I'd chosen, and let a drop of the liquid fall on her finger and rubbed it on my left wrist. She said some words in her language and handed the bottle back to me and told Doreen that I was to hold the bottle in my right hand for a few minutes. I did.

Then she took the second bottle I'd chosen and rubbed a drop from it on my right wrist, asking me to hold the purple bottle in my left hand for the same amount of time. Finally, she took the third bottle of Indigo and placed a drop from it on her middle finger, anointing the center of my forehead in the area known as the third eye. I then cupped the bottle in both hands as directed and felt a current moving through my body that was calming and exhilarating at the same time. I sensed something wonderful was taking place at a subtle level that was important.

When the process was complete, Tia Minnie found a small bag for the three bottles, holding them out to me. "Take these home. Use them every day for three to ten minutes. They will bring the healing you need." I thanked her and she reached out her arms to give me an embrace. It was a very precious moment.

The two women chatted, and Tia Minnie told Doreen that I'd chosen well, naming the exact colors I'd taken. We said good-bye and made our way back to Roland's house. I marveled that by giving the gold coin to Doreen I had not only made a friend, but received far more in return than the coin could ever be worth.

Back at the house, I shared my experience with the others at dinner. Roland smiled.

"I told you that Doreen would warm up to you once she saw who you were! Tia Minnie is a real treasure. I've used her bottles, and they've helped me. Her work with minerals and color is quite something."

I agreed. "I was really fascinated by the whole thing, but I don't understand how they work."

Roland answered me. "The minerals and color respond to the electromagnetic field of your body. By holding the bottles, glass becomes the conductor and subtle cellular changes take place. Do you see the synchronicity at work here? We have talked about the electric and magnetic field from one point of view, and here you see a completely different application by a woman who isn't even thinking about why her process works. She comes to it intuitively."

Roland was very serious as he continued. "The reason this is coming at us from so many different directions is that it's time for these things to happen. This is the era of electromagnetic healing and discoveries that will revolutionize some of our technology. It's tied to the electric and magnetic fields of earth that are undergoing change to make these things possible. And it's one of the reasons why we need to clarify our own inner perceptions, so that we can take advantage of the opportunities that will be presented."

Chapter 11
❧ *Beyond History* ❧

Next morning I awoke earlier than usual, feeling that I'd slept better than I had in years. I took a walk in the garden and then headed to the workshop area. I didn't expect to find anyone there, but Nathan had also arrived before the others. He was at the back of the room, and as I approached, I saw an odd shaped sphere that looked like a tiny flying saucer moving by itself over a piece of wood on the table. I had seen tops that spun on the table, but this was hovering above, and I asked Nathan how that was possible.

"It's moving in relation to the magnetic strips beneath the wood, using a combination of aerodynamic principles based on shape, weight, material, and attraction."

I couldn't take my eyes off of it. It seemed magical.

"It's very graceful."

Nathan nodded. "Yes. Things that work with the natural flow of energy are extremely graceful. You can tell this is not a mechanical device operating on fuel. It's very riveting, isn't it?"

Looking at Nathan, I realized he was the one person at the workshop about whom I knew very little.

"Nathan, how did you get interested in all the things you do? What was your start?"

He laughed. "Well, growing up in the projects of Philadelphia was a tough experience. As an African

American, I had to give a wide berth to a lot of people who had no interest in seeing me make anything of myself. Fortunately, there were two individuals who really believed in me. One was my grandmother, and the other was a sixth grade teacher who turned me on to science. I was hooked forever. That's why I tend to get so impassioned about things.

"I know first hand what can happen if somebody takes an interest in you. It's become a pop phrase, but it really does take a village to raise a child. And the villages I saw raised drug addicts and gang members because very few people felt adequate or capable of making a difference. There was no structure, no framework for kids in the inner city. So gangs became the family. Guns meant power, and drugs were the escape. There was poverty, but more than that, there was hopelessness.

"My grandmother was a tough lady. She never believed anything couldn't be achieved. We were going through a lot of shifts when I was born in a search for our own identity. For a lot of us, the stereotype of colored and black were inadequate. Blood became our term. It was our blood and sweat that built a lot of this country, our blood that was spilled on the streets of America. We became brothers and sisters in a nation that wanted our labor but not our character. It was a way of trying to pull ourselves into a unified force."

"How did you escape what so many other people didn't?" I asked.

Nathan laughed heartily. "I told you my grandmother was a tough old bird. She would have invoked the wrath of God if I'd gotten off track. But more than that, I always had a sense that I was here for something bigger than my surroundings. Somehow I had the foresight to look further down the line to see what was happening to people who got into the gangs and became the addicts. There were very few of them who didn't end up dead or in jail. So when my grandmother told me I had to pay attention in school because it was a way out, I believed her."

"Where were your parents?" I asked.

"They worked constantly to bring in enough money to support the family. My grandmother lived right next door, and that's what saved us. I have two sisters who have also done well. One's a teacher, and the other's a lawyer. We're active within our communities and work with those left behind, because none of us forgot our roots. We know we were lucky. If things had been different, we might have been part of the tragedy rather than the triumph."

I shook my head. I had no idea that Nathan had overcome such a challenging beginning. "I'm sure glad that you got the right guidance, because it would have been such a waste not to have the benefit of your brilliance, not to mention you."

Nathan smiled at me. "Thanks. I'm glad it turned out that way, too."

After breakfast, Roland started the morning session by going over some of the things we'd talked about the day before.

Fiona spoke up. "Roland, there are a few things I would like you to clarify. Yesterday you said we all had to give up our history in order to do this work. Please elaborate on that for me."

Roland paused before speaking again. "In answer

to your question, it is the collective history that each of us holds on to that separates us from the rest of life. We nurse grudges that have been played out for centuries. You can look at the obvious examples of this in relation to what's happened in Eastern Europe and the Middle East as well as other places around the world where people act out ancient hatreds toward one another. But we all experience levels of this collective unrest, just not necessarily to that extreme.

"When one culture or dominant group forces its will on another, control can be exerted for as long as restrictions are in place. But if the change is imposed from the external world, and nothing is done to clear the underlying cause or misconception, when the restriction is removed, the issue will burst forward again in full fury. You cannot legislate love. It has to come through the release of fear, and this requires education and tolerance."

"Until each of us gains clarity within ourselves, the collective is contaminated. That's why we have to bring the level of accountability down to the individual, the smallest cell. If we build from the individual level, we will have a foundation that can withstand attack. The more each of us contributes to the light body, the larger our possibility will be."

Lillian spoke up. "When I went around the world in search of the Goddess images, I found something quite extraordinary happening in Yugoslavia before all the madness was unleashed. In a little town called Medjugorje, there was the visitation to some of the local children by an apparition of the Virgin Mary. The children were told things and given about seven signs that would signal certain world events. They were not allowed to tell anyone, but the revelation was written and sealed, to be revealed later. The children were devastated by the information, and continued to pass the message from Mary to the people that they must return to prayer and love one another so that the prophecies would be avoided. A local priest who knew of the prophecies even forbade his parishioners to leave the church one Sunday until they forgave each other for past offenses.

"There were healings and continued conversations with the apparition for several years. Pilgrimages are still made there by people from all over the world who want to be healed. But the reason for my telling this story is that the hatred and horrendous conflict between Bosnia, Serbia and Croatia was predicted. The Blessed Mother offered the gift of her love to heal the wounds of a society that would soon be ravaged by war.

"This shows me, as much as any other example, the existence of the mystical element within our midst. As I searched for the Goddess figures of old, I saw the incredible weaving of mystery throughout cultures everywhere. This has been the inspiration for my paintings, because the great mystery is always there, just out of reach, veiled by the face of fear. It is the great dance of life between the Sacred and the Profane."

Fiona added her comments. "I met a wonderful Buddhist monk during my work in documentaries, who had experienced the horror of Vietnam, watching his fellow monks setting themselves on fire in protest to the war. His message is very eloquent. We must *be peace* in order to *have peace.*"

Roland agreed. "Yes, I know of him, also. He was very clear that we have to give up our need to hold on to the individual and collective history that has impaled us. We must allow the present moment to be our reference point, and trust that whatever we need from the past to help navigate through the future is already encoded in us. We can give up the details. We can drop the pettiness. When we do, we become clear channels, opening the way for light to penetrate us without contamination."

My experiences on the Labyrinth came to mind, as did the extensive conversation I had with my Labyrinth companions regarding food. I expressed my feeling that as we change our diets to reflect healthy eating patterns that enhance the physical body, we become clear conduits for higher electrical frequencies. By clearing the emotional body through positive thinking, we refine our field of perception and are able to maintain the higher vibrations, becoming vessels of light in the process.

We were all quiet for a few moments. There was a lot to think about. Then Roland spoke.

"As we do the breath, sound, and color exercises, we are engaging in the first part of a clearing process that is essential for what comes later. In a sense, it is as though we've all learned the alphabet, which was the prerequisite that brought us to this point. Now we're having to learn to read and to string those letters together to shape meaning. We have to relate thought through a universal medium that everyone will understand... given that they've also learned the alphabet."

Nathan spoke. "This is why numbers are universal

symbols. Language forms idiomatically, but numbers are identifiable no matter what you speak. And numbers are the alphabet of sacred geometry, which is the foundation of the universe."

Mark commented. "So, what I'm hearing is that as we practice connecting energetically through the breath, we'll feel the subtle differences within ourselves and the information fields surrounding us. And as we communicate with each other through the exercises we've been doing, we'll be able to generate some pretty cool stuff!"

"Yes," said Roland. "We're engaging in the first steps. There are other exercises that will be beneficial, and I'm going to refer you to people whose work will be helpful in refining your perception. What we're trying to do is set a process in motion, and as our intention is clear, we'll get all the help we need along the way."

Mark noted that according to research there is only ten percent of identifiable matter in the universe, and that we as humans are only supposed to be using about ten percent of our brain at this time.

"True," said Roland. "However, there is ninety percent of the brain that is attuned to ninety percent of dark matter in the universe that cannot be defined because it vibrates at a different frequency! The work we are doing is going to expand us into that, and we're going to awaken to a whole new dimension of possibilities. The purpose for all of this is a new prototype. In effect, we are moving toward becoming fully human. We're just not there yet."

Throughout the day we went over everything we'd learned during our week in New Mexico. When the afternoon session was finished, I went with Nathan and Fiona to Sulfur Springs to enjoy the experience I'd missed earlier in the week.

Trees surrounded the area, and the mixture of heat, pine, and late afternoon emitted a gentle fragrance that was restorative. We had to climb over a series of boulders and walk a weathered path to get to a place where the springs were contained in a natural pool that looked like a large cup. The odor of sulfur rose from the water, and as I breathed in the sounds and smells of this peaceful place, I felt sad at the prospect of leaving New Mexico.

All three of us were quiet, soaking in the hot springs. Fiona and Nathan had forged a strong friendship, and I was happy to be invited to join them, as they were the two I knew least.

As we started to talk about things, Fiona commented about how much she enjoyed visiting all the different places in the world where culture expressed itself so differently.

"How so?" I asked.

"Well," she responded. "In Ireland, everything is very tightly structured. We're very, very close to one another, but everything you do is prescribed by your parents, or the priests and nuns, or the neighbors. You can plan your whole life out for forty or fifty years, and there'll never be any change.

"I wanted to see what other possibilities existed, because my parents brought me to America for a visit when I was just a teenager, and I was fascinated by the lack of structure I saw here. So when I decided that I couldn't stand having my life planned out neatly ahead of me, I chose to live in the States. It was a very traumatic event at first because I had to make my own decisions, and I didn't know how. At home you didn't need to think for yourself."

"How interesting," I commented. Reflecting on my conversation with Nathan in the morning, I observed the dramatic difference in their early environments. He saw lack of structure and felt there was a need for it, and she was enmeshed in structure that plotted one's entire future. Yet, out of the unstructured world Nathan lived in came gangs who filled the need for "belonging" to a group that would make decisions for the individual, albeit negative ones.

Nathan laughed. "So we both escaped entrapment. Just different ends of the spectrum."

"True," I said. "And what is the special ingredient that made both of you different from the many others who did not break free?"

We all thought about that question and Fiona answered. "For me there was such a thirst to know about everything, from the time I was a little girl. I never took anything I was told as gospel. I had incredible curiosity and wanted to find things out for myself. And beyond that, I had a sense that I was meant for something bigger. That set me on a quest that pushed me into film making."

"Yes." Nathan agreed. "I also had a strong sense of destiny. There was something beyond my surroundings, and as much as I was helped by the influence of my grandmother and my teacher, there was an aspect in myself that was able to recognize that help. A part of me was always observing and was not connected to the events that unfolded in my life. I later came to recognize this aspect in Buddhism."

"So," I said. "From the time we were little, each one of us yearned for something beyond the world of appearances, and beyond the details of our historical and biological roots. I think we're talking about the *Essence of Soul*. For some reason we had knowledge of that at an early age, and were not content until we got connected to the right path. In essence, we have always been on a quest for the Grail."

We looked at each other reflectively as a moment of insight dawned. After returning for dinner, we met the others in the dining room. It felt like the Last Supper, and none of us wanted to go home. Lillian would be returning to Taos, so she didn't have to leave the magic of New Mexico, but for the rest of us, there were large metropolitan areas to contend with. Having found the mountains made it that much harder for me to go. I decided to spend time sketching their beauty on my way out of the valley. I wanted to emblazon it forever in my memory, and reprimanded myself for not bringing a camera.

We gathered for our last formal meeting as a group in the workshop area of Roland's house. Those of us who needed to confirm our travel arrangements had done so, and Roland went over the various points we'd discussed throughout our stay. We did the breathing, sound and color exercises, with the added provision that we would make an effort to link up with one another through this process daily.

The vibrant colors I had seen running between us were highways of light, stimulated by the synchronization of our intention, just as I'd seen with the bottles at Tia Minnie's adobe when she played certain tones on her flute. There is so much more to energy fields than any of us knows, and we were making an attempt to create subtle energetic bridges, connecting links with each other that were not dependent on any outside form of communication.

We had agreed that our group purpose was to strengthen the inner connections we were developing with one another. We would form a phone tree and talk twice monthly. For those of us on the Internet, we'd keep in touch more regularly through e-mail. Lillian, who was not yet "wired," said she was going to finally take the plunge, as it was now apparent that the Web was here to stay.

"I think as a closing note," Roland said, "it would be good to check our schedules and see if there's a chance we can meet within the next month; either here or some-where we can agree upon."

As it turned out, everyone was supposed to be in the Bay Area for different events around the end of the month, except for Lillian, who was happy to come to the coast for a visit. I offered to make arrangements for a gathering where we would exchange ideas and map a path for future exploration.

"Good!" Roland looked at each one of us as he had done when we first came together, and I felt the swelling of love, as well as a lump in my throat. I had formed a strong bond to people who, prior to the gathering, were strangers. Yet, in this setting, and through our sharing, we became very close. We shared a common quest and were kindred spirits.

We laughed and chatted amidst ourselves, saying our goodbyes and planning our next get-together. The New Mexico portion of my journey was complete.

Chapter 12
❧ *Freedom, Art and Architecture* ❧

Returning to the Bay Area was an adjustment. I was not the same person who had gone to New Mexico. I felt inner assuredness and strength in my own function and purpose that had not been there before. I bumped into and challenged the parts of me that were eager to remain separate, and looked at my patterns in relationship, including the desire to make someone else into a hero.

I saw how I kept myself in too tight a container, and through the wisdom and sharing of the people I'd met in New Mexico, I opened to bigger possibilities. I had communed with the mountains and trees in a way that would make it impossible for me to relegate humans as the only highly conscious life force on earth, and I was gifted with the grace of something much bigger, as a focus. Now it was back to the mundane details of living.

As I made a promise to myself on the trip to New Mexico not to take my lap top computer, I hadn't checked my e-mail in a week, so I logged on to the Internet and found several messages waiting. One was from an old friend, whom I'd known back in the days when I was director of a foundation. He was the research director, and we'd become good friends.

Kenneth was passionate about life, and everything he did was done with flair. He presently worked for a foundation in Boston, and was busy researching world economic cycles. In addition, he was an avid painter, writer, poet, and lover of ideas. He had been very impacted by Zen Buddhism, and had a gift of making life an art. From Scots heritage, he wore a tweed cap jauntily over his thinning red hair, and if I were to define him, he would be the epitome of a Renaissance Man.

His message was succinct. "Great One! I'm coming out June 2nd. I will be at St. Francis Hotel in San Francisco for a conference. Love to see you. Have the 12th free all day. Let's play!" Today was the ninth. I immediately put in a call to the hotel and left a message that I would be free. Kenneth was good for me because he always encouraged my creativity, had a lighthearted attitude, and appreciated who I was. After the disappointment of leaving New Mexico, I needed this.

Roland had taken a late flight to San Francisco, and was staying with friends on the Peninsula. There was a possibility that he would have to be hospitalized, so he had no idea what the duration of his time in the Bay Area would look like. On the day of our departure from Sulfur Springs, it was clear that Roland was in pain. We had done a healing circle to give him the sustenance he would need to get through the hospital experience, but for now, there was nothing to do for the rest of us but wait to hear from him.

My phone rang. It was Kenneth. "Aah, Great One! How have you been?"

I loved the way he called me 'Great One,' a joke between us that began during our days at the foundation when I was Executive Director and he was Research Director. I had the ultimate say-so, and therefore, I became the Great One. We laughed so many times relating incidents from those days. The possibility of the intended goals had been brilliant, but the outcome was merely tax evasion. As one of our colleagues had said, some wealthy men had polo ponies, and others had foundations. When I realized I was nothing more than a glorified tax write-off, my days as director were over.

In hindsight, I had not been happy about accepting the position, as it was a departure from my own work, and I had a feeling of moving off course from my intended goals. However, I was persuaded that it was a practical decision, as I needed the income, and the salary offered was generous. The focus was also intriguing. We would study the causes of war and peace within an individual, society, and the world, to determine at what point crisis became a catalyst to breakdown or dynamic growth. We set into motion some wonderful studies that Kenneth initiated, but when it came time for publication, the founder wanted nothing released.

I remembered going to the office, dreading each day. I was making lots of money, but was empty inside. The work that looked so promising became a major frustration, because we couldn't do anything with it. In the evenings, my first act was to fix a drink to numb out. I had become a glorified paper pusher, and it didn't sit well with me.

My creativity came to a complete halt, and I found that the extra money made was spent rather than saved. By the time I extricated myself from the position, I felt totally compromised. It took a couple of years to regain a sense of flow with life, but I'd learned a valuable lesson. Whenever I went against my inner knowing for the sake of money, everything dulled. I was agitated, frustrated, disconnected, and the money never made the difference I thought it would.

Each time I retracted and opted for a simpler life, things harmonized, and I felt inner peace. I didn't know how this worked for other people, but I was clearly aware of the need for integrity to and from myself. I could see the parallel of these choices to my dream recently of the two cups...one vital and the other dull and lifeless.

"Great One! Are you there?" Kenneth was waiting for a response.

We agreed to meet on the morning of the twelfth for breakfast and a day of museum hopping in San Francisco. I liked that idea because the Legion of Honor had recently reopened after years of remodeling, and I'd heard good things about what they'd done.

I drove to the City, and parked at Union Square. Kenneth was waiting in the lobby of the hotel, brimming with enthusiasm. It was good to see him, and as we ordered breakfast in one of the hotel restaurants, we shared what we'd both been doing in the interim since we last spoke.

"God, I haven't seen you in nine years!" He looked as vibrant as ever.

"How can that be?" It didn't seem possible that we had not connected in person for that length of time. With Kenneth, even if we didn't speak for a year, when we did reconnect, it was as though no time had lapsed. Before electronic mail, our communication was confined to Christmas cards and infrequent letter exchanges. Since I'd joined the virtual community, we checked in with one another frequently.

I thought about the fear expressed by so many people toward the Internet, as though it were some major threat to life. In truth, it was an opportunity to connect with people all over the world in an instant. My introduction six months previously had blown me away. For the cost of a local phone call, and my monthly server fee, I was able to connect with people I hadn't been able to keep up with, because making the time to sit down and write letters became increasingly remote as my schedule expanded. However, when I was using the computer, I could just sign on to the Internet and write a quick note, or send pertinent information that I wanted to forward to someone.

The electronic medium reintroduced the art of letter writing, as e-mail often replaced phone calls. It was less expensive than calling long distance, and more fun than leaving messages on voice mail. It was also great to click on to your service, to find that you had mail. I loved getting personal letters and found this just as enjoyable.

After filling each in on what the other was doing, we walked to the Museum of Modern Art, several blocks away. I liked going to museums during the week because they were generally less crowded than on weekends, but since the San Francisco Museum of Modern Art was very popular, we had to wait in a long line.

The museum itself was a work of art. The use of wood, steel and concrete blended together into an abstract that was very satisfying. We went to the top floor first, where the latest art was housed. The collection was slim, but there were some interesting pieces. I was especially drawn to a huge object that was big enough to walk into. It was painted a deep blue violet and you could not tell where the entrance went as your depth perception was completely cut off. It appeared infinite, and evoked fear of the unknown or willingness to confront the void, much like a dark hole.

I was mesmerized by the piece, and as I walked around to the side, I saw that it was the shape of a bell, or in reverse, a chalice. I was intrigued by yet another coincidental element that added to my understanding of the Grail. This one was not mental; it was experiential. It was one thing to think of moving into the void. It was quite another to be confronted by it in physical form. Kenneth, who had wandered around the floor while I stood pondering the meaning of this piece, came back and pulled me over to another exhibit.

"You'll notice how we're evolving through art," he commented. "Look at this series of black paintings. On the surface, you would say they are just black paintings. They are different in size and shape, but nothing more distinguishes them." Then we walked over to a display of long steel structures. The backdrop was a white sheet, with various fragments of steel scattered on the floor of varying sizes and shapes. Several other art pieces demonstrated the same quality.

"You see, we're coming to the point in our development where we are willing to explore the void. In the metal piece, objective reality is pulled apart. In the black paintings and your bell, nothing relates to the physical world of objectivity. When we go downstairs, you will see, that as paintings evolved over time from Impressionism to modern art, we have gradually been altering the elements of reality to approach the Infinite.

"In Impressionism, the attempt was to go beyond what was realistic – to the finer qualities constructing that reality, while still maintaining the integrity of the vision. When we came to the Cubist era and Modern Art, you see the elements of the painting distorted to expand our concept of structure. What is visualized is no longer one image. The pieces are split, like atoms. This in some way paralleled the atomic era."

Kenneth was animated. "Visually, consciously, we were willing to distort reality in order to bring about another perception of it. Then as we moved further into modern art, you see the absurdity of our pictures. Art takes on a more playful, bizarre, sometimes cynical quality. We are looking at the absurdity of the reality we have created, and we are moving against it. This period correlated to the drug era and its alienation from the status quo.

"We moved from reactionary art to pop art. This was the art of the '80s that was done to objectify the new reality of materialism. Big bucks, often stark statements, but countervailing, rich use of color, broad strokes, often remarking on something undefinable. This was a time when we were moving from one world to another.

"Now, there is a transcendence to art. We are willing to go beyond all form and look at nothing. We are willing to explore the possibilities of visions that lead us to inner dimensions, and in doing so, there is great promise for revelation. We have moved beyond physical order into the formless form." He paused for a moment.

"It is interesting that just as we're willing to move art into a space that no longer needs to objectify reality, funds to the arts are cut. As we are willing to move into inner space, the perceived threat to material reality is met with the removal of financial backing. In essence, the material world is saying, 'I will not let you go beyond me!' But it can't be stopped.

"There are too many people who are being led through the material realm to its ultimate end; annihilation. There is nowhere else to go. The material world in and of itself is like the dog chasing its tail. There's nothing to catch, and once the tail is caught, what's the dog going to do with it? You can't wag your tail and chew it, too."

We laughed. He was so passionate in his perception that it was easy to understand his vision of reality. As we moved down to the main floor, I could see what Kenneth meant. Here was the evidence of art's evolution. We just happened to start at the top, but as we came to the bottom, the paintings were tighter or more ordered in their arrangement. Modern art truly moves the willing mind into spaces that reflect the play of consciousness and shifting realities.

Our venture to the museum took much longer than we had anticipated, and although Kenneth thought it had a long way to go to be world class, he appreciated the architecture and the attempt. He hoped that San Francisco would invest in modern art, as it had always been viewed as a leader in new thought. I hoped so, too.

I was excited by what I'd seen. The art on the top floor had inspired me, especially the bell/chalice, because the potential for humanity from an artistic perspective was clearly hopeful.

"Are you up for another museum?" he asked.

"I don't know if I'm up for an in-depth tour, but we can certainly go over to the Legion of Honor and see what they've done."

The Legion of Honor is located on one of the most beautiful pieces of real estate in San Francisco. Bordered by a park and golf course, the majestic building overlooks the entrance to the Golden Gate Bridge, and you can stand in front of the museum and watch huge steamers going in and out of the bay on their way to or from the Orient.

To me, The Legion of Honor, including its surroundings, is an example of human ingenuity and natural beauty combined. It evokes a sacred trust. Modeled after the Legion of Honor in France, it was placed in one of the most beautiful natural settings on earth. Human and divine conspired to bring about a complete work of art.

The human spirit is uplifted by beauty, and during the splendor of the Renaissance, architecture evoked the Divine. Using sacred geometry in design and construction, Masons were versed in the art of placement and worked throughout the western and Islamic world. Divine proportion guided the construction of buildings as it did the construction of nature.

The art of placement, now popularized through the ancient study of Feng Shui, and the art of geomancy, was integrated into building designs, utilizing sacred geometric ratios. The purpose was to evoke awe and direct the focus of the soul to the great mystery of life. Buildings based on sacred geometric proportions have the ability to instill perceptual attunement, as well as a subtle shift in the physical resonance of the human body.

When I visited Paris years before, I was very moved by the architecture. In traveling through the old sections of the city, the buildings became symphonies of stone. One could walk down a street and suddenly encounter a shape that was completely different, yet totally in agreement with neighboring structures. The result was symmetry.

I remember writing in my travel diary:

"What remains with me are the buildings as evidence in form of man's co-creative abilities. In California, we look at natural beauty; the creation of God. In Paris, man's ability surrounds you, and it is in harmony with the Divine. As much as the French have accomplished in production of goods that appeal to the senses, they have also done through architecture for the harmonizing and elevation of the soul. These buildings are a study in grandeur, as they enfold one and impart a sense of utter safety. The closeness is not claustrophobic, it is nourishing, and this is in part due to the use of geometrical shapes and blending of architectural styles. The buildings have become works of art, and are adorned to reflect the best of man's abilities.

"The buildings called me to question my own creativity, to determine where I could reach further, to explore more. Looking at this from a present-day perspective, we have few buildings that evoke the Sacred. Since the Renaissance, we have moved in a downward spiral, losing connection to the art of placement, concentrating instead on economic function and cost-effective use of space."

Kenneth interrupted my reverie, asking what I'd been thinking. I told him, and he was eager to share his own perceptions. "You know what this is all about, don't you?"

I indicated that I didn't necessarily know, and he continued.

"We are being awakened to a New Renaissance. There are too many pieces beginning to emerge that can't be explained away. Your search for the Holy Grail is one aspect of many making themselves evident as we move into the 21st Century. A resurgence of interest in the Grail, the Celts, the Labyrinth, Sacred Geometry, all are western reminders of the living reality of the Divine. In the east, there is equal awareness through different forms. One major piece of this is the emergence, world wide, of crop circles wherever grain is grown."

I was surprised that he included the crop circles. I only knew a little about them and told him I'd read in the newspaper that they were a hoax.

He laughed. "If you only knew how much dis-information we're fed in the news, you wouldn't pay attention to much of what's being reported. From where I sit, I get to see a lot more than I want to know. But that's another story.

"In relation to the crop circles, they are a phenomenon that has been occurring in cereal crops everywhere crops are grown in the world. They are sacred, geometrical forms that have been appearing more frequently in the last few years, and have become increasingly complex over time."

"Well, how do they get there?" I asked.

"It may be a phenomenon of the earth. We think of earth as this piece of real estate that we should cover up with buildings and roads, and never give a thought to the fact that it is a living organism. Earth is as much alive as any one of us, and she has incredible intelligence. She is Gaia, and she's speaking to us!"

Kenneth reminded me of Roland. He was on a roll, and I marveled at how I attracted these very impassioned individuals into my life.

He continued. "In genuine crop circles you will find that the stalks of grain are bent, not broken. The crop is still able to grow, and that's one of the ways you can tell the genuine ones from the hoaxes. Also, there is an incredible vortex of energy within the circles. We've measured them, and are able to get some remarkable readings on our monitoring equipment. What we're surmising is that sacred geometry is being utilized because it is a universal code. It crosses all language barriers. Scientists from every country can study them, and the designs are basic building blocks of the universe, as well as ancient symbols found in Egypt, and other former, advanced civilizations.

"So we figure that Gaia is making herself known. She's telling us to wake up and get off our derrières. Some of the investigators believe that we're being given clues to the next step in evolution for humanity, and that these circles are also a signal that we are being recalled to a greater circle, which includes earth and other planets. We're being reminded that we belong to a much bigger sphere, and that we have to grow up and act accordingly. There is a certain protocol required before we can be brought into the cosmic family."

I had nothing to say. I hadn't known that Kenneth was interested in crop circles. He told me he developed an interest through one of the projects he headed regarding earth anomalies in relation to economic cycles. Here was another element that signaled we were currently involved in a time period of major change.

We walked into the museum and went downstairs to the new section that had taken approximately five years to complete. I had missed visiting it, as it was always my favorite museum in the City. However, when we got downstairs, I was truly impressed. They had done a magnificent job! I found the new galleries very satisfying, and the addition of a pyramid of natural light lent airiness and spaciousness to the lower floor, which had always been very dark.

After viewing the collection briefly, we went for a late lunch at the Museum Café. The food, the view, and the company were perfect. I was curious about Kenneth's earlier comments regarding news coverage, and asked what he'd meant.

He shook his head. "You don't want to spoil a wonderful day with that. Just know that approximately thirteen conglomerates own all of our print, radio and television media, worldwide. You are seeing a consolidation of power in the most potent force on the globe – information. That's why it's so important not to allow over-regulation of the Internet. That will be one of the last vestiges of freedom of information available to any of us."

I looked at him and repeated what I believed we

all had to do. "You know, Kenneth. I'll never forget a statement that I think was attributed to the Dalai Llama, that we all have to find freedom in an unfree world. I truly believe that the illusion of freedom is just that. Everything in the temporal world leads to entrapment.

"We've got to find our way out of it through the inner doorway. That's why I'm on this quest for the Grail. It's an inner point of reference that is going to help release my attachment to fear, and to the world of appearances. There will always be something to ensnare me, or mislead me outside of myself. And I can also mislead myself and others if I don't clarify what and who I am."

Kenneth was circumspect. "You're right in what you're saying, at that level. But, we cannot ignore this kind of activity, and we have to maintain the right to freedom in communication, because it is a vital link to truth and what we stand for as a nation."

I nodded. "That's one of the reasons I think I'm learning to link up on inner levels with others through the meditation, sound, and color technique I told you about. We may not always be able to depend on other forms of communication. We stand on the brink of marvelous possibilities, but there is always the force of fear that will try to derail it."

Our mood was subdued, and we finished the rest of lunch in silence. We browsed through the gift shop, took one last look at the Rodin sculptures, and walked outside. I felt better as I reflected on the overall enjoyment of the day.

As we stood outside the museum, both deep in thought, soaking up the beauty that surrounded us, I was amazed that here I was in San Francisco, when three days before I'd been in New Mexico. While there, I felt I was in the only place that would ever matter. Standing here, I was immersed in my surroundings, and grateful that this was the city of my birth.

How quickly perception can shift. How fickle we might appear to be. Everything is but a present moment; New Mexico was no better, San Francisco no worse. They were two experiences, as was Paris. To put them into boxes would be to lose the possibility of what they really were. They were elements that contributed to a fuller perspective of life, of earth, of placement. And in it, the differences were sharp contrasts to refine my own understanding.

If I could use this knowledge in the future as a guideline, I would be well rewarded. I did not have to set things up into adversarial positions with one another – not people, not places, not circumstances. If only all of us could move out of the trap of definition in relation to better or worse. We need to come to 'is-ness,' as in, *It all just Is.* Our task is to walk between the worlds, overcoming the tendency to polarization of either/or, embracing instead the possibility of 'and.'

Chapter 13
❧ Frequency and Perception ❧

I returned to my normal routine and after several days of 're-entry,' was fully back into the swing of life in the Bay Area. I shared the experience of the mountains with Luke and Helen. Michele and I had talked and seen one another a couple of times, and at one of our meetings in our favorite coffee house, she told me that I was visibly different since I'd been away. She asked if there was any romance between Roland Ivory and me.

"You look like you're in love," she said.

"If I'm in love, it's with the process. I've waited for this my whole life, and now it's coming to me. I've always felt there was something magnificent ahead, and I think I'm beginning to see a glimmer of it." I felt very lofty.

"Well, I think that's wonderful, but there's nothing wrong with a little romance." She smiled devilishly.

I told her that I had no idea how Roland was, because I hadn't heard from him, and assumed I wouldn't see him until our arranged meeting as a group at the end of the month.

"I'll bet he calls before then." She was still at it.

I told her she was an incurable romantic, and she said that she was just a by-product of her French her-itage. We talked of other things, paid our bill, and hugged good-bye.

I had begun work on the summer newsletter and

planned to gather more data the next day. In the morning the phone rang, and it was Roland.

"Hi. I'm finished with the tests and am planning to go to Sausalito this morning to be with an old friend I'd like you to meet. Any chance you can join us later in the afternoon, say about 3 o'clock?"

"Well, yes. But first, how did everything go?" I was more than curious.

"Things actually look okay. I'm on a new drug and seem to be tolerating it well, and the other tests they did showed that the damage is still isolated, so I'm relieved. It gives me more time to find other solutions. I'll be meeting with Mark's friend in a couple weeks when I go to Oregon, and I'd also like to talk to the healer you know."

I told him I'd called Bob Sherman, who said he would not be on the road giving workshops for a while, and would make time for Roland whenever he wanted to get in touch.

I agreed to meet Roland at the home of his friend, and driving across the bridge toward Sausalito with the top down, I felt exhilarated. Roland had driven to the city with his friends in the morning, and took the ferry from San Francisco to Sausalito.

Sausalito was a jewel of a town located at the southern tip of Marin County, perched on the hillside of the bay, with a spectacular view of the Golden Gate Bridge and the San Francisco skyline. Driving along the main road of town was like meandering through the French Riviera.

The address I'd been given was one of the floating houses that Sausalito was famous for – a group of houseboats moored on an inlet of the bay. There had been an uproar about them years ago related to zoning and taxes, and there were some people who thought they were an eye sore, but a corresponding outcry from the community was loud enough to save the renegade floaters, and they were allowed to remain.

I passed some old familiar landmarks that reminded me of other times back in the late '60s when we would come to places like Zacks to party on the weekend. We would go to Buena Vista in the City, have dinner at the Old Spaghetti Factory, and come to Zacks for dancing. A lot of memories came to mind, and I recognized their effect on my body and my mood. How powerful our thoughts are! They really do have the ability to change our state – for good or ill.

I turned on the street I'd been told to look for, and drove toward the dock. I parked the car and walked down the plank that led to the walkway by the houseboats. Some looked like floating works of art, others were junky boxes on the water, and some were artfully arranged and very inviting.

I found the houseboat with a large outside deck, where wooden boxes filled with an array of exotic flowers greeted me. It amazed me that these would do well on the water, but the garden was thriving.

Engrossed in the fragrance, I looked up to see Roland standing on the deck near the front door. My heart leapt, and we exchanged an unspoken hello. He looked worn, and I could see that exhaustion was etched around his eyes, but his spirit was not diminished. He greeted me warmly, and brought me into a home that was the essence of charm and simplicity.

A woman emerged from a side door and moved

graciously into the room. I was completely taken by the countenance of our hostess, a woman in her eighties. She was dressed in a long, flowing skirt with blouse and shawl of beautiful azure blue that matched her eyes. Her name was Anna.

This gracious presence, Anna, was a woman who had come from Russia with her parents when rebellion turned her country upside down. She studied chemistry and moved on to physics, where her specialty became earth frequencies. She was fascinated with the effect of frequency on living organisms and had been involved in many pioneering studies to demonstrate correlations between sound and illness in humans, plants and animals.

Anna also had a passion for music and was an accomplished violinist. She played in a local symphony orchestra and was a member of a small group that worked with experimental sound. She also had a private practice helping people harmonize their body frequencies.

I sat down on one of her comfortable, overstuffed couches and noticed a beautiful tortoise shell cat in the corner, who looked at me with great composure.

The interaction between Anna and Roland was familiar and affectionate. They obviously had tremendous respect for one another, and I felt honored that he included me in his time with her.

Roland turned to me. "Anna has worked on projects related to sound for many years, and she has come up with interesting insights based on the results of her investigation. I thought you'd like to hear about them."

Anna looked at me and asked what I knew about

frequency. I smiled, and admitted that I knew very little about it.

"You could say that the body is a collection of particles," she began. "If the frequency is changed, the particles are rearranged. Because we vibrate at a particular frequency, we are shaped as we are, and the internal working of the body moves in and out of chaos.

"When you alter the frequency rate externally, the frequency within the body has to correspond. It either speeds up or slows down. Your brain is attuned to the frequency of your heartbeat. And your heartbeat is attuned to the frequency of the earth. You see, it is all one living, integrated system. If the frequency of the earth changes, the frequency of your heartbeat will adjust to attune itself."

I was somewhat confused. "So what does this mean?" I asked.

Anna smiled. "Well, that is the big question. As we see that the frequency rate surrounding the earth is rising, and the magnetic fields are dropping, we know that in the greater scheme of things, earth is responding to something that is occurring in the universe. Just as our heartbeat moves with the heartbeat of earth, earth's pulse is responding to stimulus from the larger body to which it belongs. So, the great detective story for cosmologists and astrophysicists is, 'What is going on?'

"Our concern is how what is happening out there is impacting us down here. There appears to be a shift of sorts, and as the frequency changes on earth, we experience a similar adjustment."

I wasn't quite sure what she was getting at. "What

can we do about that?" I asked.

"The importance for individuals during this process is to recognize that what they are experiencing is not necessarily generated internally. In other words, they aren't causing the feelings they are experiencing. The whole cosmos is in transition, and we are registering the results of that transition in our bodies and psyches."

I thought about the impact of 21 comet fragments on Jupiter years before that were supposed to be more powerful than any explosions we'd had on earth, and asked if that could also be part of the process.

"Yes. That's a good example in two ways," Anna replied. "First of all, let's pretend that a person is Jupiter. After the impact, was Jupiter reacting to itself, or to what happened to it?"

I thought for a moment, then responded. "Well, obviously Jupiter reacted to the impact it experienced."

"Exactly." Anna continued. "That's what is happening to people right now as this shift in frequency occurs. The intensity of what's surrounding all of us is like a storm, and no one is causing it. For those who are prepared and understand what's going on, this time period can be very dynamic, but for those who are not, it can be quite difficult, requiring very careful navigation. Without knowledge, people tend to react rashly, and this poses problems within a society."

Roland looked at me. "So you can see the purpose for doing the exercises we started in New Mexico to maintain a clear perspective and center ourselves."

I nodded, and he asked Anna to explain more. "What's your take of the second example of Jupiter?"

Anna looked out the window, and continued. "The ripple effect of that explosion is moving throughout this galaxy and beyond, and we don't know yet quite what that means to us on earth. But, it is a vibration, filled with information. We have yet to find out how the sound waves or radiation will impact us."

I was curious.

"How do you see sound impacting us?"

"Ah," said Anna. "That's a good question. Sound is the binding factor of all life. We can put particles in a test setting, and by exposing them to tonal fluctuations, we can actually see them rearrange themselves into different patterns through the microscope. They move as the frequency alters, and form geometric shapes, because that is the encoded sequencing of life.

"Certain dissonant tones excite the particles, and they seem to move chaotically. Then as another sound is introduced, they move into a formalized geometric pattern. Chaos occurs as the particles move from one pattern to another, and in a sense, that's what is happening to us now. We're moving between two states of being.

"We have been aware for some time that the frequency range of earth is undergoing change, and with increased solar flares and the explosions on Jupiter, we've been working to determine what effect all of this has on living organisms. We're concerned with the dynamics of frequency on cell life."

I thought about the crop circles and asked if they were possibly connected to the changes.

"Yes. There is a good possibility that the shift in frequency is contributing to those occurrences. It would be like an eruption on the surface of the skin because of internal discontent. But in this case, there is an additional component. The patterns that are being formed are not haphazard; they are quite precise, so it would seem that another level of intelligence is also acting in concert with the appearances.

"We don't know what effect the shift in frequency has on us, our environment, or the stability of our atmosphere. But the magnetic field dropping is causing a lessening of the shield around earth, and that means we are subject to many more forces from the rest of the universe."

I remembered what had been said by the man I knew at the lecture Roland gave, about the government being involved in high-frequency testing, and asked Anna if the reason for those tests had anything to do with the earth shield.

"Partially," she responded. I'm not involved in those projects, but I do know about them. The government is experimenting with the work of Nikola Tesla, who was a brilliant scientist. His knowledge of electrical fields was far ahead of his time. He was regarded as an eccentric while he lived, but now his work is being taken seriously, as many of the things he predicted are coming to pass."

I wanted more clarity about the conspiracy theory. "I heard this project was secretive and about using sound as a weapon."

Anna laughed. "My dear, most research is done with the intention of creating a weapon. Whether it's to cure a disease and becomes a weapon against a virus, bacteria, or used against other people, everything we do in research is really an action against the status quo.

"I'm much more interested in the restorative possibilities of sound. Don't waste your time on conspiracy. You only become bound by the fear it generates. Look to the countervailing potential, and explore that."

Anna looked at me for a moment, and then spoke again. "Are you aware that fear and love are both frequencies? she asked. "When we measure the effect of fear, it is very disruptive to the body. It causes a chaotic reaction to particles. When we measure the benefit of love, it has a harmonizing and rejuvenating effect. So, don't get caught in the web of fear that permeates this planet.

"There is more you can do to alter that frequency by maintaining a state of harmony and fluidity. You see, even in the use of terms we are given insight into movement. Hardened by fear. Softened by love. Frozen in terror. Renewed through joy. Each of those statements correlates to what actually happens within the body. When you concentrate on loving, everything benefits. When you give in to fear, you are speeding up the process of decay within your cells."

Anna was a wealth of information. She made me think, and I was able to correlate what she spoke of to other things I'd learned.

"In another sense," I interjected, "I can relate what you're saying to what Roland told me when I went to New Mexico, about one individual in a plane being able to shift the negativity of another."

Roland explained to Anna what I meant, and she nodded. "Yes! That's exactly the idea. If more people move into a framework of clarity and hold the charge of loving, there will be an even more dramatic demonstration of the effect it has on frequency around us. Remember that these are actual components of encoded information, and they vibrate at different rates. They have a tone and color related to them."

Roland smiled at me. "Do you see why I wanted you to meet this woman? She is truly remarkable!" He looked lovingly at Anna, and moved to embrace her. The feeling in the room was charged with wisdom, respect and honor.

Anna spoke again. "Also, acting out of love does not mean giving up your rational mind or buying the notion that life will be nothing but roses. It means that you yourself choose not to react fearfully, regardless of how things appear to be. Fear plus fear begets more fear. Fear plus love equals neutrality, and love plus love does amazing things in terms of healing. The possibilities are quite astounding!"

Anna smiled conspiratorially. "You know, it doesn't cost anything more to act lovingly, but it does cost dearly when we operate from fear."

She excused herself for a moment, and Roland looked at me.

"So what do you think?"

I shook my head in wonder. "I cannot believe she is in her eighties. She is one of the most vibrant, clear-sighted individuals I've ever met. Thank you so much for giving me this opportunity to be with her."

Roland smiled. "She is a living example of what she preaches. She has been able to maintain a high frequency through a loving response to life that shows on her body. The woman does not look a day over sixty, if that."

"Oh, I wouldn't even put an age to her," I responded. "She's ageless and timeless, and that's what I want for myself, as well. I truly want to master the ability to maintain that frequency of love, as she calls it."

Roland nodded. "You will. That's why you're involved in this process."

Anna returned with a tray of cookies and lemonade. After we finished them, Roland suggested it was time we leave, and she walked with us out to the deck.

The warmth that came from her affected me physically. I could feel myself immersed in the glow of her love. "Come back again, my dear," she told me. "You are welcome any time."

She turned to Roland, with love and tears in her eyes. "Ah, my boy. What can I say to you? My heart is with you."

She waved to us as we walked away, and I looked back once more to hold the vision of her in my mind. Roland was quiet as we made our way back to the parking lot. Finally, he turned to me.

"Thank you for coming. I wanted you to meet one another, and I think you'll get some valuable insights from what she told you."

"It was a privilege, Roland. Not only for what she told me, but also for the possibility that's ahead of me as I'm getting older. Women don't have a lot of role models amongst elders who give us something to look forward to. Getting older in this society means being used up, and for females, where our value has been so tied to our sexuality and attractiveness, it's a devastating blow to face being thrown away just because we aren't twenty- or thirty-something. Clearly, Anna defies all the stereotypes. She is someone for me to emulate."

Roland seemed surprised. "I wouldn't have thought you felt that way. You don't strike me as a person who would even consider giving up."

I shook my head. "No. I'm not. But now that I'm moving into middle age, I am fully aware that I'm entering an arena where I'll be viewed as a thing rather than a person. I have seen it happen to others, and I've talked to my women friends who are older. It's a crummy feeling. Inside you feel the same as you always did. When I check in with myself, there's no age difference. I feel no age. Just because the physical body changes, the core of me hasn't. If anything, it's getting richer. Yet, because the outer will no longer reflect youth, I'll be devalued. I don't like that, and resent the idea of cosmetic surgery to make me look like something I'm not."

We stopped. Roland took my hand in his. "Listen to me," he said. "We have a light within us that doesn't ever have to age. Anyone who is looking only at the physical, external body isn't anyone you'd want to know anyway. You are right about this culture. We don't appreciate age, and it isn't just relegated to women; men experience it as well. But, you know what? Who's responsible for that? If you allow yourself to fall into a stereotype, any stereotype, you are abdicating your responsibility to make a difference in the world.

"If you move with that fear-based attitude toward aging, it can become a self-fulfilling prophecy. You have to move beyond what the outside world says, and pay attention to what your cellular level, gut instinct knows. Some people age more rapidly than others. For whatever reason, they lose the life spark, and gradually decline. However, there is nothing that says we cannot be vital, alert, and involved until the day we die. They do it in other cultures. It's expected. And they live lives that uphold the wisdom of elders as a priceless commodity. We have fallen into a shallow mindset that glorifies a particular physical look, with an awful lot of people being swept along like sheep. It absolutely does not have to be that way!

Roland hardly paused for breath. He continued. "So what I'm saying to you is, be one of a vanguard. Encourage people of all ages to develop their interior life so that they are rich and full. Then, when the years pass, they have a substantial heritage. My God, if all people develop is their body and their face, and the whole focus is on attracting and keeping somebody based on physical appearance, they damned well better be worried about aging. But when they've done what Anna's done, and what we're doing, there's no reason to be afraid. I think you need to share that with people!"

I hadn't realized how much the whole age thing impacted me until this moment, and I could feel the tension in my body dissolving to tears. Tears of fear. Tears of sorrow. For all the things I thought I ought to have done, and didn't. For the fact that I took my youth for granted and didn't make the most of it, whatever "it" was. Losing the freshness of tight skin and gorgeous hair was not an easy pill to swallow. It did require dependence on other aspects of one's nature. I thought I'd dealt with it well, but saw how inadequate it made me feel as a desirable being.

"Furthermore," Roland interjected, "I think you are an incredible woman!" He smiled and pulled me into his arms, holding me tightly as I cried, and then he looked at me mischievously and asked if I'd taken my Geritol for the day. His question completely disarmed me, and we laughed uproariously as we walked to the car, making stereotypical comments about age all the way.

"You know the one I hate most?" I said.

"No. What?"

I puffed up and said in a saccharin voice, "May I help you with your groceries to the car, ma'am? That has bugged me ever since I was twenty-eight, when the grocery clerks first started asking. At that point, I felt like I was no longer attractive. Now it makes me feel like I'm old. I mean, do I look like I can't carry a grocery bag?"

He laughed. "It's a courtesy! You see, there is the whole thing of perception again. Somebody else would be offended because they weren't asked. Do you see how our inner pictures dictate reality? You have a viewpoint based on your perceived lack, and somebody else says something to you, unaware of that lack. They are coming from a completely different place, like the grocery clerk. Because it connects with your inner fear, you react out of fear, and the end result is anger or frustration. Something offered from an entirely innocent perspective is blown completely out of proportion.

"Now multiply that many times over, and you have the misunderstandings all over the globe that lead to war. Your unresolved fear leads you to revolt against grocery clerks, whom you assume are out to "get" older people over the age of twenty-eight, and they in turn determine that you are a crazed group of fanatics and call in the National Guard, and well, you see where we're going with this. It's an absurd example of a very real problem. This happens all the time. Can you see why it is so important to stay clear with yourself, to stay attuned?"

I looked at Roland, amazed. "You know, just talking about this with you has completely diffused it for me. I don't think I'll ever react that way again to a grocery clerk. In fact, I think I'll probably find the situation comical."

"That's another point!" He was on a roll "It's important to have somebody to talk things over with. We all need the benefit of another vantage point. And it's important to inject humor, because these kinds of things get built up inside of us as we take ourselves too seriously, and become self-conscious. Humor can break the charge. It makes us see how ridiculous we are, not in a judgmental sense, just from a perspective of clarity. When we can move out of self-consciousness, out of fear into laughter, we make room to love again."

With that, he took the car keys out of my hand, opened the door to the driver's side, and quipped, "May I help you into your car, ma'am?"

We laughed again, and drove away.

Roland had dinner reservations for us at a gorgeous little hotel on a hillside in Sausalito, overlooking the bay. We had a superb meal, enjoying the incredible view, and one another. I felt more comfortable with him, as I'd shared a part of myself that made me vulnerable. His reaction had been supportive and informative, and he helped me to move beyond an issue that blocked me perceptually. These were the ingredients that contributed to a rich relationship, and I was grateful to be at a stage in my life where I could do this rather than being bound by the old dictates of gamesmanship.

We finished dinner, paid the bill, and walked to the verandah of the hotel. The night sky was rising, stars were peering through the pale evening light. The skies in New Mexico were awesome by virtue of sheer natural beauty. Here, the twinkling lights of the City skyline blended in the sparkling waters of the bay, reflecting a different kind of splendor.

Chapter 14
❧ Fear and Transformation ❧

Roland had an extra day before he had to return to New Mexico, so we decided to go over to the coast for lunch. I was to meet with Bonita later in the day, but enjoyed the prospect of spending additional time with this man who was becoming very special to me. Not only was he instrumental in opening new avenues to exploration, but helped me ground awareness of things I already knew, and challenged me to use them more appropriately.

We drove over the mountains of the peninsula to a seaside town called Half Moon Bay, which had remained a sleepy little farm community in the midst of major expansion everywhere else in the Bay Area. Half Moon Bay worked hard to retain its authenticity, and was famous for its Pumpkin Festival in October. The people were friendly, and the pace unhurried.

We found my favorite little restaurant in the quaint downtown area where the food was good, and you could talk without being drowned out by loud music. We ordered our lunch, and Roland asked me how I was doing with the morning and evening exercises we'd done in New Mexico. I admitted that it wasn't the same without the group, but that I was keeping my agreement.

"I want you to meet with a man named Fu Hsi who's developed a technology that's going to help revolutionize our lives. He's a brilliant physicist from

China, and has discovered a method for releasing memories encoded in the body and re-encoding healing information for optimizing soul evolution. This ties in to the work we're doing in preparing the body to benefit from the change in frequency that's occurring. His work is still in the experimental stage, but the results so far have been very promising, involving cell renewal, rejuvenation, and enhanced physical and mental capabilities."

"Oh, that sounds like another fad, Roland. That can't be real." I was skeptical.

He looked surprised. "I'm not interested in fads or hype. This man is the genuine article, and his work is an example of the kinds of things that are going to start popping as the shift in frequency accelerates. He's part of what I was telling the group about in New Mexico. We all have to be alert to possibilities, because they are definitely happening. This is about what we can do right now to enhance the quality of our lives and life in general. As we're ready, some remarkable individuals and opportunities are going to present themselves to us."

He looked at me with the same intensity I'd seen many times before. I hit a passionate chord, and he responded in kind. I realized that my reaction was out of habit, since there was so much in our area that promised what Matthew from the bookstore and I jokingly referred to as, 'How to gain instant enlightenment, make a million dollars, live forever, and have the best sex of your life in three easy steps.'

My yearning was not for a magic bullet. It was for meaning. I wanted to expand awareness in ways that would contribute to my overall understanding of life, and allow me to contribute more fully and effectively as a result. I told Roland this, and he assured me that the research now being done in science was among the most grounded and exciting of possibilities happening on the planet.

"We are finally coming to a place in our understanding scientifically of the many things written about in ancient texts. We are being able to prove the validity of certain spiritual passages, ancient prophecies, and glyphs that have been left for us as a road map.

"It was understood then that a time would come in the future when humans would develop the faculties to understand what was stated in code. And what we're finding is that all of these messages left to us are indications of the building blocks of life and the universe. The language is mathematics, and people like Fu Hsi have spent their lives working to decipher what's here for all of us to read. We need to develop the eyes to see and the ears to hear, because the ladder between the so-called heavens and earth is in place... and we're climbing it!

"We have to reach a level of development where the brain can contain this information. It's like the story of the elephant we used in the workshop... there has to be a framework in which to put what you are perceiving. That's why all these pieces are essential. We have to clear our physical body, our emotional baggage, and our mental constructs that limit possibility. If we don't, we're not going to know what's in front of us, because it won't register. There will be nothing to anchor it to.

"We send probes out to other planets looking for

life, and are disappointed when we don't find what we expect. What we should be looking for is consciousness, but there is no framework for that yet. We cannot see that anything exists other than the surface of a sphere. Do you understand what I'm getting at?"

I nodded. "I think so. It's just swimming around on the periphery of my mind, and I catch glimpses of it, but it's not something that I can hold on to. Keep going."

He continued. "Now that we're developing super computers able to take reality to any number of dimensions, we begin to see the building blocks of the universe in a way that is far more textured and subtle than we were able to envision before. We may not know what we're going to find, but through mathematical exploration and the capability of seeing the results on screen, our flow of information is expanding by leaps and bounds. We're being shown a picture of what consciousness at different levels looks like that will alter our perception of life.

"That's one of the reasons why this time period is so exciting. We're on the brink of major breakthroughs in knowledge. So many pieces are going to be provided that will help us see the whole context of life in a remarkable and entirely new way. We have never had this kind of leap in consciousness during our recorded existence, and it's largely because of technology that we're able to do it, but we have to make sure that we reach a level of maturity and wholeness to handle what we receive, or we'll be like the sorcerer's apprentice, manipulating technology without the necessary wisdom to accompany it."

I looked at him. "So, what you're saying, if I'm

hearing you correctly, is that with this technology we will be able to set up our probes to look for other dimensional realities on planets that may show us something quite different than what we think we see?"

Roland nodded. "That's right."

I was excited by the possibilities. "If we can do that on other planets, couldn't we do it here? I mean, you hear people talk about ghosts and weird feelings in various places. Could it be that there is another level of activity that is occurring simultaneously at a different dimensional level, including the one I witnessed in Germany?"

He smiled at me. "Good point! No reason why not. If this process can work in space, it should be duplicable here. You're collapsing the data even further by including the possibility of past and future coinciding with the present. Can you see the incredible potential of what's ahead, and why this is such an important time for us to get ourselves together? We're on the verge of discovering things that are going to shake up many of our cherished ideals, or of finding out why we have them in the first place. This is a time period of revelation in the largest sense of the word!"

My mind was racing. "So, Russell's concern about education goes way beyond even his idea of it. We have to develop another perceptual context for people because we're moving out of our old models that have been the basis for learning. Things that are happening in the field of sacred geometry, and other areas I don't even know about, are opening the door to a major shift in consciousness, and our perception of what the universe really is."

Roland nodded as we got up and walked to the cashier. "And that's where electrical frequencies and magnetic fields come into play."

I looked at him. "How so?" I asked.

"Because the magnetics are what lock us into place and retain history. They are the binding force. The electrical field is what offers new information, so if the magnetics are dropping, the old structures are being loosened. With the rise of electrical frequency, we're experiencing major shifts that require us to develop an ability to comprehend what we're seeing. Without that capacity, we're going to mistake the new data and miss major opportunities for expansion of human consciousness."

"Oh!" I exclaimed. "You mean like in the movie Pocahontas, when she saw strange clouds in a dream that she felt would change her destiny, and then in actuality the ships came in to the inlet with their billowing sails. She had no context for sails, so she saw them as clouds."

Roland laughed. "Well, I didn't see the movie, but, yes, that's the idea."

We walked through the little town and headed for the beach, which wasn't far. The fog hovered off the coast, but the weather was still warm and there wasn't any wind. We found a place where the sand was thick and we sat quietly. I looked at Roland, who was gazing out beyond the ocean reflectively, and I picked up handfuls of sand, feeling its softness and substance as I let it drizzle through my fingers. It was amazing that these tiny granules could be building blocks for many things, and that the sheer number and weight of them in concentration provided the boundary between land and sea.

Roland looked over at me. "Do you remember being buried in the sand when you were little?" He asked.

"Oh, I certainly do." I said with disdain. "I hated it. I couldn't move, and I felt so helpless because it was packed in around me. Actually it terrified me."

Roland smiled. "Being buried in the sand is a pale comparison to being in one of the King's chambers in the pyramids, but the feeling of helplessness gives you an idea of what the ancient initiates went through. The whole purpose of perceptual deprivation is to give you an opportunity to face your worst fears and neutralize them so you are freed from any preconceived attitudes that limit possibilities."

I shook my head. "I'm not willing to experience that kind of initiation. It really petrifies me." I shuddered at the thought.

He looked at me strangely. "If you don't, you're not going to complete the process that's so important for the next phase."

He began digging a hole in the sand. Soon he was on his knees, using both hands and arms to carve out a body cast in the sand.

"What's that for?" I asked warily.

"For me. You can bury me in the sand. I haven't done this since I was a kid, and it'll be fun. I always felt like I was part of the earth when I was buried. It's a unique experience."

The hole was quite deep and Roland took off his shoes and socks, positioning himself to fit within the sand-cast. He began mounding the sand over himself and asked me to help. I was reluctant at first, but got into the idea of making a sandcastle out of him. Soon, all that remained visible was his head. Roland made sounds and hummed, and when I asked what he was doing, he smiled.

"I'm contacting the earth and asking to feel the wisdom of the sand. As I become one with it instead of fighting against it, there's a great deal I can learn. You experienced that unity in New Mexico with the mountains. This is just another avenue of participation. Being buried doesn't have to represent a negative. In Vietnam and all the other wars we've had, foxholes saved a lot of people's lives."

I'd never thought of that, and after he'd been lying quietly in the sand for thirty minutes in a private reverie, I walked over toward him as he opened his eyes.

"I want to try it." I was curious and thought perhaps I might feel differently now.

Roland laughed. "Sure. Just help me out of this, and you can have your turn."

After he emerged and shook himself off, I laid in the space he created. It was warm and I could feel my toes embracing the sand. Roland promised not to leave my side and to help me out whenever I wanted. He then proceeded to cover me with tightly packed sand, and as I felt the weight, I was afraid. I didn't know if I could go through with the process, but Roland spoke to me softly, like a loving parent.

"I'm right here. I'm not going to leave you. If you're afraid, you can get yourself out of the sand, but I'd like you to follow my voice and work through this fear, if you can. First of all, breathe rhythmically. Practice all of the things you've learned in the past."

Terror welled up in me as I heard the sound of waves crashing on the shore. I was transported to a time when I was about four, playing in the sand close to the water's edge. Huge waves came in on the beach and I was knocked over again and again, unable to stand up or catch my breath. The water began to pull me out from the shore to the sea, and I didn't know how to swim. The people I was with were busy with something else, and they weren't paying attention. Someone finally saw me, and rushed over to pull me out of the water's grip. I gasped for air and coughed up seawater. It was a terrifying experience that gave me a healthy, or unhealthy, respect for the ocean.

Suddenly, I was transported to another incident when I was about three years old. I had been with an older group of children while visiting with friends of my parents. I remembered having followed them from room to room, asking questions. Suddenly, they grabbed me and rolled me up in an area rug on the floor and stuffed me in a closet. I was terrified and cried hysterically, screaming at the top of my lungs. It was so hot, and I could hardly breathe. After a while I heard the closet door open, and my father, who had been downstairs, pulled me to safety. I remember him holding me very close in his arms, enraged at the older children. It seemed that I had pestered them, and they wanted to get rid of me.

Then a third image came zooming into my mind. I was in a tomb. It was in an enclosed area where there was no way out, and my panic became sheer terror and numbness. I was being buried alive, and the only way out as I could see it was death. The enormity of that realization froze me in a state of horror, and as I recounted it, I began to gasp for air. Roland was right there, stroking my forehead. He asked me what I'd seen and I told him about the three visions. Since I was stuck in the last one, he addressed that.

"I want you to see that there is another way out of this enclosure. Are there any cracks in the walls?"

I was moaning now. "Yes, very small cracks."

"All right," coached Roland. "See yourself as moving from being in a body to being pure energy. Visualize yourself as a beam of light, and move through a crack in the wall."

I was amazed at how this shift in perception affected me. Suddenly I was freed of my fear, free of restriction, and I was able to move through the cracks to the area outside. When I turned to look at the building I'd been in, there was a gigantic pyramid! No wonder I had no interest in going to Egypt. I'd been buried alive there!

"Now," continued Roland. "I want you to feel your essence and the essence of the sand becoming one. See it as a protective mantle around you, and remember to breathe. Then move where the vision takes you. I'm right here, and I'm not going to leave you."

Immediately, I thought of my father. He had been there to save me from the rug, but died several years later, and wasn't by my side. The issue of trust around men and abandonment became a predominant theme throughout my life. I breathed into that realization, and stabilized my breath.

The sand felt warm and inviting now, and as I moved into and through it, I could feel the heartbeat of earth. Images of beauty replaced my terror, and once again I felt connected. The fear of being buried was gone, and I was able to send gratitude and love to this part of earth that housed me and aided in the healing of old wounds.

When I felt complete with the process, Roland helped me out of my cocoon and held me tightly in his arms, like a protective and loving parent.

"You did it! You confronted your fears and overcame them. I think you'll be able to look at the idea of being buried in the sand with neutrality from now on."

He continued to hold me for several minutes, and I was able to feel tension falling away. It was as though I'd held myself so tightly for eons because I couldn't trust that anyone else would be willing to hold a part of the structure with me.

When I felt at home in my body again, I looked at him incredulously. "I can't believe it. I never expected to have those kinds of feelings. It was really amazing, and I felt so many things coinciding at different levels. That was very cathartic, Roland. I feel as though I've released a major block."

He smiled at me, and we walked down the beach together, hand in hand.

"What you experienced was a graphic example of what's occurring in our daily lives right now. This is the process of initiation we're all being called to, whether we're ready or not. That's why it's so important to understand what's happening, because it's preparing us for the coming shift in frequency, and we've just scratched the surface!"

Chapter 15
❧ Of the Head and Heart ❧

Roland and I returned to the Peninsula, and I called Bonita to see if I could bring him along for our walk. She was delighted, as I had told her about him before.

When we arrived at the Center, Bonita greeted us out front, and she and Roland had an immediate affinity to one another, which pleased me. She told us that two unexpected guests had arrived on their way to give a seminar in Santa Cruz. As we walked into the Center, I gazed upon a handsome man with a turban and long beard, and a beautiful blonde woman. I recognized their light immediately, and to my surprise, Roland chuckled, and was embracing both, like long lost friends.

"Well, my old compadres, what are you up to?"

It turned out that Roland and the couple, who were from New Zealand, had known each other for twenty years. They'd done seminars together in the '70s, and whereas Roland had gone on to write about vibrations and earth changes, they were leaders in the field of music and sound. They presented the music and message of indigenous cultures, especially the Maori of New Zealand.

The woman, Amina, related that the Maori tribes of New Zealand were now willing to release the story of the singing stones that they felt responsible for. These stones, indigenous to New Zealand and

Australia, were being released to the world to awaken other stones. A book had been written about them recently, and they were considered the elders in the mineral kingdom, sent forth to awaken the record keepers. From this contact, the human kingdom would be included, and the wisdom of the ages would begin to unfold. It dawned on me as they spoke, that in the Islamic tradition, the Grail was thought to be a stone. I was also aware of the synchronicity... all kingdoms were part of the awakening process. It was not just humans who felt a stirring.

Amina's partner, Hart, sang for us. They asked Bonita to share the power of her voice with them, and she did some of her sound work, which impacted all of us. Everyone felt that sound was the next important wave of unfolding human potential, and Roland shared the importance of his latest research in relation to each of us becoming templates for the new tone.

Amina smiled softly, and looked at Roland with great compassion.

"Darling Roland, you are making it all so technical. You can quantify and measure, and you can set an outline if you must, but the expression of light that will emerge must come from the heart. The beauty of our interaction with the Maori people is that they are so in tune to the earth that they don't need blueprints. There is a living template, as you call it, anchored in their hearts. All we need to do is open ourselves to receive."

Hart came to Roland's defense.

"Well, Amina, in western society, people need graphs and plans to follow. They don't all have the luxury of living as we do."

Amina smiled at both men, and shook her head. "Left Brain. You need to listen more with your hearts. Move into the circle, and out of the line."

She got up from the pillow on the floor where she was seated, and kneeled down in front of Roland, who was also sitting on the floor. Placing her hands on his face, she cradled it like a mother would cradle her child's face. She looked at him with such an expression of tenderness that I felt a lump rise in my throat. She then hummed a melody, and tears came pouring down his cheeks. He crumbled into her arms; deep, haunting sounds rising from him, filled with years of unexpressed emotion.

Everyone was still, and it took a good ten minutes for Roland to regain his composure. Here was the isolation I had seen in him, the loner just beyond the veil. I felt my own aloneness and the yearning for reunion to the Source of life, which Amina had so eloquently portrayed without words. Indeed, the heart knows.

Bonita broke the silence. "I think for myself, there has been so much structure imposed upon me throughout my life, that I need a simpler sense of form. I am so internally motivated to go out and accomplish and do, and I find myself being embroiled in one workshop after another, always thinking I should be doing more, and the truth is, I've done it all. I just want to bring my voice forward in a way that is authentic for me, and if others can gain something from that, terrific!"

Amina spoke again from deep conviction. "It is quite all right to approach this unfoldment in whatever way works best for each of us. We just have to be careful that we're not falling back into patterns that keep us small or confine our spirit. Reaching out to heart with heart is a risk. It's much safer to analyze it all. But we're not here to be safe."

She smiled broadly, and the child in me wanted to rush over and lose myself in the comfort of her nurturing arms.

She continued. "There's more we can do for one another with a touch or kind word than with all the instruction manuals in the world. All this talk of frequencies and energy fields is fine, but it distances a lot of people who don't understand, and it smacks of the need to be special.

"Is there something happening on earth right now? Certainly. Has it been predicted to occur? Yes. Do we need to prepare ourselves? It's helpful...but all we really need is a willing heart. The message that we're receiving in New Zealand is to simplify, to make this process very simple. We have a voice. We have ears. We can breathe. We can dance. We can touch one another. Simple steps...with heart. We need to concentrate more on the being, rather than the doing."

Roland nodded his head. "Yes, you're right. Thank you, Amina."

His eyes were full, and they both stood and shared a long embrace. You could feel the love swirling in the room, and we were all touched. She had one last statement to make.

"You know, we're all created with magnificent potential. The Creator has a clear intention for each one of us, and all we have to do is stand aside and allow ourselves to be played as the instruments we are intended. If we can overcome self-consciousness, and allow our authentic tone to come forward, we will move from being isolated notes, and gather together as a symphony."

Bonita was excited by Amina's statement. "I have been trying to put together community sing alongs... not with the idea of singing old songs, but of bringing each person back to the power within their own voice, and letting them have a place where that voice can be heard. It is a very powerful possibility, and expressing together in community is quite remarkable."

We spoke more about communal voices, and then it was time for Hart and Amina to be on their way. We had less than an hour together, but they were now part of my inner landscape, like the mountains, and I was enriched for knowing them, and would miss seeing them.

After they'd gone, we three spoke of the synchronicity of their arrival. Roland commented that it was just what he'd needed. We sat in silence and meditation for the remainder of our time together.

Driving down the hill, Roland took my hand in both of his. He looked over at me, acknowledging Amina, and the importance of her statement.

"It's easy for me to get caught in the trap she spoke of. Words can be an incredible tool, but they can also be a weapon and a shield."

I nodded, for much of what she'd said applied to me as well. Roland and I were two of a kind, and we both sensed the connection. There was an eloquent silence between us as we drove the rest of the way to the home of his friends.

As I dropped him off, he turned to me, a curious look on his face. "I just had a thought," he said. "Are you busy tonight?"

I told him that I didn't have any plans, and he suggested that if his friend, Fu Hsi, was available, he'd like to take me over to meet him. We agreed that he would call if it was doable, and I went home.

My life was moving as if it were an art form. I had the privilege of meetings some remarkable people, and it had come about since I paid attention to the inner prompting that began years ago. The inner teacher, who guided so much of my life, had given me several directives through the years, and brought me to this moment in time.

The first was to voluntarily simplify my life. The second was to be aware that I was not here to be safe, and third, to give up my history. All of these directives were now coming into focus with clarity that had not been evident at the time I received them. Each of these messages were portrayed to me by others, in various ways, and my purpose was to pick up the cue and take appropriate action. As I did, the next step unfolded. When I did not, the roadblocks in my path made the journey more difficult, and I would confront the same issue again and again until I found resolution.

In the mandate to find the Holy Grail, the journey I experienced was not at all what I'd expected. It was far richer and layered, way beyond an historical perspective of a tangible object from antiquity. This process was the Grail. I was unfolding to become a clearer, more objective version of myself, able to hold a tone and to resonate in such a way that I would portray a living light. In my vision of the Grail's content, I could see a liquid light of golden white that seemed to be a much more appropriate color for blood than the red that shocked me every time I saw it.

Where this journey would lead was not clear. It was all about unfoldment, and my guess was that this was a lifelong process. Showing up for the journey, being ready to listen and follow the next request. These were the elements that made it worthwhile. I became a painting, and a symphony. All I had to do was stay attuned.

The phone rang, and Roland was exuberant. "Fu Hsi can see us! I'll have the use of my friend's car, so I'll pick you up at seven o'clock, okay?"

I had a quick bite to eat and got ready, wondering what part Fu Hsi played in the quotient.

Fu Hsi lived in the east bay. The little town of Lafayette was nestled in the hills, and his particular location was way up meandering roads to a house that looked like a temple from China. The curved arches of the roof were an interesting contrast to the surrounding area.

We entered a serene courtyard, with two beautiful carved red wooden doors greeting us. Roland rang the doorbell, which sounded like a gong, and I was quite intrigued. The wide door opened, and we were greeted by a man in his fifties, smiling warmly and welcoming us into his home. Again, I felt an immediate connection, as I had with the couple from New Zealand. He introduced us to his wife, and it was as though I'd known her forever.

Fu Hsi had been born in China 57 years ago, into a family of physicians, both western and eastern. He knew at an early age that he had a mission to accomplish in life, and at age seventeen, his work began in earnest. He was guided to get an education in science, and went on to become a successful businessman in

the aerospace industry. He was an avid student of philosophy and metaphysics, and throughout his life, he
was guided in decisions by an inner teacher. When he
was seventeen, he began writing every night as directed, and was informed that the basis for his work
would take 40 years to complete. Now, at the age of
fifty-seven, the last pieces of his technology for the
future were being put in place.

Fu Hsi was in a unique position to speak to scientists, educators, businessmen, and people involved in
the world of spiritual pursuit, because he had tra-
versed all arenas. He believed that there was a unifying theory of the universe that pulled everything
together, and that the base was formed by decoding
God's encoded information in what he called the
"vacuum." This information manifests itself as sacred
geometry.

We listened to him for a couple of hours. There was
so much to absorb, and it was difficult to comprehend,
but what came through this man was well-reasoned
logic merged into heartfelt action.

"The most important thing is integration," he said.
"We cannot come to this from one direction alone. We
need to have a technology that will bring the two elements of science and humanism, including religion,
together. We have works like the Bible from western
tradition that represents the manifestation of God's
logic, and hidden in the I-Ching from the east is God's
encoded logic itself."

That reminded me of something Bonita had said in
relation to her work with sound and music.

"Fu Hsi, I have heard that the I-Ching mimics the
DNA, and that there are people working on drum-

ming the sequence patterns for optimizing health. Is that something you know about?"

He nodded. "The I-Ching is a very important work that anybody interested in integration of health should learn about. There are books that explain the process well. However, one must attempt to understand the logic represented by the trigrams and hexagrams of the I-Ching through inspiration!"

Roland asked Fu Hsi to tell me more about the exercises he developed.

"Well, it's a process that measures the encoded logic from your body and gives us information that we can put into the computer to get a print-out of the areas of body/mind and soul/spirit where help is needed... where your strengths are, what herbs, homeopathics, and minerals you might be lacking. It is a very sophisticated program that I have developed over many, many years."

I was confused. "I don't understand. How do you get this information?"

Fu Hsi smiled. It was obvious he had to explain himself all the time to people who were unable to actually see his vision.

"By taking certain pieces of information that hold encoded logic, such as your name, your birth date, and acupuncture point readings of your body, I have devised a program on the computer that will take this information and give about a two hour read-out of the entire mechanism that forms the template of your body/mind, and soul/spirit, with the intention of optimizing your soul evolution.

"From that point, we can design certain body postures and movements that will allow you to activate the template and accelerate your soul evolution toward the Divine. I also have classes and lectures that allow you to understand the mechanism of wholeness. When your brain has the information, it can pass this new understanding through the body.

"You cannot do anything without the participation of the brain, and the template gives us an idea of the structure we're working with. The postures and movement connect the body to the template. The classes and information give new insights that activate the encoded knowledge of the body, and replace them with something that is more complete.

"This is wholeness, and it will alter aspects of the physical body and the genetic structure. All of this information is lodged in the cranio-sacral part of the body, and you learn to become a self-correcting universe through the process."

I found this quite astounding. "Roland tells me that you are working with the exercises on an experimental basis so far. Have you found changes in the people who have been involved?"

Fu Hsi smiled. "Amazing results! We have a lot of older people in the program, and they are finding their bodies becoming more youthful, they are gaining more mental and physical agility, have more emotional stability, and are opening themselves to expanded possibilities in life. The whole concept of age is being thrown out the window.

"The fellow who is doing the exercises with people comes from a Tai Chi Master family background. He couldn't believe when he first did these exercises. He said he knew his whole life that there was something more that would bring everything together in the body, and this is it! I'm not bragging. It's been my life's assignment. I didn't ask for it, but I have to tell you that since the last pieces have come together, I have a true understanding of God that I never had before. There's no more separation.

"I used to worry about how I would get this process out to people. I spent millions of dollars perfecting it. Now, no worry. It's going to find its way. I'm not concerned anymore because I have become a prototype of what this process is all about... and it's about overcoming our separation and returning to wholeness."

Fu Hsi's wife came out with tea. He and Roland talked at length about their research findings, and when it was time to go, these people became two new precious additions to my life. I had much to think about as a result of this meeting and the one earlier in the day. There were so many paths to the top of the mountain; it was hard to know which one to take. It seemed important to remain open to the messages of each, and then move forward with the aspects that were most closely aligned to one's own temperament.

Driving home, Roland and I discussed the importance of information to the brain, as Fu Hsi had suggested, and the power of moving from heart, as Amina had demonstrated. Our task was integration, and as both of them had said, the purpose was a return to unity, a return to Love.

Chapter 16
❧ Before Our Time ❧

Roland left the morning after our visit with Fu Hsi. He was doing a book tour the following week in the Midwest, but would return for our gathering at the end of the month. I found myself missing him, and didn't want to, so busied myself with other activities.

A week before the gathering of our group from New Mexico, I received a call from an old friend, Herbert Rothenberg. He invited me to lunch at his home in Los Gatos, a wonderful old town in the foothills of the coastal mountains near Silicon Valley. Herbert was a past professor of ancient philosophy at Stanford University and now worked on research projects with various institutions. His wife, Iris, was a noted horticulturist, who promoted projects about soil and organic farming.

I drove to their beautiful home nestled in the hills for lunch on the appointed day, and was welcomed by their overstuffed sheep dogs, Whimsy and Pickles. Iris came out to herd her canine children into the house, and greeted me with the special warmth for which the Rothenbergs were famous. She took my hand and led me to the garden that was her pride and joy. It was truly magnificent, with flowers of a size and vibrant color that were seldom seen. The health of the garden was evident, and bees, butterflies, ladybugs and other insects were busy at work doing their jobs.

I commented on the noticeable difference between her garden and others, and she laughed.

"People always kid me about having rocks in my head...but it's because of the rocks in my soil that the plants do so well."

Iris was known in the area as a champion of the earth. She believed that we had stripped the vital nutrients from the soil, and that only through a process of re-mineralizing could we hope for plants and crops that would be fully alive. She worked with a group who was intent on using glacial rock in pulverized form to enliven the earth. She said overuse of pesticides, fertilizers, and lack of crop rotation depleted soil, and was tireless in her efforts to educate others, speaking to groups all around the world.

I once asked her how she had gotten interested in her pursuit.

"You know, because of my name, I became interested in flowers at an early age. From there, I began to notice the difference in the quality of plants, and by asking questions, I found out why they fared as well as they did."

Iris knew at an early age what she wanted to do with her life. She earned several degrees in horticulture, and found that standard farming methods did little to enhance the quality of life, its primary concern being economic. Nutrient value was no longer a consideration, and the caliber of seeds deteriorated, insuring that food was losing its vibrant energy.

When she had completed her extensive education, she joined a collaboration of other concerned individuals who investigated the possibility of alternative farming and growing methods. They established organic farms during the past thirty years, and as more reports of depleted food quality in conventional farming came to light, people were more aware of the need to eat organic food rich in nutrients to strengthen their bodies.

We walked through the garden to the back of the house where tables and chairs were placed strategically for conversation amidst a mini-paradise. A grotto with lush flowers and a waterfall spilling over gigantic moss covered rocks emptied into a reflecting pool that housed the family's fish collection. These were also their pets, and Iris had names for each of them.

Herbert came from the kitchen to meet us at the French doors leading into the dining area. He had a n apron around his waist and a big smile on his face.

"Ah, my dear, so good to see you. Today I am the kitchen crew. We will be having lunch soon."

Herbert, the distinguished educator, was also a magnificent chef. He had every cookbook in the world and would often do imitations of his favorite cooking shows. His humor was equaled only by the meals he created.

During lunch, the Rothenbergs asked me what I'd been doing since we last saw one another several months before, and I told them about the directive to find the Grail, my meeting with Roland, and the subsequent journey to New Mexico. They were both intrigued by the details, and after lunch we moved to chairs in the garden, continuing our conversation.

Herbert asked me if I understood the significance of why we were doing the exercises, and I told him that since there was a new frequency pulsating on earth, we needed to make ourselves ready to receive it.

"Yes, that's true, but are you aware of what has happened historically when there have been major shifts on the planet?"

"Well," I responded, "there were major losses of different species."

"True." Herbert leaned over and lifted a pipe from the table nearby and filled it from a pouch of tobacco he had in his pocket. He then took out a metal object and tamped the tobacco in place, and meticulously lit the pipe, puffing elegantly as he spoke.

"When the basic elements that sustain conscious life are destroyed, everything tied to that system loses consciousness. We have records of ancient civilizations that had reached very high levels. Events occurred that wiped them out, and after each great cycle, we were left with simplistic human beings."

I looked at him. "So what you're saying is that when this shift occurs, we will lose our level of knowledge as a species?"

Herbert nodded. "If we are tied to the external reality of the planet, yes. However, all the great teachers of the past came with a message to humanity that they did not need to be bound by their environment. Many great sages throughout the world had the ability to defy our idea of reality, and as they purified their mental and physical being, they defied our idea of death and decay. There are those whose bodies did not deteriorate for hundreds of years after they'd gone on. They were able to do things in life that were thought of as impossible or miraculous, because they were not bound by the level of consciousness they found themselves in. They were internally rather than externally referenced."

I looked at him, a light bulb going off in my head. "So this is why religion teaches that we have to look to another world for our sustenance. It is to keep us from being perceptually bound by events. And, if I'm hearing you correctly, you're saying that we have the possibility of liberating ourselves completely through this shift in perception."

Herbert smiled. "Exactly. You spoke earlier of two cups that were presented; one the cup of remembrance and the other of forgetfulness. We don't have to forget if we can develop and maintain a level of consciousness that is not bound by apparent physical reality. There are other frequencies we can attune to."

Iris added more insight. "That's why the initiates of ancient cultures had to go through such great trials. They had to be tested to see if they could maintain a higher state of awareness in spite of every fear and temptation being presented to them. When they referred to higher mind, they were referring to a higher frequency."

She smiled and continued. "That's why food was an important part of their process. If they didn't have the quality of sustenance to support their physical bodies, their mental capabilities would have been compromised. Refinement was and is very important, so you can see that my interest in soil has many different applications, because high energy food enables us to move into peak frequency!"

Herbert looked at us, puffing his pipe contentedly, and then continued our conversation.

"It all boils down to valid advice given to us so that we can overcome what would otherwise be our undoing. The more tied we are to external events, the more vulnerable we are to being affected by the changes that will occur. The more centered we are in a state of non-attachment, the less the external ebb and flow will matter. Our consciousness can then rise above physical reality."

I was being given more clues as to why this process of finding the Grail was of vital importance. We were in a unique position to exercise the divine portion of our nature, and to move beyond external limitations, thereby freeing ourselves from the cycle of necessity. It was all up to us individually and collectively.

Iris spoke again. "However, in the process of moving beyond the limitations posed by events, we must never forget that our purpose in overcoming the earth is not to reject or abuse it. The idea is to move beyond the world of appearances, which is very much tied to perception. But we have within us elements of divinity that cares for all life, so we are also here to contribute and replenish.

"We can restore balance where we have caused imbalance, and to move through life without concern for anything other than ourselves is missing the point. This is one system and we have the responsibility to make every moment of life an elegant statement of co-creation."

Herbert agreed. "You know, a lot of the problems we're facing are of our own doing. There are cycles within cycles, but we are certainly pushing the envelope to hurry them along. There have been highly advanced civilizations in the past who moved the window beyond their understanding, to their own detriment. They became the lost civilizations spoken of in ancient texts."

I was curious. "Do you really believe that there were civilizations who had our level of technology?"

Herbert smiled. "Of course. There is documentation of their existence scattered throughout the world. After the burning of the great library of Alexandria in Egypt, we lost a tremendous record of civilization that preceded what we call ancient times. However, I know for a fact that certain groups and individuals have documents proving and chronicling the existence of major civilizations prior to the time we deem civilization to have begun. The richness of this planet's history predates anything we know of."

"That's quite a bombshell," I exclaimed. "Have you discussed this with others?"

Herbert laughed. "There are a number of us who delve into archives, but the desire to retain history as we know it has a strong following. And the groups who know better have a deep investment in not letting there be a different history."

I was extremely curious now. "Herbert, what are you getting at?"

Again he chuckled. "No, not now. You have enough on your plate, and this is another story. When you're at the point on your journey where you run into questions for which there are no historical answers, we'll talk more about it. Right now, I think it's important that you find your way to those questions, and I don't want to dilute your process."

I left the Rothenbergs, my head filled. Here was more to think about, and I'd learned that it couldn't be done in a day or a week. This process required germination, just like any other creative endeavor, and I had to sit with the various pieces of the elephant that were laid out in front of me. In my case, they were all the clues about the Grail.

Chapter 17
❧ Sun, Moon and Earth ❧

In the week before our get together, I saw many of my friends whom there hadn't been time for since going to New Mexico. I shared the information and exercises with anyone who was interested.

When I worked at the store, customers came in with tales of change occurring in their lives at rapid rates, of sleepless nights, or exhaustion when waking. They talked about relationships and the need to deal with issues that they'd avoided forever. Everyone, without exception, commented on how intense the time period was, and that they had a sense of urgency about preparing themselves for something, they just didn't know what.

Some people were making amazing break-throughs. Others, who were locked in narrow view-points, were having a particularly hard time. It was an unrelenting period that was not affording anyone much slack. The issues might differ, but the intensity was the same.

At the end of the day, my friend Michele called. "There's a special meeting at the Planetarium in San Francisco tonight. I know it's short notice, but I think you would be interested in what's being discussed. Can you come?"

I noted that there was nothing I had to do that evening, so agreed to meet her at six o'clock, so that we could be at the Planetarium by eight.

It was still light outside when we arrived, and we were fortunate to find a parking space near the Museum of Science in Golden Gate Park. During our drive to the City, Michele had talked about the speaker who would lead us in an unusual discussion about the sun, moon, and earth.

He was born in the early 1900's and was raised by a Native American woman after his parents were killed. She was apparently very wise, and taught him many skills that white people rarely learned. He had gone into mining and was an expert tracker who was able to locate minerals, or people anywhere in the world with equal ease.

He had also studied with some remarkable teachers throughout his life, and was full of incredible stories. Michele said that whether or not they were all true, he had a compelling presence that spoke of an underlying knowledge that was uncommon. I looked forward to hearing what he would have to say.

We found the meeting room where a dozen people were already gathered, and Michele introduced me to some of them. In the course of conversation, they asked about my interests, and I told them about my search for the meaning of the Grail. It was close to 8 o'clock, so as others filed in, we were asked to take seats in chairs that were arranged in a semi-circle facing a movie screen.

Our discussion leader, Walter Cleary, was a stocky man of medium height, whose face spoke of a long, eventful life. He had riveting blue eyes that veiled something beneath the surface, and it was evident that this man knew much more than he would ever tell.

His voice was deep and he spoke engagingly. After

some preliminary information, he paused for a moment and looked at the group thoughtfully. He then posed a question to us.

"Are you aware of the reason for self knowledge from a planetary perspective?"

He looked at us inquiringly. Several people offered opinions, and he nodded. Remembering what Herbert had said about the loss of consciousness when a planet goes through major shifts, I spoke up.

"I think, in relation to consciousness and planetary evolution, it has something to do with the need to prepare for higher frequencies so that we aren't tied to the consciousness level on earth."

He smiled. "Good. But why? For what purpose?"

I looked at him blankly because I didn't know the answer. No one else did either. He flipped the switch to an overhead projector, and a picture of the sun, moon, and earth hovered above us. Then he began.

"There is a symbolic story about earth that involves its relationship to the sun and the moon. In this account, the moon is the infant child of earth, and in its formative period requires sustenance from earth to live. This is accomplished through a magnetic pull exerted on souls who live lives dictated by attachment, or magnetic attraction. Energetically, the moon feeds off them, and they in turn are caught in a cycle of rebirth until they break their attachment to the magnetic pulls that bind them.

"Only when souls free themselves from addictive behaviors and magnetic pulls of the past, are they able to overcome the force exerted by the moon. Then they can move toward the light of the sun. These fully actualized human beings become the sun gods we often hear about. And, they may choose to come back to earth voluntarily to help other souls find their way into the light."

Someone in the room mumbled. "That's not a very comforting story!" The rest of us laughed.

Mr. Cleary continued. "That is why all religions warn souls to purify themselves and move to the light. As individuals overcome the magnetic pull, they are released from bondage, and this can only be achieved through inner work and soul development.

"This was the reason for the chambers of initiation in ancient times. Individuals could be placed in reso-nant chambers where the magnetic fields were very low. Through the increase in electrical frequency they were able to shed their attachment to everything that bound them to the past. As they did, they moved toward enlightenment, represented by the sun, and added to the collective body of light."

Michele raised her hand. "What does the magnetic element have to do with being recycled in life and death? What do you mean in layman's terms?"

Mr. Cleary paused for a moment. "Are you famil-iar with astrology?"

She nodded. "Yes. I don't know a lot about it, but I have some idea."

"In the pure sense, astrology and astronomy are one science. There was a split of the two over philo-sophical discrepancies, but astrology is the study of the movement of planets in relation to one another. It measures the level of tension and accord between these huge bodies based on mathematical tolerance. As planets come into alignment they are either in har-monious or stressful relation to one another. In other words, the tension between the two planets is either beneficial or problematic."

"When you view this from the pure light of science, there's nothing strange or esoteric about it. It's merely a mechanical process of physics. Now, when we look at the moon in relation to the earth, it exerts a pull, because the dynamic between the two is magnetic. When we look at the sun in relation to the earth, the influence is electric. They have a very different effect on one another."

He moved a pointer to the moon and demonstrated the connection visually. Then he made a more sweeping movement between the sun and earth.

"So, getting back to our story of the sun, earth, and moon, the reason why the moon is able to feed off of souls is because they are pulled by the magnetic force it exerts on them, so long as they are attached to illusion. You see, in an interpretive sense, the moon is the mask – it deals with what appears to be, rather than what is. When people live lives unconsciously, they are pawns to this force.

"In our story of the sun, moon, and earth, we talk about the moon being the child of earth. Taking that to an individual level, we might say that the personality is reflective of the moon. On the other hand, sun represents our true nature in Spirit. And the earth represents the self, whose job it is to mature the personality through its own connection to Spirit. It must evolve from the limited and isolated idea of self to the unlimited and inclusive Oneness of Self."

A man sitting in the middle of the room interrupted. "Can you give us an example?"

"Alright." Mr. Cleary thought for a moment. "Let's

take a person who lives a life unconsciously, meaning he's not paying attention to anything other than what appears to be in front of him. Issues come up in his life, and he finds someone else to blame for the problems. When he is faced with something he doesn't understand, he merely blocks it. He runs in an endless cycle of repetition, never making much headway because he is always reacting to circumstances – relating totally to his personality, never to his Spirit. The self is caught in an immature response pattern, and does not actualize because it does not turn to Spirit for guidance. He is therefore bound by magnetic attraction, and will die in the same mode in which he lived."

"What do you mean by being bound by magnetic attraction?" I asked.

He paused. "Bound to circumstances. Bound to base reactions, anything that is fed by history and has nothing to do with the present moment. The magnetic attraction is whatever pulls us to the past. It is the binding factor. So, as he is pulled by his personality, which has no connection to anything greater than its own logic, he is caught in an endless loop, because there is no room for vitalizing information to enter. He is closed. There is nothing electric, or spiritual, in the worldview of this individual. He is stuck in rote responses based on memorization and familiarity, never thinking for himself. He is bound by fear, denial, and conformity – so the magnetic field binds him. Do you understand?"

I nodded. "I think so. This is what is meant when we're told we must give up our history. When we are polarized to all the things from the past that are based on misconceptions or hurt, and we nurse grudges, we are unable to allow for movement forward in our body or our psyches."

Mr. Cleary agreed. "Until you neutralize all relationships, with anyone or anything that has a negative influence in your life, you are bound by the law of magnetic attraction. You cannot move forward. If there was a sieve, each binding attachment would hold you back because it is an energetic limitation.

A hand was raised, and a neatly dressed gentleman gave his impressions. "If I am caught up in my desire body, which is another way of describing the magnetic field, I can be bound by addiction. I may be obsessed with drugs, alcohol, sex, or anything else that I am unable to handle in moderation. This tells me that I'm ruled by my desires, and until I can release my over-attachment to the things that bind me, I am enslaved by them."

Mr. Clearly was visibly pleased that someone else really understood what he was talking about. "Yes!" he said. "And furthermore, when you are bound by the desire body, you can feel it in your physical body. You are pulled down. Addiction radiates from the lower part of your anatomy. It grips you, and the appetite for whatever you are affixed to, is insatiable. It is never satisfied, and is lustful.

"The higher frequencies operate without binding you. They are light and radiate in the heart area upward. They are supportive, nourishing, and give a feeling of fulfillment.

"You can demonstrate for yourself where you are operating from by paying attention to whether you are pulled down by something you are doing, or elevated by it. It is physically demonstrable."

Someone asked if Mr. Cleary would write the points he made on the board, putting them into humanistic terms, and he did.

1. Personality is only a mask of who we truly are.

2. If we rely on personality as our source, we are limited because we are relying on something that has no source other than its own reflection.

3. As an individual, or self, is bound by the personality, he must go through a cycle of repetition and rebirth because his identity is anchored in illusion and attachment.

4. As the individual, or self, turns to Spirit for its source of nourishment and identity, it is lifted up to what is real. It is released from the bondage of addiction, and concentrates on what is fulfilling at the highest levels.

5. When self identifies with Spirit, personality is able to reflect the soul's true nature, which is light.

6. This state of being is eternal, beyond the field of life and death.

7. Rebirth is no longer necessary unless the soul chooses to come to shed light for others who are still bound by the field of illusion.

Mr. Cleary went on. "As the story continues, the need of the moon to devour souls for sustenance is completing itself, because the moon is coming into its own maturity, and no longer requires feeding from earth. As the moon becomes autonomous, earth's magnetic field drops, and the barriers that keep souls from moving toward the sun are removed.

"Earth moves into a new dynamic relationship

within the solar system, and we on earth are placed in the same physical conditions that initiates dealt with in the temples and tombs long ago where the magnetic fields that bound them to limitation were removed."

"So," I said, "does this mean that people will have an opportunity to give up their historical issues more readily? Are we coming to a place in time where the personality will be given more assistance to grow into maturity?"

Mr. Cleary shook his head. "We'll have the opportunity, but not everyone will be able to take it. Remember that many of those who underwent the process of initiation long ago were unable to make the transition because they had not adequately prepared to respond to higher frequencies. Unless one does the internal work required to face fears and doubts that bind us to the past, we cannot make the leap forward, and will be short-circuited in the process, so to speak. Here again we see why we are told to neutralize relationships and overcome the magnetic pulls that bind us. We cannot work with higher frequencies until we're truly ready. Otherwise, we're playing with fire."

Everyone was very quiet. The information was a bit overwhelming. Mr. Cleary continued.

"This is life-altering information, and you have to hear it in many different ways in order to digest it. When you expand your consciousness, you open yourself to higher frequencies that connect to subtle energy bands which are attuned to higher vibrations and dimensions. It is in these bands where many of the answers to our major questions will be found."

A woman from the opposite side of the room spoke. "Does this mean that we will be able to tune in to conscious life in the rest of the universe?"

"Yes, it does. We'll be able to pick up signals that we couldn't hear before because we were tuned to the wrong dimensional frequency. But more importantly in the moment, we're going to pick up subtleties within ourselves. We're opening to an area of highly sensitized perception, and as a result, there will be amazing revelations available to us."

This was totally fascinating! Mr. Cleary was reinforcing all the information about higher dimensions and the importance of the magnetic and electrical fields that I had heard in the past month. There was so much to absorb, and it was a little overwhelming to figure out how to make the transition to more enlightened frequencies.

It was suggested that we take a short break, so Michele and I walked into the hall, looking at the display of planets and their orbits. It was amazing to think of the influence these gigantic bodies had on one another. There was the moon, so close to earth, operating as a satellite, yet getting ready to become autonomous according to the story.

One of the men who had been in the group was gazing at the constellation of Orion on a map, and I noted that he had an Apollo/NASA logo on his upper sleeve, with a picture of the moon and earth on either side of a big "A," and the constellation of Orion in the center.

"Did you participate in any of the moon landings?" I asked.

He turned to us, smiled, and nodded his head.

"It must have been quite an experience to be part of history in the making," quipped Michele.

The man laughed. "More than you know, madam, more than you know." He winked at us and went back into the room.

"That was a strange reaction!" I looked at Michele and we both shrugged our shoulders. After a trip to the ladies room, we returned to our seats for the remaining discussion.

Mr. Cleary continued. "There are bands of information penetrating the earth and its inhabitants right now. Individuals are finding each other formally and informally. Ideas are implanting themselves into certain people's minds, and they're drawn to discover something, just as one of you mentioned about searching for the Grail."

He looked over at me and nodded.

"There's a purpose to that calling beyond the obvious that has to do with increasing your awareness and adding to the bigger pool of knowledge. If people are willing to act on the insights they're being given, and share this information, others will be more aware of something they may have felt, but discounted."

A young man looked up eagerly. "Does this have anything to do with awakening a birth vision in each of us, something we were born with, but forgot?"

Mr. Cleary smiled at him. "You may be noticing a lot more people who suffer from depression or agitation now. That's not a coincidence. It's part of the Dark Age we find ourselves in, and because we've lost the connection to the vision we were given before birth. It is bound in the magnetic field and can only be released when we move into that arena with an ally to retrieve it."

"And what is our ally?" Michele asked.

Mr. Cleary smiled. "Light. It is illumination that allows us to penetrate the dark and find what we've lost. Yet, the magnetic field does not relinquish its prize easily. We have to prove ourselves worthy."

He looked over at me. "And, this moves into the arena of your quest for the Holy Grail."

I was surprised! "So," I asked, "Is there any other help for those of us on this quest?"

"Yes," he said, "The help comes from those who have gone before, and this brings us again to an opportunity present when we break the hold of the magnetic field."

"What's the opportunity?" I asked.

He smiled. "There will be a new birth... of what, we don't quite know, but it's a new *Source of Light*. Ancient prophecy says there will be a second sun. Many religions refer to it as the arrival of, or the return of, the Son of God. The native people call it the return of Great Spirit. No matter how it's named, it is the penetration on this planet of new, or renewed Light that will change the way we see reality. It will subject us to the higher laws of physics."

A woman who was sitting next to Michele was very excited. "This dovetails into the research I'm involved with. We are noting shifts in the behavior patterns of dolphins and whales. There will be more soundings from them, and their tone will shift to the new frequency. The mineral kingdom will demonstrate its deep earth wisdom in ways that will astound us. I'm only skimming the surface. This is a coinciding movement by all of earth. We, as humans, are only one portion of this process."

I was speechless. As I thought about what everyone said, I began to see the whole interplay of light and dark, positive and negative. From his story about the sun and moon, I recognized the components that had set up hostility toward the feminine principle many centuries ago, because in most traditions, the moon was thought of as female, whereas the male was represented by the sun. The feminine aspect was the negative, magnetic force, whereas the male was positive, electric. The two elements were necessary for existence, but the magnetic aspect is what attracted life, and held it in form.

From this perspective, if the soul seeks to avoid death and rebirth, then the magnetic element is to be feared. The soul would be engaged in a battle to overcome earth and woman, because they would be viewed as binding. We can see through this view how the roots of ignorance translated into acts of destruction toward an earth viewed as hostile or corrupting, and toward women, the vessels of life.

We are afraid of the dark because it represents the absence of light; and we are afraid to face our dark or shadow side, because it deals with the magnetic aspect of our nature. Out of ignorance, everything that polarizes us to the magnetic field has historically been seen as 'evil,' whereas if the moon is a child of earth, requiring nourishment for life, the whole process is about a natural evolution of growth.

Delving into the dark, or magnetic part of our psyche, is an important stage of development. Avoidance does not lead to deliverance. It leads to neurosis. Only when a soul is fully prepared, and has viewed the limitations that bind it, can there be successful movement toward the sun, or Spirit.

By releasing the fear of confrontation with self, the Self can emerge, and according to the story Mr. Cleary told, there is assistance in the process, because the duration of the moon's dependency on earth for sustenance is coming to conclusion.

This information has the potential to unlock the mysteries of many of our myths. When I realized the intention of the original concepts to liberate the soul from the cycle of rebirth, which is a magnetic process, everything made sense to me. Females, moving to the rhythm of the moon in their menstrual cycles, become highly-charged magnetic forces. The fear of the feminine is the fear of being absorbed, devoured, and regurgitated into the life process again.

In the Tibetan texts, souls are warned not to be attracted to events occurring on earth as they depart life, because their focus will pull them to that which attracts them. This is a metaphor for the magnetic pull, and is why all traditions advise souls to 'go toward the light' when they die. This directive does not deal with a mythical fairy tale scenario; it refers to the actual mechanics of life!

I thought about the little Scottie magnet dogs I had as a child. One was white, the other was black. When they would move in certain ways, they were locked together. When I would turn them in a different direction, they would repel each other. If this could happen with my little animal magnets, what could be the power of the earth's magnetism, in relation to the pull of the moon?

Mr. Cleary looked over to me. I must have been mumbling. He asked if I had something to add to the discussion, and I told him what I perceived.

He nodded in agreement. "That's about right."

"There is so much fear and superstition generated around all of this. Why didn't the ancients just tell people, plainly, what was going on?" I asked.

The man we had encountered in the hall laughed out loud, and he and Mr. Cleary exchanged knowing glances. Mr. Cleary looked at me, and a smile crept over his face.

"Have you ever heard of the story about the elephant?"

My mouth opened in amazement. Here was reference to what we'd spoken of in New Mexico. I nodded, and he continued.

"These people didn't even know the world was round, or that there was much beyond their own villages! The ancients, and a few initiates through time, brought the knowledge forward in ways the mentality of each age could accept. As times changed, the message was updated, but the encoded logic in all the spiritual texts is based on the same fundamental principles. When we advance to a level, where we can decipher the sophisticated codes left for us, the mystery of each will be unraveled.

"The ancient texts are all brilliant renderings designed to speak through time. Incidentally, they were also given as individual pieces of a larger picture. Until all the texts from the various backgrounds are brought together, the full picture is not going to emerge. Each was given a slightly different perspective, and the integration of them all will present what we might call a whole elephant."

Mr. Cleary answered questions, and as the discussion came to an end, he left us with these thoughts.

"Paradox is everywhere. One thing that is vitally important to remember, in relation to Light, is that you are to find your own light.

"When you move toward the light, you must be careful that it is not a false source, because when you follow a True Source of Light that emanates from the Self, you are liberated. If you follow the main stream, you will be regurgitated back into life, remembering nothing of the journey you have experienced before.

"I cannot impress this strongly enough upon you. Listen to the very word, enlightenment... *in-light*-en-ment. Light is not from an external source! This is part of an agreement that leads us to the arc, or the Ark of the Covenant, and that's a topic for discussion at another time."

As we left, I was filled with questions, and my mind was doing somersaults with the information. Michele was also pensive. I broke the silence.

"What do you make of the man from the moon? He and Mr. Cleary seemed to know something they weren't sharing."

Michele chuckled. "Well, there's more to all of this than meets the eye, that's for sure. Perhaps one day we'll find out."

I laughed. "One thing that is certain, my friend. Going to lectures with you is never a dull event!"

Chapter 18
❧ Reunion ❧

In preparing for the reunion of our group from New Mexico, I decided we should begin the day by walking on the Labyrinth. Everyone had expressed interest in the process when I told them about it during our week together. I completed arrangements for our time together, now just days away, and when Roland called that evening to let me know he'd be arriving from his book tour in the Midwest the following afternoon, he was pleased with the plan. I felt an inner glow when I heard his voice, but didn't want to reveal my feelings. The purpose of our gathering was too important, and it wouldn't be appropriate to focus on anything that would divert attention from our collective goal as a group.

Roland was staying with his friends in Woodside, and everyone else in our group was in the City. We agreed to meet at the Cathedral on the morning of the 25th at eleven o'clock.

On the day of our gathering, the weather was drizzly rain, but since it was Tuesday, I wasn't worried that we would have problems finding a parking space, or dealing with crowds in the church. Roland drove up with me, and it felt very comfortable being with him, as though we'd been doing this forever.

By the time we got to the Cathedral, Lillian was already waiting in the vestibule. The others came up the stairs from a different direction, and all of us collected in the awesome presence of stones, marble, and stained glass that framed this beautiful expression of faith.

I explained the procedure for walking the Labyrinth. Each of us found a unique space within the massive cathedral to spend time in prayer and contemplation. We would walk the Labyrinth when it felt appropriate, and then spend time alone to reflect on what we'd received. Roland asked us to keep in mind our purpose, as individuals and as a group, when we made the journey.

In the front section of the church was a beautiful stained glass window of a woman looking serenely at the viewer. The quality of the glass was better than in the rest of the church, and I was drawn to pray quietly in front of this restful image. She seemed to speak to me... *"I am the Lady of the Night. I am the Grail. I am the defiled one, now being redeemed. I am the feminine face of God, and it is through spirit that I am where healing will occur. Open yourself to the grace of my presence, and bring my voice forward. It is time for reconciliation."*

I was moved by those thoughts, and the energy of light and love filled me.

Lillian, Fiona, and Mark were already moving on the Labyrinth. As I looked for the others, I could see Nathan studying the different panes of glass with writing on them, and Roland was seated in one of the pews, head bowed in prayer.

A few other people, who had been on the Labyrinth, now completed the process. I walked over to it, just as Nathan did. We smiled and bowed, quietly, taking our place at the entrance, and we began the spiral journey toward the center.

Five of us were now moving around the Labyrinth at different points, some walking slower, some with greater speed. The feeling was very powerful, because we were surrounded by elements of ourselves in one another. Roland joined us, and a feeling of completion came over me. It was as though a huge energy vortex opened, and we were in a time warp, enacting something we'd done before in another time and space.

We were on the wheel of life, searching for our appropriate spaces so that we could bring something to light. Intuition was our only guide, for the memory of what we were here to do had been erased, and we were having to find our way in the dark, the connection to one another our psychic lifeline.

I had no idea what the others felt, but as I breathed and intoned our sound, I felt a reverberation from the Labyrinth. It was as though something else had emerged, and when I looked at it, not as a flat sphere, but as a multi-dimensional shape, we were walking around the inside of a vessel, leading us into the center where the six-petaled flower awaited. As each of us arrived, we took a place on one of the petals, or stations, that *felt* right. We held out our arms and joined hands with one another.

Roland spoke for the group.

"We are engaged in a process to release ourselves from fear and the unconscious actions that have kept us locked in limitation; that have held us in bondage to war and peace, life and death, and all the other opposites that focus on separation. We are here to help one another make the leap necessary to portray the living light. We open ourselves to the Divine Light of the One Source for the greater purpose of becoming fully conscious, so that we may be of service in the Grail."

The feeling was very powerful as he completed the prayer, and we began breathing and toning, letting the waves of sound and color move between us, as it had in New Mexico. Only now, something was breathing us, and the colors and sounds that emerged were absolutely awesome.

Out of the petals came colors in points of light, and the star we had envisioned, became real. The hexagram, or Star of David, became the Star of Bethlehem, and then the Star Tetrahedron. It was this great star that rose each time a major change in the consciousness of the world was about to take place.

We were catapulted into a sacred space, invoking a sacred symbol, and unbeknownst to us, we were part of a much bigger movement occurring around the world that was heralding a new age.

These were the End Times, and there was much yet to be completed, but a promise of the future was in front of us. We all felt it, and the vibration in the center of the Labyrinth was *pulsating!*

We were riveted to our spaces, and the tones that emerged from us made my body feel as though everything unnecessary was falling away. I was shedding my old skin, and in its place was something made of light. As I felt the clearing, both inside and out, I merged with the crystal tone of a bell. As our collective voice rose, all the bells of the church began to ring-in the noon hour.

The sun, which had been hidden by a cloud cover, now burst through the colored panes of glass, and showered rainbow colored hues across the carpet. It was a magnificent crescendo, and when the bells stilled, our process in the center of the Labyrinth was complete.

The purpose of our gathering was forming in my mind. We were opening to reunion of the lost and distorted parts of us that had caused terrible division in the past. Life unfolded in western culture from a doctrine of separation, and the many horrors, visited upon one group by another, could be traced to these misconceptions.

Science was providing an understanding of the role electric frequency and magnetic fields had played, and we were able to see how the two together formed life; one binding to the past, one moving toward the future. Without the two, there was no life. Without matter, the substance from which all life is formed, there would be no manifestation.

When I thought of the mountains, the animals, the beauty of natural creation, there was nothing evil about it. Through limitation, however, we had translated words incorrectly, altering doctrines that would shape our lives. I had seen how certain terms changed meaning in some of the biblical passages, and it filtered through my mind that, in the beginning, man was given *stewardship* over the earth, not *dominion*. The difference between stewardship and dominion is monumental! It contains the seeds of enlightened direction, or brute force!

I could see the beauty of indigenous cultures who had not been bound by these limiting perceptions, revering the earth that housed and fed them, and the sky that gave them light and air. I could feel the unity with my acknowledged kin – the mountains, not out of some unnatural preoccupation, but because we were all spirit, housed in living matter. We sprang from, and returned to, the same life pool. Our consciousness was attuned to different frequencies, but we were all of, and from, *one source.*

I felt that the Labyrinth mimicked an aspect of multi-dimensional consciousness and brain wave activity, and the message was that we were being reformatted and rerouted, opening to vaster possibilities within ourselves. This meant reconciliation and reunion with our disparate parts... right and left brain, male and female, Jew/Christian and Moslem.

Those of us who came from this western pool of consciousness had to find our way back to the Source and recognize our interdependence and potential. We had to reflect a divine marriage between heaven and earth, overcoming the myth of separation.

As we walked our way out of the Labyrinth, I saw one of the panels on the wall. It showed the founding of the United Nations here in San Francisco. Now, a birth of a new, unifying force was occurring, and there was no more appropriate place for its delivery. We are all the elements of a new Grail – a new covenant between Creator and Creation. We are being asked to grow into our role as fully human, to embrace life in its entirety as our companion on the journey.

I could see the factions coming together; east and west, north and south... the elements were repairing. Where division had taken place, like a zipper coming apart, the elements were now returning, as the zipper was drawn together. That which had reached its apex in the outpouring was now returning unto itself. The outward breath was being drawn inward, and through my mind flashed the words, *"I sent you into the world as one who became two, and now I reclaim the two and make of you one."*

Years ago, when I was director of the foundation dedicated to the understanding of the dynamics of peace, criteria had been set to find a common ground of agreement, for you could not negotiate until you had a place from which to begin that was mutually acceptable. In that state, a framework for discussion was possible.

Within our own species, in extreme situations, we may only be able to start at a negotiating place that acknowledges we are each human. As humans, we may only be able to come to the point with other species where we can agree that we are all born of the life force. But, from these points, we have a basis for beginning.

Another thing I learned at the foundation was that in order to speak together effectively, we have to define terminology, because semantics plays a strong role in reaction. If we don't agree on what we mean by the same term, we are bound to misunderstand one another.

What I think of as God may mean something very different to someone else. So we need to tell each other what we mean when we refer to something. For example, when we say, 'I want to be happy.' Happiness to me, means 'I want to be free.' This seems so basic, yet is often taken for granted. This simple oversight is often the basis for lack of agreement.

As we did our return walk around the Labyrinth, I saw the interrelationship of earth to the cosmos, and to what Mr. Cleary had talked about.

The indigenous cultures were coming forth with their stories, because it was time for the fabric of earth to be re-woven, and humans were ready to hear another view of creation. As the magnetics dropped, we could pierce the other dimensions and pick up subtleties that we had never been able to perceive before. As we shared our various vantage points, the picture of the elephant came into magnificent clarity for everyone.

This was the purpose of the Grail – to re-form us more appropriately in the image of our Creator, to make of us a *whole* vessel – *a Holy Grail* – in which the most precious seed of the Sacred could be housed, and nurtured.

I completed walking the Labyrinth and sat down on a bench along the side of it, looking up at the stained glass windows for 'direction.' Nothing in particular struck me, except way at the top, I saw $E=MC^2$.

We left the Cathedral quietly, and once outside the church, we decided to have lunch at the Cliff House on the edge of the Pacific Ocean. This was where my regular Labyrinth companions and I had gone after our first visit. Arriving after the lunch hour, my friends from New Mexico and I, were seated immediately.

We went to the restaurant on the top floor because the view was spectacular, and we could order sandwiches, salad, or breakfast. We each sat quietly, engaged in our own reverie, yet not separate from one another. Fiona spoke first.

"I saw the importance of media and film in this unfolding process. We have spent so much time dwelling on negative themes that we have helped cement the imprint of fear into the consciousness of society, and we have done very little to glorify the human spirit.

"It was made clear to me that I am to involve myself in film and media projects that give people hope, and to make films that celebrate life, rather than degrade it. What I was shown was the preciousness of children, and that we cannot treat them with indifference, as though they aren't affected by what they see, because the quality of what they see on television has a big impact on them."

Nathan spoke up next. He was very stirred on the Labyrinth to do more work with sacred proportions. He said he wanted to involve himself in the riddle of the crop circles, and other earth and planetary anomalies, that would lend further insights into the process that was unfolding. He smiled at us, more present than ever before.

"I experienced strong feelings of love throughout my whole body, and I could feel my heart open. I mean *really feel it*. This has never happened to me before, and it was awesome!"

Mark nodded. "I know what you mean. I saw myself expanding outward, reaching out to all the people in my life who have hurt me, and those whom I have hurt. Suddenly, we were all one circle of energy, and I felt as though I didn't need to protect myself from them anymore. I forgave them and they forgave me. What had been a whirlpool of dark, swirling energy, turned into a vibrant light, and all my anger, judgment, and fear was swept away in its presence.

"There wasn't any separation, and I felt connected to everything... an incredible feeling of love replacing the pain. I will never forget that. It's like, whatever happens, I can handle it. As long as I keep focused on that light, and allow myself to be love, I can really help heal the world.

"I am going to use this in my life. From now on with clients, I'm going to tell them what I see is possible for them, because I know it will make a difference. They're not coming to me accidentally, and I'm not in this to be safe. There is nothing gained by me playing small, and I really get that this is a time of incredible movement. I'm going to do my part to help it along."

Lillian smiled. She spoke in her husky voice.

"I went back to the faith of my grandmother, and the power of prayer. So much is possible if we remember to ask for help, and prayer is one of the most important things available to us. I could see the possibilities through millions of voices raised in prayer each day, like making the world one big temple, or mosque, or cathedral, and remembering the sacred all the time. Prayer will change our relationship to the way we view spirituality. It isn't just a once a week affair. This is a daily act of being in love.

"I've always painted the figure of the Goddess veiled or hidden, because she has been submerged. But on the Labyrinth, she was passionate and vital, and I could feel myself responding to her fertility. My paintings are going to emerge differently now that I've experienced this. She was always in hiding before, but she has been welcomed to come forward. My Goddess, is she powerful!"

We chuckled at her radiance. Then, Roland looked at me. "What about you?"

I expressed what I'd felt, but told them that I didn't know what to do with the vision.

Mark smiled. "I sense that if you go home and take time to sit with what you received, you'll be led to your part."

It was Roland's turn to share his insights, and he was reflective in his comments.

"I felt very humbled by the process, and recognize that I've got to take some serious time off for myself, and concentrate on healing. I've been so intent on getting things done that I've lost sight of some of my own needs. As much as I want to reach out right now, my journey has to go inward. I'm going to cut down on my speaking and workshop schedule, because this is time for me to be with me. The gift I was given on the Labyrinth was myself, and I'm grateful. So, that's my focus for the next few months, at least."

We were fairly quiet throughout the remainder of lunch, and as I looked at each of these people who made up a part of my soul's purpose, I recalled how they had been strangers a month ago. Now, we were a family, and had an indelible bond that was forever. We knew that the adventure we began in New Mexico was on-going, and that there were many curves on the road ahead of us. Our process was not one that insured an infallible life or fairy tale endings. It provided each of us the wherewithal to establish a place of internal stabilization, and to overcome the fear that was so predominant in many people's lives.

We were strengthening ourselves and drawing upon the support of one another in our quest, whatever that might become. We were willing to show up for the possibilities presented, and to give the best of ourselves, moving out of self-consciousness into unified reality.

As each of us clarified our intention and cleared our own 'baggage,' we could act as conduits and vibrant mirrors to one another, encouraging and supporting the bigger picture. There were presently six of us who would show up for one another, in whatever way that was needed, whether in the physical body or through communication. Each of us knew that there were five others who were vitally concerned and committed to our individual and collective progress. Whether it was Lillian's emerging feminine through painting, or Fiona's films uplifting others, they could count on the group to support the vision.

As Roland needed rest, we would encourage that as well, for the purpose was wholeness. If each of us felt whole, we could make a major contribution. We did not need to shrink back, because we were no longer isolated. We were a collection of notes and were creating a symphony, with the power of our Creator guiding us.

As we walked to our cars, we passed the huge cavern on the side of the cliff where the Sutro Baths used to be. It had been a gigantic building with an ice rink, multiple swimming pools and other things, overtaking the cliff and surrounding area for many years as a testament to man's dominion over nature. Eventually, the elements reclaimed their own, and the splendor of the natural setting drew people to investigate the cliffs and caverns that had once been covered by a monolithic structure.

The beauty of the setting far outstripped the arrogance that tried to tame it... and we all remarked how we felt that same hand was at work with each of us, paring us to the core of our being, so our True Essence could emerge.

We stood in a circle above the cliffs, the sea crashing rhythmically onto the shore below, renewing our vows of love to That which had created us. No words were needed, we had said enough. Hugging each other, tears of joy and sorrow at being parted, we prepared to go our separate ways to the lives and commitments we had created.

Chapter 19
❧ Vision of the Grail ❧

Roland left our gathering with Mark, as they would be going to Oregon together later in the day. He came over to me as I was getting into the car, and pulled me into his arms, holding me tight. A lump rose in my throat, and he looked at me with knowing eyes. "Soon," he said. "I'll see you soon." He squeezed my hand and left.

I drove home, full of my experience on the Labyrinth, and filled with the possibility of what might be in the future. Our group had come together with an idea of solidifying our intention collectively, but what emerged went way beyond any of us.

At home, I processed my feelings about Roland. I recognized that he needed space to heal, and that this was not a time for relationship with anyone but himself. If there was to be something more for us, it would develop naturally. I didn't have to rush anything, or push for something out of fear it would go away. It pleased me to observe the shift in my own pattern of response. There was no need to panic for fear of not having. I had a deeper understanding about relationship, and a great part of that was thanks to him.

My heart was expanding. The love I felt was complete and unconditional. I wanted for Roland's well being, regardless of what that meant. I could give him the space he needed, because I cared for him. I didn't need to possess him to prove to myself that something belonged to me and wouldn't go away.

What a feeling of freedom! How joyous to care enough to let someone go. I'd heard about it before, but never understood what people meant by that. Now I felt it firsthand. No strings. No conditions. No bargaining. Just letting someone go to their greatest good.

I looked out at an expansive universe, not a confining one. I knew in my heart that I could go on with confidence, knowing that in spite of all appearances, I was always provided for and loved. My task now was to determine where I was headed in my own journey. There was much to digest.

I reviewed everything I'd experienced – from the beginning of the journey through the powerful finale on the Labyrinth. I reviewed my notes and thoughts, putting all these things in perspective.

As I'd researched and opened my mind to the possibility of the Grail, it moved beyond the Silver Chalice from which Jesus presumably drank at the Last Supper, and the Holy Grail in the legends of King Arthur and the Knights of the Round Table. The Grail became an object throughout history, that all cultures held as a touchstone to something that would transform us into what we are meant to be.

The requirement of the Grail in all traditions, whether searching for a cup, a stone, or a sacred geometrical formula, has been the willingness to risk the self to the unknown. As in the tales of would-be knights, courage and depth of intention had to be proven before the possibility of knighthood was bestowed upon them. This was similar to the journey of initiates in more ancient times. Knighthood was only the second stage of a process. And it was intriguing that those on the quest were called knights, because the correspondence to *night* was unmistakable. Night represented the shadow side of our own nature, which had to be explored before we could achieve wholeness. Night was also the domain of the moon, corresponding to the feminine principle.

The Knights Templar truly were in service to the Queen, because she was the fallen one, represented by the moon. Their search for the Grail was a search for the Light, the Sun, or Son, that would reunite the King and Queen and restore order to the kingdom of earth. Their shining armor reflected light, and they became potential messengers of reunification.

What occurred historically was something quite different, leading to major rifts and destruction, through misplaced focus on the material world. Idealism became fanaticism, and the journey of reunification became mass exploitation. As Herbert said, the loss of the ancient library in Alexandria during the Crusades marked a major rewriting of history.

All of the stories passed down through time and events are the personification of multiple processes that take place individually and collectively... from the cellular level to the psychological, to the cosmic. One aspect of the Grail quest mirrors the process that earth undergoes in relation to the dual forces of electric and magnetic fields.

The Grail, in this context, might refer to the quality of forces surrounding earth. As they become more finely tuned, a resonant frequency is able to penetrate the core, and the responding tone is an uplifting of consciousness.

On the other hand, when we are bound by fear, and exploit our environment, the changes happening to earth can conceivably wipe out consciousness. Again, the paradox.

Stories throughout history attempt to bring a merging between the world we can relate to as humans, and the world as it is unfolding within the cosmic realm. As our technology allows us to approach the mysteries with less fear, we begin to move with curiosity toward greater understanding and insight, seeing correspondence within the stories of old to their scientific counterparts. What is occurring is a merging of the various pieces.

At the dawn of a new era, the co-creative purpose for which we have been intended, comes more clearly into focus. If we continue as separate entities, bound by our own will and singular viewpoints, we are polarized to fear, because we constantly have to protect our position in relation to the multitude of other positions facing us.

If we insist on continuing to see God as the father, who is jealous, petty and possessive, we are binding ourselves to an egotistical viewpoint of a Creator who could never have achieved the magnitude of creation surrounding us. As we relegate all things not male, and not human as inferior, we are putting ourselves into a constant position of dominion rather than stewardship, and we miss the opportunity of dynamic partnership and collective initiation that *is* possible.

The function of the 21st Century is to work with the concepts of union, or in many cases, *reunion*. This is a century that will require true understanding of the Grail in relation to its wholeness... neither male nor female, not positive or negative. This is the century of *and* with events occurring that will make us aware of our need for inter-dependence, for we are not alone in the universe.

Many of our stories will undergo change, and new myths and archetypes will be created that tell of the events that brought us to this point. We face the dawn of recognition that our need for differentiation has set us into adversarial roles and has caused us to feel isolated.

The development of individuality makes way for an era of partnership, where the power of unification will be explored. A focus on *more than self* opens the door to consideration for another. In the expression of two, the role of a third – the child, becomes a precious contribution to life, rather than a thoughtless blunder.

My mind was flowing with possibilities presented by the Grail! In reviewing what I'd learned about its meaning, I recognized one thing clearly. Through time, the Grail made itself evident whenever there was a significant change in consciousness about to take place. The shift of the millennium certainly qualified as a dramatic time of change through all the major prophecies, and I wanted to participate in the unfoldment process in whatever way was appropriate for me.

I went to bed early, not talking to anyone or doing anything distracting because I didn't want to lose the potency of the insights. During the night I dreamt about the Grail. In my dream there were two cups standing side-by-side. One was silver with a crescent moon and five-pointed star over it, and the other was gold, with the sun and a six pointed star hovering above. As I watched these two cups, a third cup rose from the earth between them, and it had no color.

Invisible hands raised each of the other cups, and the contents of both were poured into the third cup. As this occurred, there was a merging of colors. The new cup became opalescent, with sparks of gold and silver glinting from it – radiating the most beautiful light I'd ever seen.

As the other two cups moved into the distance, the sun and moon also seemed to blend together, and over the third cup, the two stars converged into a new star. It had eleven points with eleven more points shining behind it. It was magnificent! While I watched, I heard the words... *"This is the new dispensation; the portal and gateway to reconciliation as the two become one. It is the return of the Beloved."*

As I saw this vision unfolding, I was shown a picture of the globe, with focus on the western world. There was a golden key that appeared with numbers looming in front of it. A spiraling light hovered over the Middle East, and then zoomed like a laser beam onto Jerusalem.

Bring forth the star of reunion, and I saw the star that had formed over the cup... it is the star of renewal. Light streamed down, and from the earth there was a glow of beauty we had never seen before, and a magnificent tone emerged from the connection. There was new growth and vibrant health everywhere, and the earth was honored, as though she was a bride.

More words came. You have worshiped the sacrifice. You have elevated destruction, but this is the time of resurrection and reunion. In places of worship, a magnificent star of light became the focus. We were merging into a holy alliance of heaven *and* earth. The cup in front of me was big enough to hold all views because it was the original One from which everything had come, and to which everything was now returning.

Just before I awoke, I heard the words... *"Reverence for Life!"*

This dream was more profound than any I had before. I wrote down each aspect because I felt it was significant.

As I was sorting through my thoughts, the phone rang. It was someone I had never met who had read my newsletter, and wanted to subscribe to it. He turned out to be a scientist from the East Coast who was working on the exploration of DNA. From the way he spoke, it was evident that he blended science with spirituality, and I had an impulse to ask him if he was familiar with the Grail. He responded that he was.

"What do you believe it is?" I asked.

There was silence, and then he answered.

"When an individual is able to move to a place within themselves that no longer holds judgment, anger, and defense... in other words, perception without fear, then compassion can be generated. And, when the heart resonates compassion, the tone that is set up within the body is implanted into the DNA, creating a perfectly braided spiral that looks like an endless stream of liquid light, or golden fleece. This becomes a Grail that is holy, without end, and sets a tone for all of life."

Compassionate heart. Liquid light. Resonant tone. I was amazed at the correlation between his description of the Grail and all of the clues I'd been gathering since the beginning of the quest. Something major was unfolding, and I was being put on notice to pay attention.

Bonita and I had our weekly walk scheduled earlier than usual. At nine o'clock that morning I arrived at her home. We took our normal hike around the mountains, exchanged ideas, and returned to the Center, where less than two months before, this quest had begun. Bonita suggested that we meditate, so sitting in spaces that felt appropriate, she intoned the sounds, and drummed a beat that would lead us to a quiet space within ourselves. As the sound subsided, and I moved deeper into my silent prayer and I heard *the Presence* whisper to me, as I had that day in the Center six weeks ago... *"Write my story."*

"Write whose story?" I thought. "The Grail? The Labyrinth? The group?"

"Write all of it."

"How, in the newsletter?"

"Write it as fiction. Go home and start writing. Ask for help in prayer. I will guide you. This process is not just for you; it is for others as well... Write my story."

Driving home I wondered how to go about doing what I was told. I felt a sense of excitement. I talked to myself, and decided that if it didn't work out, I could just throw my writing away, but perhaps there was something that would be valuable to others from the experiences of the past months. If I could capture even a fraction of it on paper, it might awaken someone else who had more insight to add to the vision, or become a framework for future work.

When I arrived home there was a message from Mark. He bought a couple of books about the Labyrinth after lunch, and decided on his way to Oregon that after Roland finished his time of healing we should all go on a pilgrimage to the Labyrinths in Europe. I thought about what that expedition might lead to, and wondered if it was something I ought to do. There was no doubt in my mind that this was a continuing adventure. But for now, I had an assignment to complete.

I sat at my computer, took a deep breath, and began typing. I had the first sentence in my head already... *As I trudged up the hill, noting my breath, I felt an overwhelming sense of gratitude for life and I had a strange sensation that things were about to change in a most remarkable way.........*

Glancing at the clock on my computer, it was 11:11, and the music playing in the background was a flute version of *Amazing Grace*.

Glossary of Terms

The following words, arranged alphabetically, are used within this book in the context described below. There may be other definitions of the terms, but in relation to this story, the following definitions are correct.

After the Rapture Refers to, in this story, to a time, after the shift of energy occurs, that will transport us from one level of awareness to another.

Agent Orange was a very powerful chemical defoliating agent used in the Vietnam War to eradicate all plant life in a given area so that the enemy could not use the vegetation for hiding places.

Archetypes refer to the underlying patterns from which everything of a similar type is cast. In Jungian psychology, archetypes are related to the collective unconscious that binds all of us, and from which the psyche draws its notions. Much of Jungian dreamwork is based on the collective archetypes that allow an individual in Switzerland to view the same image as someone in Iowa – without having any conscious frame of reference for that image. This is said to be drawing upon a universal archetype that psyche knows, while the personality may have no frame of reference for it.

Ark of the Covenant refers to the vessel of preservation and regeneration in holy agreement between human and the Divine that is found within the soul.

Astrophysicists refers to scientists who study the physical relation of form and essence or matter and radiation of planetary bodies. It is a division of astronomy.

Attunement refers to bringing ourselves into harmony with a larger reality.

Auric fields relate to the energy pattern surrounding a physical entity that emanates from that entity and gives information related to the health, well-being, and level of development. It cannot be viewed directly, but must be seen through vision attuned to subtle energy.

Blessed Mother is another term for the Goddess, the feminine aspect of God, as referred to in the Catholic Church as the mother of God, or the mother of Jesus.

Caldera is the remnant of a volcanic eruption that is shaped like a huge basin.

Celtic lore refers to the stories that were handed down through Celtic tradition and have become the basis for many myths. The Celts were a group of people who inhabited large portions of western and central Europe in ancient times and had a major influence on the pre-Christian traditions of the British Isles. The myths of King Arthur and many other heroic legends arose from the Celtic tradition.

Chakras are energy centers that are located along the spinal cord of the body and appear as magnetic colored wheels of light that correspond to body functions. For maximum health, the chakras are supposed to rotate equally and radiate strong vibrant colors that relate to the particular energy centers they represent.

Collective unconscious is a term in Jungian psychology referring to the inborn unconscious psychic material common to all humankind that is a result of all experience that has preceded present time.

Cosmic vision refers to a larger view of reality than that which is bound by our space/time definition. It includes other worlds and possibilities.

Cosmologists are the philosophical and astronomical scientists who deal with the structure, origin, and evolution of the universe.

Cosmos refers to the world or universe as an orderly, harmonious system.

Craniosacral refers to the region of the brain that houses the parasympathetic or autonomic nervous system.

Crop circles are the increasingly elaborate geometrical forms found in cereal grains throughout the world that seem to spring from an intelligence that we do not as yet understand, and are pointing out fundamental elements of the building blocks of the universe.

Dimensions, as used in the book, refers to the ability to see within a given space. A straight line has one dimension, and with each dimension, more is visible and adds complexity. We see three dimensionally in our current world model with the faculties we have developed to this point. When we move to higher dimensions, we are able to see greater subtleties and possibilities.

Druids refers to the ancient wisdom keepers of the Celtic tradition who had the ability to walk between the worlds and bring visions to light. They were considered the sages, and had great empathy and connection to the natural world as well as the Divine.

Earth sciences refers to the branches of science that study the earth... geology, meteorology, geography, etc.

Electrical field refers to the surrounding area of an electric particle that has been charged and in which other particles are acted upon by an electric force

Electromagnetic fields refers to the arena in which the phenomenon occurs between electric and magnetic components as they interact through currents and charges.

E-mail is an abbreviated term for electronic mail that is exchanged through computers on the Internet.

End Times refers to a specific period in which prophecy and biblical passages converge, noting an ending to life as we know it. Some see the end times as the completion of a major cosmic cycle, with tests and trials, but the opening to a Golden Age. Western religions tend to see it as a time of reckoning and tribulation. It denotes a major completion of an old age and the opening to a new one, requiring preparation.

Energy in the context of this story refers to the horsepower available to an individual or situation. There are low energy and high-energy individuals, and energy as it is used here is the substance from which action is molded.

Energy bodies or centers refers to centers of light and vibrancy within the body, also known as chakras. They can be divided into different categories, such as the head, heart, and spleen.

Esoteric refers to something that is not known at a surface level. It requires delving deeper into what may appear to be one thing, but is much more complex when viewed from another vantage point. It is often information that is available and of interest to a select few, and provides the framework for teaching that is later given to others, in more understandable forms.

Fractal refers to a complex mathematical equation that has a geometric shape and dimension arrived at through sequence following definite rules.

Gaia is the term for earth that views it as a living, self-regulating organism rather than a stationary piece of real estate.

Give Away In some indigenous cultures, the give away is a way of sharing gifts that may be tangible or intangible. It is the sign of a noble individual to share with others in this way.

Glyphs are pictographs, or hieroglyphics often found in caves, or at ancient sites that provide information about the civilization that formed them.

Gnostics seek direct knowing and to overcome the duality of essence and matter. Ancient Gnostics were called heretics, and it is said that they rejected the material world. However, modern Gnostics embrace many different vantage points, including the Jungian psychological type, where the great quest is to overcome the alienation and separation of self from Self.

God refers to the Creator of life and at times the male aspect of that Creator.

Goddess refers to the feminine aspect of the Creator

Grail Seekers refers to those who seek understanding and reunion with truth, beauty and goodness.

Great Mother refers to the nurturing feminine aspect of creation.

Great Mystery refers to the unknown that houses all knowledge of what is, has been, and what will ever be. It is also the *All That Is.*

Great Spirit is the creative force of the Source of Life.

Grids refer to the subtle energy patterns that ring the earth like a web.

Healer refers to someone who has an ability to facilitate healing in someone else either through prayer, laying on of hands, or through other means that allows the body to return to vibrant health.

Heart chakra is the energy center located near the heart, often referred to as the center that reflects our ability to love and be loved. When it appears to be closed, it means that there has been a major hurt or trauma to the individual that has caused them to "shut down" that portion of their feelings.

Hermes as used in this story refers to the great Egyptian personification of will, wisdom, and action. He was often referred to as the messenger of the Gods, and can be correlated to Mercury in other systems of categorization.

Hexagram is a six-pointed star that refers to the sexual union between spirit and matter that perpetuates life in the universe. It was originally an Indian symbol, but became the official symbol of Judaism, often known now as the Star of David.

Holy Grail refers to the sought after unity of soul and spirit...the attainment of the peaceable kingdom that can only be achieved after a spiritual quest.

Indigenous cultures are native to a particular area or region and often predate the onslaught of European expansion and belief. They are very often rooted in reverence for life and unity with the earth and all its inhabitants.

Initiates refer to a select group of individuals in ancient and modern times who are on a spiritual quest that requires moving through all manner of tests to overcome limitation within self.

Internet, or Net, is the interconnecting network of information that allows people to find data from myriad sources by using a special phone connection and service to their computer for which they usually pay a nominal fee per month.

Kiva is the sacred space and spiritual gathering place for many native cultures. The kiva is usually a deep circular pit in the earth that is aligned to energy vortexes, allowing for heightened awareness and insight. It may be open or enclosed.

Knights Templar were a religious order founded in the Middle Ages "in honor of our lady" to uphold the Goddess, named then as Mary Magdalene, and to provide safety for trading routes through Islamic territory. They became first class warriors who were feared by everyone, and were later hunted and killed by a petty French king who invented stories of heresy against them to repossess their land and wealth. They have been associated with Masonic principles, and were guardians of the Shroud of Christ. They were very definitely knights of the Grail who have kinship in principle with alchemy, the Catarrhs, Gnostics, and the Rosicrucians.

Kokopeli is a legendary hunchback figure of the southwest tribes whose likeness is found everywhere in that region as he plays the flute and is the bringer of joy and fertility.

Labyrinth is a geometric shape that is found in different sizes throughout the world and seems to be a place in which an individual can move into an altered state of awareness to confront aspects of their psyche and spirit.

Life science refers to the study of living organisms and their interrelationship such as biology and genetics or botany and ecology.

Living Light references the aspect of Divinity that is present always and moves through the world to heal and enlighten.

Lotus position refers to a standard yoga sitting position in which the right foot is placed on top of the left thigh and the left foot is positioned over the right thigh for maximum strengthening and elongating of the spine.

Magnetic field refers to an area surrounding a magnet, electrical current or any other "charged" particle (including planets) in which the magnetic force acts upon these elements.

Mandelbrot & Julius Set refer to the life and death of a fractal. Shown in a colorful video presentation, this equation comes to one point in its life of balance and then moves into another set until its death when balance is once again achieved. Theoretically, all life mimics this process.

Metaphysical refers to that which is beyond the physical realm, and often is linked to cosmology and the supernatural. It is a highly abstract branch of study that seeks to understand first principles; cause rather than effect.

Medicine is a term used by some tribes to refer to energy and can either be good or bad, depending on the intention of the originator or recipient.

Mysticism is the comprehension of God or spiritual awareness through direct comprehension rather than through any form of intermediary.

Myths refer to stories that have been devised

around timeless truths that project moral lessons in an imaginative form, often encompassing archetypes.

Namasté is a Sanskrit term that is used as a spiritual greeting. Loosely translated, it denotes that "I bow to the God in you from the God in me."

Nikola Tesla was a brilliant inventor and scientist who lived in the 19th Century and worked with electromagnetic fields, doing revolutionary work that we have not yet been able to duplicate successfully.

Pentagram is also known as the pentacle and is a widely revered esoteric symbol, denoting devotion to things pertaining to the earth and the feminine. It was cast down as an evil symbol during the Christian ascent, and was relegated to witchcraft and evil by the church.

Physicist is a scientist dealing with the field of matter, energy, motion and force.

Polarization refers to the sharp division of groups into opposing factions and also refers to a magnetic pull to a particular state or condition.

Power Animals are used by Native Americans to denote attributes within an individual related to particular animals that seem appropriate to that individual.

Primal tones refer to original sounds that bring us back to our most basic instinct and sense of connection to all of life.

Profane refers to lack of reverence and degradation of that which is sacred.

Psychic level refers to the plane of intuition that hovers beyond the rational mind and allows an individual to sense things that are at times paranormal. However, it is not necessarily spiritual and must be approached with caution.

Quantum physics is the study of how everything relates to everything else, with the intention to bring about a unified field theory that will describe the movement of everything that exists.

Renaissance was a time that bridged the medieval to modern world and was a period when art, literature and education flourished. When used in present day, it denotes a rebirth and renewal of whatever it is in context to.

Resonant chamber refers to an enclosure or space that holds a particular sound that allows for altered realities to be experienced.

Resonant frequency is a tone that carries a band of information.

Root chakra, or the first chakra, is related to survival. This is the energy center that is the foundation of emotional and mental health, and the one in which many people have issues, or get stuck. Without the first chakra, there is no life, but it is important to develop refinement through the other energy centers of the body for balance and well-being.

Sacred Geometry refers to the mathematical principles that govern the working of the universe and as such, invoke awe within humans because it is a study of divine proportions.

Sarasvati is the Hindu goddess of wisdom and the arts.

Sari refers to a single piece of material that is worn as dress by the women of India, wrapped around the body, and draped over one arm.

self *(with a small "s")* refers to the individual, or lower self, that identifies with its own perception and view of life cut off from any sense of larger context.

Self *(with a capital "S")* refers to the higher or

greater Self that is connected to the larger context of life, recognizing itself as individual, and yet interconnected to all of life. It is this part that often is referred to as the Inner Guide, or Conscience.

Shakti refers to life energy, or the feminine aspect of creative energy.

Shaman is the word that described Siberian healers, but is used now to indicate any individual who has great healing ability and wisdom. We mistakenly refer to Medicine men and women of our Native American tribes as shamans because it is the new word of choice.

Silver Chalice refers to the cup from which Jesus drank at the Last Supper. It was later taken and hidden, transported throughout the world through the centuries, and believed to have vast healing and miraculous properties.

Spirit is another term for the power of the Creator of Life that moves through us when we are open to receiving its blessing.

Spiritual center refers to the indwelling space within each individual that is connected to a greater plan and purpose of life, regardless of the details in the moment that might appear depressed.

Star of Bethlehem is another term for the pentagram

Star of David is another term for the hexagram

Star Tetrahedron is a geometric shape that is considered to be the key building block for the third dimension.

Stonehenge is a series of standing stones found in England that are associated with the tales of King Arthur and the Knights of the Round Table as well as Druids, who were supposed to carry on their sacred rites at the site.

Synchronicity is a term coined by psychiatrist Carl Jung, and denotes meaningful coincidences.

Template refers to a model or framework that provides guidelines for action and can be copied by others.

Third Eye refers to the spot over the nose area in the mid portion of the forehead that correlates to the pineal gland and sensory awareness. It is the location of the sixth chakra, or energy center.

Trigger points refer to issues that ignite our vulnerable areas and cause us to be touchy when someone confronts them.

Vanguard refers to individuals on the leading edge of new thought.

Vibrations are the feelings one gets from a particular place or person. It is an energy level that imparts information.

Vision Quest is modeled after the Native American practice of going into the wilderness with minimal food to spend time with the elements and oneself. It is during this experience that many people confront their fears and move into meditative states that lead to the potential vision of their life purpose.

Vortex is a whirling pool of energy that draws things to itself.

Wisdom of the ages refers to the great insights that have been handed down through civilization's many changes, and remain beyond the limitation of mundane thinking. The timeless truths are unchanging.

Zen Buddhism is a branch of Buddhism that encourages enlightenment through meditation and direct, intuitive insights.

Resource Guide
Listed below are books, tapes, periodicals and individuals that may be helpful to you in your continuing journey of spiritual unfoldment. I have also listed other information in relation to the chapters where mention of the subject material was introduced. Not all chapters had new information, so are not listed.

Chapter 1: A Strange Assignment

A Dictionary of Symbols, J.E. Cirlot, Routledge & Kegan Paul Ltd. 1962
The Chalice and the Blade, Riane Eisler, Harper & Row, San Francisco, 1987
The Elements of The Grail Tradition, John Matthews, Element Books, 1990
The Krater and the Grail: Hermetic Sources of the Parzival, Henry and Renée Kahane, University of Illinois Press, 1984
Mystical Way & The Arthurian Quest, Derek Bryce, Samuel Weiser, Inc. 1996
The Secret Tradition in Arthurian Legend, Gareth Knight, Samuel Weiser, Inc. 1983
Man and His Symbols, Carl Jung, Anchor Book-Doubleday, 1964
Memories, Dreams & Reflections, Carl Jung, Vintage, 1989
Portable Jung, Joseph Campbell, Penguin 1976
Alchemy, The Golden Art, Andrea De Pascalis, Gremese Intl. 1995
Conscious Dreaming, by Robert Moss, Crown, 1996
The Holy Bible From the Ancient Eastern Text, George M. Lamsa, Harper & Row, San Francisco 1968

Chapter II: The Labyrinth

Labyrinths Ancient Myths and Modern Usage, by Sig Lonegren, Gothic Image Publication, 1991

The Mystic Spiral Journey of the Soul, by Jill Purce, Thames and Hudson, London, 1974

The Spiral Labyrinth Journey: A Pilgrimage Into the Sacred Erotic Earth, by Nityaprema, Sacred Enterprizes, Unlimited. 1994.

Walking A Sacred Path, by Dr. Lauren Artress, Riverhead Books 1995

Article in New Age Journal, "Walking the Labyrinth," by Lynn Murray Willeford, June 1995, p. 79

Labyrinth Letter, a quarterly newsletter from Jean Lutz, 10550 E. San Salvador, Scottsdale, AZ 85258-5744 (602) 860-0854; Website: Labyrinthltr lists a few public places where you can walk the Labyrinth in the United States:

1. Grace Cathedral, 1051 Taylor St., San Francisco, CA 94108-2277 (415) 776-6611

2. Riverside Church, 120th Street & Riverside Drive, New York, New York (212) 222-5900

3. Trinity Cathedral, Cleveland, Ohio (216) 771-3630

Gnosis Magazine No. 40, Summer 1996. Special Issue on Hermeticism

Gnosticism The Path of Inner Knowledge, by Martin Seymour-Smith, Hidden Wisdom Library, Harper San Francisco, 1996

The Nag Hamadi Library, Revised Edition, James M. Robinson, Editor, Harper San Francisco, 1978

The Allure of Gnosticism, Edited by Robert A. Segal, Open Court Publishing Company, 1995

Conscious Dreaming, by Robert Moss, Crown, 1996
Diet for a New America, by John Robbins, Stillpoint Press, 1987

Chapter III: After The Rapture
A Door Ajar, A Record of A Spiritual Journey, by Alix Taylor, White Wolf Press, 1994
Angels Don't Play This Haarp, by Manning and Begich, 1995; ISBN 0-9648812-0-9
Nothing In This Book is True, But It's Exactly How Things Are, by Bob Frissell, Frog. Ltd. 1994
Sedona Beyond the Vortex, by Richard Dannelley, Vortex Society
Ariadne's Web: Issue dedicated to The Grail, Volume 1 Number 5, March/April 1996
Bloodline of the Holy Grail, by Laurence Gardner, Element, 1996
Chronicles of the Crusades, Edited by Elizabeth Hallam, Weidenfeld and Nicolson, New York, 1989
Holy Blood, Holy Grail, by Michael Baigent, Dell, 1983
Genisis: The First Book of Revelations, by David Wood, 1985 Baton Press, England

Chapter IV: The New Mexico Connection
The Celtic Tradition, by Caitlin Matthews, Element Books Limited, 1995
The Celts, by Frank Delaney, Little Brown & Company, 1986
The Druids, by Stuart Piggot, Thames & Hudson, 1968
Within The Hollow Hills, Edited by John Matthews, Lindisfarne Press, 1994

Chapter V: Rivers of Light

Alchemy, by Marie Louis von Franz, Inner City Books, 1980

Christian Meditation and Inner Healing, by Dwight Judy, Crossroads Publishing Company, 1994

Meditation, by Eknath Easwaran, Nilgiri Press, 1978

Meditation, by Grace Cook, White Eagle Publishing Trust, 1965

Miracle of Mindfulness, A Manual on Meditation, by Thich Nhat Hanh Beacon Press, 1975

Seeking the Heart of Wisdom, by Goldstein and Kornfield, Shambhala Publications, Inc. 1987

Seven Mansions of Color, by Alex Jones, DeVorss & Company Publisher, 1982

The Meditative Mind, by Daniel Goleman, Jeremy Tarcher/Putnam Book, 1988

The Present Moment, By Thich Nhat Hanh, 6 cassette series from Sounds True Audio, #F015, Catalogue, (800) 333-9185

Zen Mind, Beginners Mind, by Shanryu Suzuki, Weatherhill, 1970

Occult Geometry and Hermetic Science of Motion & Number, by A. S. Raleigh, DeVorss Publications, 1981

Animal-Speak, by Ted Andrews, Llewelyn, 1996

Animals As Teachers & Healers, by Susan Chernak McElroy, New Sage Press, 1996

Medicine Cards, by Jamie Sams & David Carson, Bear & Company, 1988

Chapter VI: Tree, Mountain, Bird, Sky

Human Energy Systems, by Jack Schwarz, E. P. Dutton, New York, 1980

The Chakras and the Human Energy Fields, by Shafica Karagulla, M.D., and Dora van Gelder Kunz, Quest

Books, 1989

The Elements of the Chakras, by Naomi Ozaniec, Element Books Limited, 1990

Wheels of Life, by Anodea Judith, Llewelyn Publications, 1987

The Message of the Sphinx, by Graham Hancock and Robert Bauval, Crown Publishers, Inc. 1996

Ancient Voices, By Steven McFadden, Bear & Company, 1992

Mother Earth Spirituality, by Ed McGaa, Eagle Man, Harper & Row, San Francisco, 1990

Kinship With All Life, by J. Allen Boone, Harper San Francisco, 1954

Profile In Wisdom, by Steven McFadden, Bear & Co., 1991

The Sacred Tree, by Bopp, Bopp, Brown & Lane, Four Worlds Development Press, 1984

Heaven Help Me! by Nancy Freier, Lightlines Publishing Co., 2000

Chapter VII: All That Glitters

The Acupressure Way of Health, by Iona Teeguarden, Kodansha, 1978

A Complete Guide to Acupressure, by Iona Teeguarden, Kodansha, 1996

Traditional Chinese Acupuncture, Vol. 1, by J. R. Worsley, Element Books, 1990

Hands of Light, by Barbara Ann Brennan, Bantam New Age Books, 1987

Light, Medicine of the Future, by Jacob Lieberman, O.D., Ph.D, Bear & Company, 1991

Subtle Body, by David V. Tansley, Thames & Hudson, 1977

The Magic of Movement, Cassette, by Francoise Netter, E-mail: Body4Mind@aol.com

Art Spirit, by Robert Henri, Harper & Row, 1984
Fire In the Crucible, by John Briggs, Jeremy P. Tarcher, Inc.,1990
Free Play, by Stephen Nachmanovitch, Jeremy P. Tarcher, Inc. 1990

Chapter VIII: Need and Greed
Energy Anatomy, by Caroline Myss, Ph.D, Six (6) cassette series, by Sounds True Audio (800) 333-9185
Pranic Healing, by Choa Kok Sui, Samuel Weiser, Inc. 1990
Emergence, by Carlos Nakai, Canyon Records Production, CD
Casino Master, by John Patrick, John Patrick Productions (800) 254-3210
Stewardship, by Peter Block, Berrett-Koehler Publication, 1993
Nothing But Good Times Ahead, by Molly Ivins, Vintage/Random House, 1993
Tierra Gitana, Gipsy Kings, Nonesuch Records, CD

To acquaint yourself with some of the present theories in education:

Debating the Future of American Education, Edited by Diane Ravitch, Brookings Institute, 1995
Dumbing Down of America, Edited by Katherine Washburn & John Thornton, W.W. Norton & Co., 1996
Dumbing Down Our Kids, by Charles J. Sykes, St. Martin's Griffin, 1995
Possible Lives, by Mike Rose, Penguin Books, 1995
Rethinking America, by Hedrick Smith, Avon Books, 1995

Schools For the 21st Century, by Phillip C. Schlechty, Jossey-Bass Publishers, 1990
The Schools We Need, by E. D. Hirsch, Jr., Doubleday, 1996
Teaching The New Basic Skills, by Richard J. Murna, Free Press, 1996

Someone making a difference in education: Marva Collins, West Side Preparatory School, 4146 West Chicago Ave., Chicago, IL 60651, (312) 227-5995

Chapter X: Revelation
Anatomy of the Spirit, Caroline Myss, Ph.D, Harmony Books, 1996
Aura Soma: Healing Through Color, Plant and Crystal Energy, by Irene Dalichow and Mike Booth, Hay House, 1996
Healing and the Mind, Bill Moyers, Doubleday, 1993
Healing Words, by Larry Dossey, M.D., Harper San Francisco, 1993
Prayer is Good Medicine, by Larry Dossey, M.D., Harper, San Francisco, 1996
Prayer As Energy Medicine, by Ron Roth, Harmony Random House, 1997
Remarkable Recovery, Caryle Hirshberg & Marc Ian Barasch, Riverhead Books, 1995
Turbulent Mirror, by John Briggs & David Peat, Harper & Rowe, 1989

Chapter XI: Beyond History
Amazing Levitron that defies gravity, Nature Company stores or order by phone 1-800-275-2877
Amazing Grace, The Lives of Children and the

Conscience of a Nation, by Jonathan Kozol, 1995, Harper Perennial

Tao of Chaos, by Stephen Wolinsky, Bramble Books, 1994

Medugorje, The Message, by Wayne Weible, Paraclete Press, 1989

Queen of the Cosmos, by Jan Connell, Paraclete Press, 1990

Woman Earth-Spirit, by Helen M. Luke, Crossroad Publishing Company, 1981

The Goddess Re-Awakening, by Shirley Nicholson, Quest Books, 1989

The Once and Future Goddess, by Elinor W. Gadon, Harper & Row, San Francisco, 1989

Being Peace, by Thich Nhat Hanh, Paralax Press, 1987

Peace Is Every Step, by Thich Nhat Hanh, Bantam Books, 1991

The Blooming of a Lotus, by Thich Nhat Hanh, Beacon Press, 1993

Inner Guide Meditation, Edwin C. Steinbrecher, Samuel Weiser, 1989

Serpent In the Sky, by John Anthony West, Quest, 1993

The Holographic Universe, by Michael Talbot, Harper Perennial, 1992

Awakening Earth, by Duane Elgin, William Morrow and Company, Inc., 1993

Chapter XII: Freedom, Art and Architecture

The Arts, by Hendrik Willem Van Loon, Simon and Schuster, 1939

The Meanings of Modern Art, by John Russell, Harper Collins, 1991

Nicholas Roerich, The Life and Art of A Russian

Master, by Jacqueline Decter, Park Street Press, 1989
The Cosmic Connection, by Michael Hesemann, Gateway Books, 1996
The Crop Circle Enigma, Edited by Ralph Noyes, Gateway Books,1990
Feng Shui, by Eva Wong, Shambhala, 1996
Feng Shui, The Chinese Art of Placement, by Sarah Rossbach, Arkana, 1983
Ocean of Wisdom, by The Dalai Lama of Tibet, Harper & Row Publishers, San Francisco, 1990

Chapter XIII: Frequency and Perception

Awakening to Zero Point:The Collective Initiation, by Gregg Braden, L.L. Productions, 1994
Geopathic Stress, How Earth Energies Affect Our Lives, by Jane Thurnell-Read, Element Books, 1995
Alphabet of the Heart, Sacred Geometry, by Daniel Winter, P.O. Box 142, Waynesville, NC 28786
Nada Brahma: The World is Sound, by Joachim Ernst Berendt, Inner Traditions
Tesla: Man Out of Time, by Robert Cheney, Dell Publication, 1981
Aging As A Spiritual Journey, by Eugene Bianchi, Crossroads Press, 1984
In Midlife, A Jungian Perspective, by Murray Stein, Spring Publication, 1983
Old Age, by Helen Luke

Chapter XIV: Fear and Transformation

The Divine Proportion, by H.E. Huntley, Dover Publications, 1970
Sacred Geometry, by Nigel Pennick, Harper & Row, 1980

The Temple in Man, The Secrets of Ancient Egypt, by R.A. Schwaller de Lubicz, Autumn Press, 1977
The Global Brain Awakens, by Peter Russell, Global Brain, Inc., 1995
Pocahontas, Walt Disney Home Video

Chapter XV: Of The Head and Heart

Song of The Stone, by Barry Brailsford, Stone Print Press, P.O. Box 12-360, Chartwell, Hamilton, New Zealand
Secret Power of Music, by David Tame, Inner Traditions
The Soundscope, by R. Murray Schafer, Inner Traditions
Music and the Power of Sound, by Alain Daniælou, Inner Traditions, 1995

The sound work of Tina Clare. For information about Sound & Community or tapes and workshops on sound and drumming, e-mail: BCLight@AOL.com

Inner Structure of the I-Ching: The Book of Transformation, by Lama A. Govinda, Weatherhill, Inc., 1981
Journey into a Science of Reality, by Wing Y. Pon, East West, 1978
Neo-Taoism, Volume One, Putting God Back Into Physics, by Wing. Y. Pon, E-W Institute
Neo-Taoism Volume Two, The Holon Method: An Inspirational Outline on Reconstructive Knowledge, by Wing Y. Pon

Classes in body movement and video lectures on the

Holon Theory are presented by Wing Y. Pon. You may obtain information about these classes and his books by writing to him at P.O. Box 32855, San Jose, CA 95152

Chapter XVI: Before Our Time
Information about re-mineralization of the soil can be obtained by writing to Don Weaver, P.O. Box 1961, Burlingame, CA 94010

Biodynamic Agriculture, by Willy Schilthuis, Anthroposophic Press, 1994
Secrets of the Soil, by Peter Tomkins & Christopher Bird, Harper Collins, 1990
Forbidden Archaeology, by Michael Cremo and Richard Thompson, 1996
When The Sky Fell, by Rand & Rose Flem-Ath, 1996

For further information about the types of things brought up in this chapter, order *The Laura Lee Show* catalog for audio tapes, and a listing of her internet radio programs at: http://www.LauraLee.com

Chapter XVII: Sun, Moon, and Earth
Beelzebub's Tales To His Grandson, by G.I, Gurdjieff, Viking Press, 1993
The Tibetan Book of the Dead, Translated by Robert Thurman, Bantam, 1994
The Tibetan Book of Living and Dying, by Soygal Riponche, Harper San Francisco, 1993
Through the Eyes of a Dolphin, by Liliana Saca, M.A., Space Frame Press, 1996
The Coast to Coast Radio Show with Mike Siegel

from 10 PM - 2 AM on AM radio. Web Page: http://www.CoasttoCoast.com, or Dreamland on Sundays with Whitley Strieber.

Chapter XIX: Vision of the Grail
Contemplative Prayer, by Thomas Merton, Doubleday, 1996
Conversations With God, by Neale Donald Walsch, G. P. Putnam & Sons, 1996
Prayer, by Richard J. Foster, Harper San Francisco, 1992
Seat of the Soul, by Gary Zukov

❧

About the Author

Kathleen Jacoby has been a spiritual seeker for most of her life. She has worked in the world in many capacities and has found that the only life worth living is one where the Spirit of Love and Compassion leads. *Vision of the Grail* is a story she was guided to write. It has elements of truth woven into fiction, and is designed to engage the reader to participate in a journey that we all ultimately must take.

Kathleen is a master storyteller. She has a gift of insight that she offers in her writing and her consulting work with individuals and groups. She is the author of two other works, *A Call To Prayer,* and *Where You Live Is What You Learn.* She is also creator and editor of a quarterly newsletter, *Seasons of the Soul,* and is a regular columnist on TheInnerVoice.com website.

Kathleen leads a weekly discussion group on America OnLine that further investigates the principles found in *Vision of the Grail.* She has been co-host of *The Millennium Café* radio show with partner, Steve Freier, where they interview individuals on the cutting edge of new ideas.

Kathleen has developed strategies for successful living, based on a spirit-filled life. She offers a tape series, gatherings and columns dedicated to this concept. Her life is a work in progress, and as she integrates the lessons life hands her, she is able to share them with others.

Kathleen believes in the potential within each of us, regardless of circumstances. She sees life as a process, not a destination, and recognizes that everything is given to facilitate a greater work in progress… the mastery of ourselves.

For additional information about Kathleen's work, or to order tapes her numerology tapes, booklets, or the newsletter, please write to her at:

Lightlines Publishing Company
760 Vella Road
Palm Springs, CA 92264
(760) 325-9200

E-mail: VisionoftheGrail@aol.com

OTHER TITLES FROM LIGHTLINES PUBLISHING CO.

(Order Form on page 289)

Heaven Help Me! A Celestial Guide To Healing
Author: Nancy Freier
ISBN 1-930126-02-6
Cost: $12.95

This inspiring book provides readers with Heavenly guidance for everyday problems. It is an answer to prayer... any prayer. Replete with angelic wit and wisdom, the insights to 190 commonly asked questions will open your heart and offer you new ways to respond to life's crises. Also included are 26 moving prayers that can change your life and how you view it. Here's what some reviewers had to say:

"I loved Heaven Help Me!"
-Meredith Young-Sowers, author of *Angelic Messenger Cards*

"This valuable reference guide is a must for every household."
-Nick Bunick, subject of *The Messengers* and author of *In God's Truth.*

"I highly recommend this book..."
-*Spiral Journey Magazine*

You Can Talk To Your Angels:
A Guide To Inner Listening
By Nancy Freier and Jim Clark
ISBN #1-930126-08-5
Cost: $14.95

Now, you can talk to your angels and have conversations with God! You know how to pray and now you can learn how to listen for the answers you seek. *You Can Talk To Your Angels* is complete with instructions, prayers, meditations and real life angelic experiences from students who have already awakened this inner listening skill. Common blocks are explained and removed, and questions answered. Step-by-step guidance and helpful tips are given for creating a personal, sacred communication with the Divine Intelligence within you - just waiting for you to tap it.

You Can Talk To Your Angels Meditation Tape
ISBN: 1-930126-05-0
Cost: $10.00

Side A: *Meet Your Angels* Meditation by Nancy Freier and Jim Clark. A guided experience in which you meet your angelic guides and teachers.
Side B: *The Great White Light Healing Meditation* by Nancy Freier and the Angels of the Great White Light. A meditation that helps you relax and heal yourself on the subtle vibrational levels using the Great White Light of God.

Lightlines Publishing Co. Order Form

(Please check appropriate box and indicate quantity ordered)

❏ Qty_____ **HEAVEN HELP ME! A CELESTIAL GUIDE TO HEALING** • by Nancy Freier; ISBN: 1-930126-02-6; $12.95

❏ Qty_____ **YOU CAN TALK TO YOUR ANGELS: A GUIDE TO INNER LISTENING** by Nancy Freier and Jim Clark. ISBN: 1-930126-04-2; $14.95

❏ Qty_____ **YOU CAN TALK TO YOUR ANGELS** • Audio Tape. *Meet Your Angels* and *The Great White Light Healing Meditations* by Nancy Freier and Jim Clark; ISBN:1-930126-05-0; $10.00

❏ Qty_____ **VISION OF THE GRAIL** • by Kathleen Jacoby; ISBN: 1-930126-07-7; $14.95

❏ Qty_____ **SEASONS OF THE SOUL NEWSLETTER** • By Kathleen Jacoby; Published quarterly. Subscription price $16/year.

❏ Qty_____ **THE INNER VOICE NEWSLETTER** • By Nancy Freier. Subscription price $24/year.

Amount of order $_____

CA residents add 7.75%sales tax $_____

Shipping Fee *(See note below)* $_____

TOTAL $_____

Shipping Costs: *Add $2.50/item to cover postage and handling to U.S. addresses. Add $8.00 for foreign shipments (U.S. funds).*

METHOD OF PAYMENT:

❏ Personal Check *(Payable to "Lightlines Publishing Co.")*

Credit Card: ❏ VISA ❏ MC ❏ American Express

Name on Card: _____

Card # _____Exp. Date _____

Street _____

City/State/Zip _____

Phone _____

E-mail: _____

We will contact you only if there is a question with your order.
Your name will not be shared with any other mail list.

PLEASE MAIL TO:

Lightlines Publishing Co. • 760 Vella Road • Palm Springs, CA 92264
Phone: (760) 325-9200
E-mail: info@lightlinespublishingco.com
Website: http://lightlinespublishingco.com
Thank you!